Friends
With
Issues

a novel

MEREDITH BERLIN

First Edition

ISBN: 978-1-957723-72-3 (hard cover)
       978-1-957723-73-0 (soft cover)

Published by Warren Publishing
Charlotte, NC
www.warrenpublishing.net
Printed in the United States

To Jordan

Marriage is a gamble, let's be honest.
—Yoko Ono

Follow your heart but take your brain with you.
—Dr. Alfred Adler

1997-1998

CHAPTER ONE
Nick Gallagher

Greenwich, Connecticut

Six months before the day he died, Nick woke up the way he usually did—jolted from a bad dream. He remembered bits of it—being with friends near his old Manhattan apartment, wandering into a gun club for shooting practice. He thought his shots were pretty good until the owner tore down the target paper and showed him how off the mark he was. The scene changed, and he was walking through the offices of a new magazine—a magazine with a lot of buzz, though it had yet to be published. He tried to offer advice to his old colleagues, but he was invisible to them. When he opened his eyes, he had that vague feeling of being useless.

Nick lived in a ten-thousand-square-foot house. He had twenty of the most desirable acres in Back Country Greenwich with a large movie-star pool, clay tennis court, and full home theater. Floor-to-ceiling windows reflected the changes of every season. The exterior was concrete. He hated the house—he thought it looked like an office park.

He glanced over at his sleeping wife and ran his fingers lightly over Susan's upper arm, gently squeezing it, making sure not to wake her. Her skin jiggled where he touched it—soft and lush. But

Susan didn't want him to look at her arms. Or the rest of her body. When he occasionally passed by her as she was getting dressed, she was already in her underwear or robe. He couldn't remember the last time he'd seen his wife nude.

When he'd married her twenty-three years ago and they were living in Manhattan, she was a petite, lean, don't-even-think-of-messing-with-me magazine executive in stiletto heels. They made love spontaneously and fiercely. In the dining room after dinner or locked behind his office door. Then it slowed down. Friends told him that was natural, but Nick didn't believe it. Not so early in their marriage. Not with Susan.

After the birth of their daughter, Kelly, Susan had said she didn't want to make love just because *he* was in the mood, especially when the baby was crying in the next room. He tried to rekindle their romance, scheduling date nights to see a Knicks game or a new Off-Broadway play. For a while, her interest perked. After the sale of his second magazine, they went from being upper middle class to ridiculously wealthy. They often traveled throughout Europe and Asia, staying only at Relais & Châteaux hotels, and made love.

He'd agreed to move to the suburbs, even though he loved the city. Susan spent the next two years decorating the Greenwich house—badly. By then the sex became so infrequent that when they did make love, she felt like a stranger to him.

"Tell me what you want," he'd urged her.

"Nothing, I'm fine," she'd said and squirmed away. "Why do we have to talk about everything?"

"Not everything. This."

They'd had the conversation over and over. Different words, different places, but always with the same conclusion. It wasn't his fault, she'd told him; it was hers. He eventually stopped trying.

Nick got out of bed and headed to the shower. Susan had done one thing right when she helped design his bathroom: six showerheads and three glass walls overlooked the forest that bordered their property. He squinted and saw a big buck standing still in the distance. It was October, and the leaves were turning.

The oaks were golden. Some of the maples were red, and delicate white birches mixed with pines ran all the way down the hillside.

After his shower, Nick toweled off, wiped the fog from the mirror, and stared at himself. Forty-eight … but a good forty-eight. He was tall. His body was tanned and muscular. He swept his light-brown hair back from his face. His sky-blue eyes were sharp and inquisitive. Beautiful women flirted with him. He'd heard the gossip: *Nick's rich. Nick's smart. Nick's great in bed. Nick could help your career. Oh, and Nick's wife could not care less if you slept with him.*

After Susan had stopped having sex with him, he began sleeping with other women, but he only picked partners who didn't want serious relationships. Susan and Kelly were his family. He didn't want complications.

Susan's voice interrupted his thoughts. "What are you doing today?"

Wrapping a towel around his waist, he opened the door to see her standing outside the bathroom. Her chestnut-brown hair was neat, considering she had just awoken. There was a little mascara goop under one eye.

"I've got an eleven o'clock with Joe Noonan in the city," he said. "He wants to sell *Sound*. I told him I'd look at the numbers."

"Just don't buy it," Susan said, arms crossed over her breasts. Nick had made $25 million on his last magazine purchase. Obviously, she didn't want him to lose it all on this one.

Nick shrugged, noncommittally. "It's turning a profit. Not a lot, but they're doing okay. About fifty thousand newsstand readers, a hundred thousand more in subscriptions. Give or take."

"Which isn't anywhere near *Rolling Stone*'s sales. And there aren't any ad pages, except for condoms or upcoming concert tours." Susan paused. "Maybe some drug-addicted rock star's 'memoir.'" She said the word *memoir* with little air quotes, and he laughed. Celebrity memoirs—the two of them could both write a book about that farce.

Nick and Susan had met when she was head of ad sales at a men's magazine. *That* woman, the one who knew how to persuade almost any company to place their ads in her magazine, the one who refused an offer to become publisher of America's most popular women's magazine because she wanted to take care of their daughter—*that* was the Susan he loved.

"Right," Nick said, taking out his razor. "I'm just going to help Joe come up with a good asking price." He watched his wife walk toward her own bathroom on the other side of the bedroom suite. "What are you doing today?"

She turned around and smiled. "Working out with Jenna, double-checking some dinner dates we have, and thinking about my next career move."

As if a new career was just another check on her to-do list, Nick thought. *One question only.* "What would that be?"

"Not a magazine," she said, offering a sly smile that said, *Wait till you hear what I have to tell you.*

He sighed. "Okay, Susan, I'm here to listen whenever you want to talk."

Susan being Susan, Nick thought, *giving just enough information to keep me interested.*

CHAPTER TWO
Susan Gallagher

Susan looked at herself in the bathroom magnifying mirror. She applied expensive cream around her dark-brown eyes. "Liquid velvet" was how Nick used to describe them. She placed her thumbs on her jaw and index fingers on her temples and pulled upward. Yes, she could look younger, but no facelift for her. She was the same age as her husband—too young for that.

She shrugged off her white waffle robe. In her bra and panties, she turned sideways to examine herself in the full-length mirror. She ignored her thighs. Too early in the morning for them. Instead, she gave her belly a critical study. Pulling in her abs, she thought, *I'm lucky. I'm really not that fat.*

Lucky because of her appetite. Susan was a foodie—nothing was too exotic for her to try. Opening a small, chic restaurant in the suburbs of New York City was a dream she'd harbored for years. Yes, she'd been a force in the magazine business, but it had come easily to her. Food was her true passion. Going out to dinner and tasting a new dish aroused her senses. She would briefly close her eyes and try to figure out what ingredients were in the meal. Was there an undertone of nutmeg in the fettucini Alfredo? Why did a disc of goat cheese taste grassier in one restaurant versus another? Where had the chef discovered said goat cheese? Was it locally sourced? Imported? If she wasn't particularly interested in the table conversation, her mind would wander further. Maybe she should learn how to make goat cheese. In France? Could she become a goat cheese apprentice to some renowned cheese maker? What about New York? There had to be goat cheese makers here.

Susan turned her attention to her calendar. There was going to be a small dinner party at Elizabeth and Danny Altman's house next week. And tomorrow night, they were going to a restaurant with Nick's friends, whom she'd never met. Nick knew the wife from his days in the TV business. Susan wasn't particularly curious about the actress-slash-wife, but they were going to a new restaurant, and *that* interested her.

She pulled on a sports bra and slipped into yoga pants. Then she put her hair up in a clip and walked downstairs to the gym where her personal trainer, Jenna, was waiting. Susan lay down on a mat and began stretching. She had finally decided to get fit. She didn't like the way certain parts of her body had become flabby. She'd heard other women say they believed in loving their bodies no matter the shape. Fine for them, but she wanted her old one back, and she was ready to try and get it. Her clothes were too tight, but her home gym had turned out far more inviting than she'd expected. Pink lighting flattered her skin, and the mirrored walls made her appear slimmer than she was. She thought department stores should use the same lighting. Women would definitely buy a lot more bathing suits.

Susan got up, stood against the wall, and stretched her hamstrings.

"Okay," Jenna said. "Let's start with the recumbent bike today." She turned up the volume of the surround-sound stereo, blasting heavy metal.

Susan covered her ears. "Please shut it off and put something else on. Jesus, Jenna! It's too early for that music."

Jenna searched through a collection of CDs and selected Steve Winwood's album *Arc of a Diver*.

"Better," Susan said and began pedaling. After ten minutes, she'd had enough. "I'm tired."

"Push yourself, Susan. You won't see results unless you try harder."

Let her try harder, Susan thought.

Jenna changed tactics and smiled. "Just another fifteen minutes."

Susan rolled her eyes but got back on the bike.

Her trainer was a five-foot-ten, twenty-eight-year-old San Diegan with sapphire eyes and below-the-shoulders straight blonde hair. Her posture was perfect. So were her boobs, butt, and legs. Susan felt a twinge of envy.

"Don't you want to look fabulous for your friend's party?"

"It's next week, Jenna. I'm not going to look better that fast without lipo."

Jenna laughed.

Elizabeth and Danny Altman's dinner party was one of the few engagements Nick would remember without Susan reminding him. He had known Elizabeth for years, and they had worked together at *The Street*, a gritty fashion magazine that earned Nick his fortune. He was looking forward to seeing Elizabeth, but Susan would be meeting new people at the party, and she wanted an instant skinny makeover. Not likely. Then there was dinner tomorrow night with the soap actress and her husband. Whatever.

When the song finally finished, Susan got off the bike. "That's it. I've got a busy day."

"We just started," Jenna said. "You need to do a cooldown and meditation." She stood, hands on hips, looking at Susan. "You seem anxious today. It'll help."

Susan made a face. "Anxious? Please. I'm never anxious. I'm focused."

She found meditation irritating. All those deep introspections and spa music did nothing for her. New Age, tinkling bells, deep breathing—just another way for people to try and express themselves in a "calm" manner. Susan thought people spent too much time sugarcoating their feelings. She had a different philosophy: Spit. It. Out. She spoke directly, a quality she knew Nick admired. If some people viewed her as scary and confrontational, oh well. "I'll do five minutes of meditation, but no crystals and forget the incense."

Jenna changed the music once more. The sound of gentle rain filled the gym as Susan lay back down on the mat. Jenna talked her through the chakras, imagining a third eye and going over her vertebrae, one by one.

"I'm not getting anything out of this," Susan said.

"Shhh, let yourself go."

Susan laughed. "That's what got me here in the first place."

In a low voice, Jenna coaxed, "Come on."

Susan closed her eyes. *Okay, let's have some meditation. Nick will buy that magazine, even after I told him not to. I have to choose a dress that's classy for dinner with the actress and her husband. Buy a bottle of wine for Elizabeth's party. I'll go to the pool with a glass of Sancerre after this nonsense is over. Bundle up and bring a book.*

It was a cloudless fall day, not many more before they would close the pool for the winter.

Is this meditating? she wondered as Jenna's voice droned on with the pitter-patter of raindrops. Her thoughts continued in fits and spurts. Her mind wandered back to that day a few months ago when Jenna had raced with her to the ER.

She had been stretching her calves in the gym when Susan got a call that her daughter, Kelly—home for the summer after her first year at Cornell—had a waterskiing accident. Jenna insisted on coming with her. Susan was surprised. Jenna could have left her to be alone with her daughter, believing Kelly's injury was a private affair, Susan thought later. But no, it was Jenna, not Nick, who'd driven with her to the hospital. Jenna who listened with her as the doctor explained Kelly had a concussion, some contusions, and a torn meniscus. Jenna who held her hand when the doctor said Kelly wouldn't need surgery. Nick met them at the hospital, relaxing once he learned their daughter would be okay, but Jenna was the one who had been there for Susan.

Today, after Jenna left, Susan ate a tuna sandwich, small bag of potato chips, three chocolate chip cookies, and a club soda. She stepped into a red one-piece bathing suit, slid her feet into sandals, and pulled on an oversized black cashmere sweater. She was annoyed to see small pills all over it. She'd paid nearly $700 for the sweater at a boutique in Soho.

The saleswoman had advised hand-washing it with baby shampoo. "Make sure to block it," she said.

Susan had glared at her. Block it? Instead, she had it dry-cleaned, which had been a mistake. Now she could only wear it around the house, and it aggravated her—even after her meditation. She left her workout clothes on top of the washing machine. Her housekeeper, Maria, would take care of them. Maria's husband, José, kept the pool and hedges looking pristine. They lived in the guesthouse on the other side of the Gallaghers' property. Susan didn't say it enough, but she was grateful to have them.

She tossed a John Grisham paperback into her canvas bag, along with a towel, her flip phone, a copy of *Vogue*—in case the book didn't interest her—sunscreen, and lip gloss. On the way out, she poured herself a plastic glass of wine to-go. Maybe it was a little early in the day for alcohol, but she wasn't a big drinker, and besides, who made the rules for what time of day she should drink?

The pool was situated below the house, carved into the hillside with a grove of fir trees providing privacy. The turquoise water glittered, sunbeams dancing off its surface. It was heated to a perfect eighty-eight degrees. A hot tub spilled over into the pool.

José had already brought out her chaise, positioning it precisely at the angle she liked, with the sun full on her face. Screw skin cancer—she wanted a tan. She looked around and smiled. Life was good. Maybe she'd swim later. Probably not. She opened *Vogue* and had just turned to a story about "Fashion in America" when a long brown-banded snake slithered near the chaise's leg.

"Shit, shit, shit!" Susan yelled. "Get the hell away from me! José! José, where are you? There's a friggin' snake here! It's a copperhead!"

José didn't materialize. Susan stood shakily on top of the chaise, her legs bare and the pilled cashmere sweater covering some of her but not enough to protect her from the snake and its venom. This thing was going to ruin her relaxation time ... or worse. Where was José? The copperhead, or whatever it was, was starting to wrap itself around the base of her lounger. Something had to be done immediately. She'd have had no problem shooting it, but she didn't have a gun. God, the thing was thick.

Quickly, she jumped off the chaise. With the snake still holding on, she used all her newfound strength to pick up the chair and toss it off the deck and into the woods. Her heart hammered, and her hands were shaking. She ordered herself to calm down, and when that didn't work, she took some deep breaths the way Jenna had taught her and a long sip of wine.

Back in the house, she used the landline to call Nick. "Where are you?" she demanded. She was excited to tell him about her scary experience and how brave she'd been.

"I'm about to walk into *Sound*. What's up?"

"I thought you'd like to know a copperhead was wrapped around my chaise by the pool."

Suddenly, Nick sounded very interested. "We have copperheads?"

"Well, it had a copper-colored head, so I assume. I got rid of it."

"You picked it up? Are you okay?"

"I'm fine. I flung it and the chair into the woods."

"Good for you. Hopefully, it won't come back."

"It better not. And I forgot to remind you—tomorrow night, we have dinner with the Fletchers in the city."

"Who are the Fletchers?"

"Your *friends*, Nick. Isabella Fletcher? The TV actress and her husband?" His absent-mindedness got on her nerves.

"I forgot about that. Crap. Not in the city, Susan. I don't want to drive back in again. Can you make it somewhere near us?"

Susan had been looking forward to eating at a little restaurant on West Tenth Street. No matter. She could research another one closer to home. "Fine. And don't forget, next week we have that dinner party at Elizabeth and Danny's."

"I'm looking forward to it. And Susan? Great job on the snake."

CHAPTER THREE
Brooke Hayworth

"Amanda, do you have all your books?" Brooke was late; she was always late.

"I have my books, Mom, and I've already missed first period. You told me you'd drive me to school over an hour ago. Why can't you ever get it together?"

Brooke fished around her shoulder bag for the car keys. There were anemic snowflakes fluttering outside. October and snow. Yesterday, the temperature had been in the seventies. She dreaded the coming cold and shorter days. But she had to stay focused.

"Mom? Mom! I'm late. I can't always be late. Where are you?"

Brooke hurried toward the garage where her daughter was already standing by the car. "Coming! I need my car keys."

"You left them in the car so you wouldn't forget. Please, let's go!"

They jumped in the car, and Brooke backed the red Jeep out of the driveway and onto Cross Highway, heading toward school. The covered bridge under the Merritt Parkway looked quaint, with trees on either side turning golden overhead. Amanda adjusted the radio dial to her mother's favorite station, WFUV-FM. Laura Nyro was singing "Eli's Coming." Brooke sang along.

When the song ended, Amanda said, "I have tennis today, and then I'm going to Zoe's to work on our play."

"What play?"

"I told you, Mom! Brooke! Brooklyn? We're putting on a play for a group of Brownies."

"Oh, that's great, honey. Do you get extra credit for it?"

"Yeah, from the English department."

"It'll look good on your college applications."

Amanda rolled her eyes. "Jesus, Mom, I'm thirteen. Maybe I'm doing something just because I *want* to?"

Brooke pulled up to the middle school, Amanda springing from the Jeep before it fully stopped. As she drove away, Brooke shut off her I'm-a-terrible-mother-and-I-made-another-stupid-comment thoughts. She had school today too. Brooke didn't practice law anymore. These days, she took classes, learning something that had always interested her: making fine jewelry.

Her husband, Tripp, worked from home now. Allegedly.

She approached Silver Ore Gold, the storefront jewelry school in town where she and other students learned to create handmade jewelry from precious metals and stones. Brooke had always loved gems: emeralds, opals, and deep-blue sapphires. She couldn't afford to work with those anymore, but incorporating the less expensive and colorful semiprecious stones—dark-purple amethysts, rock crystals, and pea-green peridots—engaged her. She fabricated silver chokers with chunky blue lapis lazuli from Afghanistan, purchased garnets for some of her necklaces, or found rough ones along the train tracks in Westport that she later polished, and hammered 18-karat gold when she could afford it. She used torches to anneal and solder metal, formed and sawed gleaming silver, then blackened her pieces so they wouldn't look dainty. She felt a sense of pride creating something original from raw material. When she worked, time and her worries faded.

Her oldest daughter, Tara, would be going to college soon. Amanda, her younger one, would outgrow her teenage sass. And her marriage to Tripp was a problem she no longer wanted to fix.

Making jewelry was something that didn't involve family—it was her accomplishment alone. Jewelry rerouted her.

The school wasn't open yet, so Brooke drove to a boutique coffee shop around the corner from Main Street and parked. Most of the original boutiques that had made the town so charming were replaced by chains—the Gap, Williams-Sonoma, Ann Taylor. It was basically an outdoor mall.

When she wanted to shop, she'd drive down the Post Road and wander into antique and secondhand stores. Even when they'd had a lot of money, she still loved discovering something unique and inexpensive. Bargains she was good at.

At the coffee shop, she ordered a large cappuccino and cinnamon bun.

She gave her order and the cute twentysomething barista behind the counter smiled at her. "How are you this morning?" he asked.

He was flirting, and she liked it. "Fine, thank you."

Sitting down in an empty booth, she pulled a heavy book from her oversized tote. *Jewelry, Concepts and Technology* hit the table with a thud. She took a sip of her cappuccino and thumbed through the pages, looking for inspiration. Taking out a pencil and sketchpad from her bag, she drew a large square locket with piercing arrows she would later etch and blacken. Maybe add a topaz here or there—certainly nothing that looked Valentine's red.

When she was done, she put everything back into her tote and pulled out her blue leather Filofax. She didn't want any of those electronic calendars, beepers, laptops—she hated all of them. Her kids got exasperated if she asked how to use them. But Tripp loved that stuff. If there was a new gadget in the *Sharper Image* catalog, he bought it. More money wasted. Did he not care that they were almost broke? They had a sprawling nineteenth-century home with a carriage house, but it cost a fortune to maintain. They could barely pay the mortgage, and his refurbished 1960s sports car had chronic, expensive mechanical problems. Their bank accounts were dwindling.

Brooke took a second look inside her bag. There was one gadget there—her cell phone. She pulled it out and called her oldest friend, Elizabeth Altman. They'd grown up together in Ridgewood, New Jersey. Now Elizabeth and her family lived in Westchester County, only forty minutes away from Brooke. When she picked up, Brooke could hear Elizabeth clattering around her kitchen in a house that was probably paid for without a mortgage. "Brooke, I can barely hear you. Where are you?"

"On my cell. The reception isn't great. I have jewelry class soon, but I wanted to know if we're still on for lunch tomorrow."

"Yeah, how about the Elm Street Oyster House in Greenwich at noon?"

"Perfect. I'll see you then."

Brooke was about to say goodbye, but Elizabeth stopped her. "Wait. How are you?"

"I'm fine," she lied.

"I miss you. We'll catch up. I can't wait to see you and Tripp at our dinner party next week. He's coming, right?"

"Getting Tripp to go anywhere these days is hard, but he'll want to see you and Danny." *I hope*, she said to herself.

"We really want to see Tripp. Tell him that."

Brooke ran her fingers through her hair. Trying to cajole Tripp to just walk out the front door was a struggle. And she had to make sure he was groomed and dressed well enough to be presentable. Just thinking about it was exhausting. "I will. Hey, how are you feeling?"

"Good," Elizabeth said. "We'll talk tomorrow."

They hung up, and Brooke dropped her phone back in her bag Her stomach cramped with anxiety at the thought of Tripp at a dinner party. She looked over at the kid behind the cash register. He flashed her another smile, and she smiled back. Men had always liked her. Ever since she was a teenager, she'd had one boyfriend after another.

So why was she still with Tripp? He'd sunken into himself. He barely spoke, walking around their house in a dirty bathrobe, living on liters of soda and chocolate bars.

The first time she saw him, she'd been a student at Tufts University. She went out with friends one night to a club in Harvard Square, and there he was, playing his guitar and singing a song by Jesse Colin Young. He didn't look at the audience, concentrating only on his instrument as he sang. His voice was deep and clear. His curly dark hair, hooded green eyes, and aloof manner were irresistible.

"Oh my God! That guy, he's so hot," she told her friends.

He sat next to her at the bar after his set, and that was that. He never really asked her out; they just started doing things together. Tripp kept just the right amount of emotional distance so she constantly tried to keep his attention. She loved his spontaneity. When she thought of Tripp from the old days, it was the memory of a Wednesday in May when they'd driven down to the Cape so they could skinny-dip, then turned around and sped back to Boston. Just because it was Wednesday. He encouraged her to go to law school. When she was accepted at NYU, he moved with her to Manhattan, and they married.

Tripp had grown up in the wealthy Beacon Hill section of Boston. His older brother, Andrew, and father were both successful attorneys. Tripp's mother, Charlotte Hayworth, left the family when he was six. She had tried to become an actress in Boston, appearing in some local TV ads, but her husband didn't encourage her. Tripp said she moved to Los Angeles so she could focus on her acting career, and then his parents divorced. Within a year, Charlotte was cast as a wholesome doctor on a prime-time comedy. After it was canceled, she landed a leading role on CBS's hit drama, *Oak Hill*. When Brooke first met Tripp, his mother had become a household name.

For ten years, Tripp and his brother had split their time between coasts. They lived with their father in Boston but spent summers and vacations with Charlotte. When he was fifteen, Tripp stole his mother's car and crashed it on the Santa Monica Freeway. An accident, the papers said. Tripp was lucky he had only broken his arm. Charlotte was quoted in the media saying, "My son needs to grow up. He has emotional issues that his father and I are trying to address." That was the end of Tripp's relationship with Charlotte. He refused to visit or take her calls.

In New York, Brooke had passed the bar and worked for Legal Aid. Tripp and a friend started a tech company and made a fortune when they sold it. The big apartment, the two daughters. Everything was fine, and then Tripp began to change. *Maybe we both did*, Brooke thought as she sipped her coffee. The man who would walk down Third Avenue with Amanda on his shoulders and Tara swinging from his arm had stopped engaging with his family. No more cheering Tara on at soccer games. He wouldn't come to parent-teacher conferences. Brooke's conversations with him amounted to who should do what errand.

"I have a coke problem," he'd told her one night when he came home from the office.

Her stomach had clenched. "What?" When did this happen? How had she not known? Before the girls were born, they'd both dabbled in drugs, but not since. A joint, occasionally. She was furious at herself for not noticing what he'd been doing.

He was later admitted to an outpatient rehab program, and she'd wavered between supporting and resenting him. She thought she still loved him, but she didn't like him. His recovery was steady, and they both tried to rebuild their marriage. They sold the Manhattan condo and bought a house in Westport.

Two years later, they'd been eating dinner when he clutched his chest in searing pain.

The 911 call, the ambulance, and the hospital. Only thirty-seven, and he'd had a heart attack. She went from resenting him to silently pleading that he wouldn't die. When he was released a few days later, her maternal instincts took over. She made sure he took his medicines, booked his doctor appointments, ate well, and exercised.

His health had improved for a few months, but over time, he became despondent. He stopped eating well and exercising. She asked him why he wasn't going to his consulting jobs in Hartford and Stamford. He said he was working from home, although he was never at a desk when she was there. As for his health, he was fine, and she should lay off. She was sick of Tripp.

Brooke pushed out of the booth and walked back to her car. The snow had stopped, the sun was shining, and the temperature was rising. She stared at herself in the coffee shop window: olive-green sweater, boyfriend jeans hanging on her hips, long blonde hair pinned up loosely. She drove toward Silver Ore Gold, focusing on the locket she'd designed.

The class this morning was on stone-setting. After it was over, Brooke stayed for bench time. She could come whenever she wanted to use the school's tools on her own designs. If she needed a little help, she consulted the owner or other students. She began to work on her piece and found herself in the flow. Hours passed like minutes till finally her stomach began growling. It was five o'clock, and the owner was shutting off the torches.

On her way home, she stopped at a market to pick up gourmet salads for dinner. Amanda was still at her friend's house, and Tara was already in the kitchen, setting the table, when Brooke walked in. "Hi, honey. Where's Dad? How was your day?"

Tara gave her a kiss and quick hug. "Dad's upstairs, working. I'm good. Making more lists for colleges. Reaches, targets, and safeties."

"Which ones?" They had visited a few over the last couple of weeks, but Tara didn't like any of them.

She put the plates on the table. "I'll let you know when I know."

Brooke nodded and opened a bottle of sparkling water. If she asked more questions about college, her daughter would only get annoyed and cagey. She wondered if Tara had the grades to get into a top-tier school. And if she did, did they have the money to send her to one? "You'll find the perfect school. And if you don't like it, you can always transfer."

"Right."

The kitchen had been remodeled a few years ago with granite counters, adding a contemporary accent to the house. But no one was making an effort to keep it clean. Rosaline, their housekeeper, was coming in only once every two weeks, and it showed.

Brooke used to enjoy making large meals for the family. Now that they were all on different schedules with different eating habits—Tara was a vegetarian and only drank skim milk, Amanda liked steak and chicken, and Tripp ate crap—she kept the fridge stocked with microwavable food everyone could just grab.

After they finished eating, Tara put their plates in the dishwasher. Brooke said, "I'm going to the carriage house to work."

"I'll go pick Amanda up from her friend's," Tara said.

"Thanks. Love you."

"See you tomorrow, Mom. Love you."

Brooke walked across the lawn to the carriage house where she had her studio. She had set up a jewelers' bench with her pliers, rulers, jars of clasps, and spools of wire, and torches. The previous owner had painted it blue. A hooked rug with a seascape design graced the floor. There was a queen-size bed, dresser, reclining chair, and bathroom with a shower. She kept some snacks and water bottles in a small fridge so she wouldn't have to walk back to the house. It would be cold tonight, but her carriage house would be warm. And so would the big house, thanks to her.

Last month, they'd received their third notice from Connecticut Light and Power. The bill was over $1,000, and Tripp was responsible for paying it. However, Amanda found it crumpled on the floor in a corner of the kitchen. When she showed it to Brooke, it took everything Brooke had to pretend not to be surprised. "Don't worry, I'll pay it. Dad probably didn't look at it and thought it was junk mail."

"And then he threw it in the corner of the kitchen?"

"I'm sure it was a mistake," Brooke said. She didn't look at her daughter; just quickly took out her checkbook and made a show of being responsible.

Brooke felt a wave of revulsion toward herself. Why had she covered for Tripp? Why didn't she tell her daughters the truth—that their father wasn't a reliable adult? Obviously, they knew it. She wasn't being fair to the girls, pretending he was okay when they could see he wasn't. Suddenly, she was too tired to work. Instead, she lit a candle and changed into an old T-shirt and sweats. There were a pad and pen on her night table. Idly, she wrote the initials *BAT*. Brooke, Amanda, and Tara.

CHAPTER FOUR
Nick Gallagher

New York City

Nick turned on the radar detector and raced his blue Porsche 911 down the Merritt Parkway, trying to beat his record time from Greenwich to Midtown. The average was an hour; he was aiming for fifty minutes. It wasn't rush hour, so it should be doable.

Sound's offices were located on East Fiftieth Street, on the twenty-second floor of the Swiss Bank Tower. The reception area was lined with black-and-white photos of Russian men in steam baths, taken in the Little Odessa section of Brooklyn. He looked more closely at the pictures. The men were maybe in their seventies—overweight, balding, and seemingly jolly.

Joe Noonan appeared minutes after the receptionist called, greeting Nick with a bear hug. The guy was six four, just a few inches taller than Nick. He had a head of curly red hair and a booming voice. Joe smelled of cologne. *Something reminiscent of high school*, Nick thought. *Brut or Aramis.* They'd met when they were both young executives. Nick and Joe were friendly adversaries, offering each other advice when it didn't hurt their respective business interests.

Joe walked Nick through halls lined with more art, selectively arranged orchids, and a few assistants talking softly into phones or clicking on their computers. From his corner office, there were spectacular views of Rockefeller Center to the west and the majestic spires of St. Patrick's Cathedral to the north. Joe's office was oddly arranged, but then, he was a true believer in feng shui.

Nick stretched out in a gray tub chair facing Joe, who was behind his antique cherry desk with all its secret drawers. The wall was covered with *Sound* covers from the last two years—NSYNC to Jewel. Nick wasn't impressed. The covers could be bolder and more reader friendly. A good editor would know what to do, but Joe wasn't particularly interested in editorial. He cared about the bottom line. Nick believed provocative covers, cover lines, and thoughtful editorial was the only way to make money.

Joe said, "I'm ready to sell."

"Why?"

"*Sound* sales are up. Advertising sales are soft, but they always have been. I want out while the magazine is still profitable."

Nick nodded. "Who's your biggest competitor?"

Joe grinned. "We don't have competitors."

Nick waited.

"*Spin*, not *Rolling Stone*."

They discussed the high price publishers were paying for prime real estate in supermarket rack space. "Subscription sales are steady," Joe explained, "but you never make money on those; besides, the post office is going to have another rate hike." Joe didn't want to live through that again. He wanted to retire and spend more time at his winter home in Hilton Head. "I'm not you, Nick. Breaking out into other media, having your picture show up in the trades—and not always with your wife." He grinned.

Nick gave Joe a cold stare. He didn't appreciate the comment about his personal life.

Joe looked away. "So, how much do you think I could get for it?" He had paid $4 million.

Nick appraised him. "Give me all your newsstand reports, the subscription numbers, earnings, taxes, payroll. I'll look them over with my accountant and get back to you next week."

"What does your gut tell you?"

"My gut tells me you made a good investment. You'll make a lot of money when you sell it."

Joe didn't hide his satisfaction.

Nick put the papers in his briefcase and walked up Sixth Avenue, past the Museum of Modern Art to Fifty-Fifth Street and Seventh Avenue for a good pastrami sandwich. At the Carnegie Deli, he fantasized about buying *Sound*. What would it be like to be in the magazine business again? What if he had a job to go to every day that consumed him? Would it be better than retirement and how irrelevant he felt?

He walked back to the garage where he'd parked his car. Tomorrow night was dinner with that actress, Isabella Fletcher, and her husband, and Nick wasn't looking forward to it. He'd met her when he was interested in creating a new talk show for ABC. His company was invested in a wide range of media. He never did the deal with ABC, but when they gave him a tour of their Manhattan studios, he'd watched Isabella sobbing it out on the set of *One Life to Live*. She was gorgeous, but her acting was terrible. When they were introduced, she shook Nick's hand and gave him a big capped-tooth smile, whispering that she hoped to get to know him better. He later had sex with her a few times in a hotel down in the Village. Once she realized he wasn't going to help move her career along, she suddenly became very guilty about cheating on her husband and said she had to recommit to her marriage. "No problem," Nick had said. He found her vacuous. That was five years ago.

Last month, he had been thinking about ABC again when he remembered Isabella liked to gossip about the network. Maybe she had some information he would find useful. He called her and suggested the two couples have dinner. She said she'd love it. Now he regretted ever contacting her. He shouldn't have invited someone he'd once gone to bed with—and her husband—to dinner. Even if he didn't care about Isabella, it was crass and unlike him. And disrespectful to Susan.

But he was eager to see Elizabeth and Danny Altman next week.

Nick had known Elizabeth since the seventies when they were both single in the city. They met at a pickup bar, drank a lot of vodka, smoked some hash, and ended up in bed. She was hot and a little wild. She was also smart, talented, and beautiful. They tried a friends-with-benefits relationship, but neither of them was comfortable with it. They left the sex behind and just became close friends. Both were from New Jersey, and they bonded over their shared love of music. When she bought a new Billy Joel or Rolling Stones album, he would come to her tiny apartment in Chelsea, and they'd dissect every lyric. Then they'd use the album cover to clean pot and smoke it.

Nick used to worry that Elizabeth made herself available to men too easily. Maybe he had simply been jealous, but he thought he was protecting her. He wished she didn't waste her time on guys who couldn't appreciate her depth or intelligence. At the time, Nick had been slowly purchasing a portfolio of small trade magazines, with his father as his backer. Elizabeth had been a freelance journalist. When either of them had a lover, they shared details. Nick liked smart, beautiful women, but if Elizabeth thought they were too needy or trying to use him, he'd listen. More than once, he'd broken up with a woman because she was right.

Nick thought Elizabeth had disastrous taste in men. The ones whom she claimed were great in bed were also the ones who broke her heart. When she met Danny Altman, a native of Cleveland and managing director at a boutique investment banking firm, Nick was relieved. Danny was the only man he had ever thought was good enough for his friend.

Years later, when he'd bought *The Street*, a gritty fashion magazine where Elizabeth had become editor in chief, their friendship deepened. Nick had four brothers, but Elizabeth was his honorary sister. She was skeptical when Nick started dating Susan, a born and bred, private-school-educated New Yorker. Elizabeth thought she was entitled and rude. Nick disagreed—Susan was ambitious, and her imperious behavior was a cover. Underneath all that toughness, she was a vulnerable, committed woman.

Now they were all married with kids and big houses in the suburbs. Elizabeth was diagnosed with multiple sclerosis and stopped working. She did a little freelance writing and editing, but she refused to run a magazine again. *But Elizabeth isn't that sick,* he thought. The last time he saw her, she'd looked radiant. If he bought the magazine, could he convince her to come back? One more success for the both of them?

CHAPTER FIVE
Elizabeth Altman

Chappaqua, New York

In the master bathroom of her crazy jigsaw puzzle of a house, Elizabeth was scrunching her curls. As soon as she finished, she would leave for her lunch date with Brooke. They had been friends since third grade, but there had also been long absences during those years.

She applied her lipstick, flashing back to the last two weeks before they'd left for college. It had been a crescendo to the best summer they ever shared. On warm nights, they would take Elizabeth's old Ford Torino and drive north on the Garden State Parkway, listening to a new singer-songwriter named Bruce Springsteen belt out "Rosalita" on the radio. They'd park at the Montvale Dairy Queen, order chocolate sundaes, and flirt with the boys who were there to check out the girls. They'd whisper to each other about the boys' bodies, muscled by summer jobs working construction. The boys would show off their new Firebirds or Camaros. Sometimes, Elizabeth and Brooke would take rides with the cuter ones and have fumbling sex in the backseats.

When they'd gone off to school on opposite coasts, their friendship drifted. During summer breaks, Brooke was no longer interested in listening to Bruce, getting high, or driving in cars with the wind in her hair. She tried to act more mature. Elizabeth found this new version of Brooke, with her self-conscious manners and precious vocabulary, phony.

After Brooke married Tripp, Elizabeth had visited them at their apartment on the Upper East Side and was struck by how large it was, so … adult. All her other friends who had been lucky enough to rent apartments in the city had roommates or lived in little studios by themselves, like she did. Their walls were decorated with posters and some hanging plants near the windows, if there was enough light to keep them alive. But Brooke and Tripp's place had oriental rugs, hardwood floors, and tufted sofas and chairs. There was real art on the walls.

Her conversation with Brooke had been stilted at first, but eventually, they found their way back into the rhythm they'd once shared. "We hit pause. Now we're back on play," Elizabeth said brightly.

Elizabeth loved Brooke like a sister, but sometimes, she hated her like one too. At the moment, she loved her—but there was something about Brooke that made Elizabeth feel … insufficient … and she didn't know why. Elizabeth had a solid, noisy, functioning family. Her eight-year-old, Claire, and six-year-old, Justin, kept her active. She adored her husband, Danny. Their marriage was still loving and erotic. She'd built a bigger career than Brooke, if that even mattered. So what was it? Elizabeth knew she was pretty. Danny said beautiful. Her copper hair had natural ringlets. Her skin always looked bronzed. Her eyes were a hypnotic green, the kind of hue most people couldn't get without colored contacts. Steroids for MS had caused her to have cataracts, and the surgery to repair them left her pupils with a particular shine. In a certain light, they appeared cat-like. Her eyes were the thing.

Next to Brooke, though, Elizabeth sometimes struggled to keep her confidence. It was as if Brooke were always the A student, and next to her, Elizabeth felt like a B. Maybe an A-minus on a good day. Brooke never had to work on her looks. Her style came easily to her. Elizabeth, who had once edited a fashion magazine (for God's sake!), felt less secure in the way she put herself together. She knew that whatever she wore today for their lunch, Brooke would look chicer. She chose a pair of all-purpose black Ralph Lauren pants, a graphic T-shirt, and a long-cut velvet jacket. But her shoes were very cool—black flats with tiny embroidered silver feet running across them. *Anyway*, Elizabeth thought cheerily, *my feet are much smaller than Brooke's.*

* * *

Greenwich, Connecticut

Elizabeth entered the Elm Street Oyster House at noon. The hostess led her to a table where a waiter took her order of iced tea. She accepted a menu and glanced around. There were a couple of businesspeople at the other tables and young women with shopping bags at their feet. Fifteen minutes later, Brooke arrived. She was wearing a vintage embroidered peasant shirt and faded blue jeans. Her hair—getting blonder by the year—hung several inches below her shoulders with wispy bangs cut long enough so if she wore her reading glasses, she could indulge in her habit of pushing them off her face. On her right wrist was a charm bracelet she had made for herself. It dangled with gold bowling pins, little bowling balls, and chess pieces. Elizabeth had seen the bracelet before and loved it. Without her trendy shoes, she would have felt matronly next to her friend. "You know I love that bracelet," she said as Brooke hugged her.

"It's yours." Brooke started removing the toggle clasp once she sat down.

"No, keep it or sell it. My birthday is in February. You can make me a new one." Elizabeth turned sideways in her chair so her feet would show.

"Great shoes," Brooke said. "Where'd you get them? And I'm sorry I'm late. There's nowhere to park around here, and I keep forgetting that Greenwich Avenue only goes one way. The traffic cop stopped and yelled at me because I almost made a turn into oncoming traffic." She laughed.

Elizabeth laughed too. Brooke looked pale and tired.

"You want to stop by Saks after lunch?" Brooke asked. "They're having a sale."

"Absolutely."

Elizabeth ordered crab cakes, and Brooke asked for the lobster salad. The waiter smiled at Brooke, though not at Elizabeth.

"He's cute," Brooke said.

Elizabeth looked at him. He wasn't so cute. She turned back to her friend. "So, how are you?"

"I'm okay," said Brooke, "dealing with the usual. Last Wednesday, I had to call 911 because I was having palpitations and couldn't catch my breath."

"Oh jeez."

"Don't worry. It was just a panic attack. Or anxiety. I don't know. It felt like a heart attack. So I was in the ER for hours. They put you in a room, hurrying up, taking blood, and then you lie there for hours, waiting for something. By the time the results came back, I was feeling better." She bit her lip. "I guess I should be happy it was only anxiety, but my body is telling me something. Like, 'Get your shit together, or I'm gonna do it for you.'"

"That's awful," Elizabeth said, "having to go to the hospital. You must have been terrified."

Brooke nodded. "And I have Lyme disease."

"Oh honey, I'm sorry." Elizabeth squeezed Brooke's hand. "You're taking antibiotics, right? How did you find out?"

"I was lucky because I got the bull's-eye rash smack in the middle of my thigh, so I was able to get to the doctor right away. Anyway, other than the rash, I don't have any symptoms, thank God. Yes, I'm taking antibiotics. The doctor says the disease should be out of my system in six weeks."

Elizabeth was about to tell her that her son, Justin, had been diagnosed with Lyme too, and he *did* have symptoms. The first few days, he'd cry from the pain in his knees, but Brooke kept talking. "My blood pressure is ridiculously high, and honestly, I feel ashamed."

"Why would you feel ashamed?"

Brooke studied the white tablecloth. "Maybe I'm responsible for some of it. Maybe if I dealt with my marriage—"

Elizabeth interrupted her. "First of all, everyone I know has Lyme. I had Lyme. My son has Lyme."

"Justin has Lyme? That's awful."

Elizabeth shrugged. "You know how it is. Your first kid gets something, you freak out. By the time your second one comes along, it's like, 'Eh, everything will be fine.' Anyway, you live outside the city, you get Lyme. It sucks, but it's true.

"Secondly, you really think you're the only one to have an anxiety attack? I used to have one with my morning coffee." That wasn't quite true, but she wasn't immune to them. Many mornings, she woke up with a churning belly. It wasn't about her marriage, but fear of what would happen if the MS progressed.

Brooke shrugged. "Please don't say anything to Danny. Tripp and I ... it really hasn't been good." She hesitated. "Sometimes, I just want out." Brooke had told Elizabeth this before. Maybe she didn't remember. "Don't mention it to anyone, but I'm sleeping in the carriage house."

"I know," Elizabeth said. Then kindly, she added, "But why?"

"Because he's a slob! He has a thousand newspapers and magazines all over the bedroom. Computer catalogs, dirty paper plates, old soda cans, and who knows what else. It's disgusting."

"Have you spoken to him about it?"

Brooke gave her friend a *What do you think?* look. "Of course. He gets annoyed and says that's why we have a maid, but Rosaline won't set foot in there. The last time we talked about it, she showed me a cut she got on her hand from a razor blade under the bed. What's a razor blade doing on the floor in the bedroom? He's gonna slit his wrists?" Brooke raised her eyebrows. "God, I hope not. I'd have to clean that mess up too." She raised her eyebrows and smiled.

Elizabeth almost laughed.

The food came, and the waiter lingered while Brooke took a forkful of her salad. "How is it?"

Brooke looked up at him with a shy smile. "Great."

"My crab cakes are good too," Elizabeth said as the waiter walked away. Turning back to Brooke, she asked, "What does Tripp say?"

"He tells me to leave him alone. You know what makes me sad? His guitar sits in the corner of the bedroom, untouched. It used to be his outlet. Now he ignores it. Sometimes, Tara will take it into her room and play. I look at that guitar, and it hurts. It reminds me of what he once was." She shook her head as if to push the thought away. "Now he only speaks to me if I start the conversation, and even then, it's one-word answers." Brooke took a bite of lettuce. "Look, I know he cares about us, but he's become incapable of expressing it." She paused. "He acts like a spoiled child who's obsessed with his gadgets, eating junk, and I don't know what else. Tara started visiting colleges, and he hasn't come with us to see a single one. He says he's too busy." She looked directly at Elizabeth. "Too busy with what?"

Elizabeth changed the subject. "How's he feeling, physically?"

"He says he's okay, but it doesn't look that way."

Elizabeth remembered how much sexual heat Tripp had given off when she first met him. He looked like a sultry rockstar who knew he had the kind of flame that brought people into his orbit. Elizabeth felt a kinship with Tripp. He wasn't gregarious. He rarely engaged in small talk, but he was interested in what she had to say.

"I'm seeing a therapist, though," Brooke said, interrupting Elizabeth's thoughts. She took a long sip of her drink.

Elizabeth's face lit up. "That's great. I'm happy for you."

"I thought Tripp and I could go together because she's a marriage counselor. But surprise, he wouldn't come. So I decided to go alone."

"That was smart. Good for you, Brooke."

"I feel comfortable talking to her. She thinks I should leave Tripp. I mean, she doesn't say that, but I know." She shook her head. "On the one hand, I want a divorce. On the other, it's not that easy for me. I feel sorry for him. And I also hate him for making me worry about him."

Elizabeth was about to speak, but Brooke put up her hand to stop her. "I know, I know, no one can *make* me feel anything. I think that's psychobabble bullshit."

Elizabeth grinned. "Me too. But I think you should feel very proud of yourself for seeing a therapist. Worry a little less about Tripp. Take more care of yourself. You're not his mother."

"Maybe if Charlotte had done a better job—"

"Charlotte is great, Brooke. Don't knock her," Elizabeth said. "Maybe she sucked as a mother, but the woman is an *amazing* grandmother. And mother-in-law. C'mon, she adds a little glitter to your lives. How many people can say they have a TV star in the family?"

Brooke smiled. "All true."

Elizabeth took her hand. "Listen, you'll work things out with Tripp when you're ready. You've been married a long time. You have kids and a connection with him. Marriage isn't easy. You know that. But, Brooke, I don't live your life. I can't tell you what to do."

Brooke nodded. "Thanks." She crossed her arms and slid back in her chair. "Okay, enough about me. How's the MS? You look beautiful, but I know that has nothing to do with it."

Elizabeth nodded. "I had an MRI last week. No new lesions on my brain or spine."

"And your symptoms?"

"I'm having a hard time with words. Sometimes, I speak perfectly, like now. No problems. Then out of nowhere, my words fail me. Can't find them, or they won't reach my tongue." She looked away. "I hate it."

"I know, Elizabeth. I know how hard it is for you. What does your doctor say? Is there anything you can do to improve your speech?"

Elizabeth shrugged. "Speech therapy. No guarantees, but it can help. I started seeing someone in White Plains."

"I admire you," Brooke said. "You don't give up."

And there was the waiter again.

"Check, please," Brooke said. She smiled at Elizabeth. "Let's get some shoes."

After paying, they wandered across the street to Saks where Brooke tried on a pair of red leather slingbacks with four-inch heels. Gracefully, she took a few steps and turned to Elizabeth. "What do you think?"

"Those are 'fuck me' shoes."

"Then you should buy them because no one is fucking me."

The shoe salesman came over and tried to convince Brooke they were perfect on her.

"Do you have them in a seven?" Elizabeth interrupted. He brought her a pair, and Elizabeth put them on. If she walked a few steps, she'd probably fall and kill herself.

"They look great on you," Brooke said. "You should get them."

In the end, neither bought them. They just picked up some makeup at the Clinique counter because there was a giveaway and they didn't want to leave empty-handed.

CHAPTER SIX
Susan

Susan looked at herself in the mirror and was pleased. Her hairstylist had come to the house and blown her hair out, so it was full but had movement. Her manicurist had done her nails in ballerina pink, and a makeup artist she occasionally used had enhanced her face in a way that would be flattering in the dim lighting of tonight's restaurant. Her long-sleeved black dress showed off her considerable chest and hid her arms. A pair of heels gave her much-needed height. Her sapphire ring was on her right hand, a simple wedding band of round diamonds on her left. She didn't need to show off her engagement ring—the Fletchers wouldn't keep their eyes off it. She took an electric-blue clutch from her closet. It would add some pizzazz. She'd bought it at TJ Maxx when she spotted Catherine Zeta-Jones in the Runway section. If TJ was good enough for Catherine, well ....

Susan had never met the Fletchers before. Isabella was Nick's friend from the TV world. He had told the couple he wanted to get together for dinner, but he didn't schedule it. Instead, he bugged Susan for weeks to set up a date with them, and she finally remembered to do it. Where *was* Nick? In the house somewhere.

She saw him about an hour ago. She called for him over the house intercom system. "Dinner with your friends, Nick. Let's go."

She met him in the foyer. Susan could see why women were hot for her husband. He was wearing cream wool slacks and a soft white V-neck sweater Kelly had bought him for Christmas. A little too F. Scott Fitzgerald for Susan's taste, but no doubt he was the kind of man women noticed.

Elle, the French restaurant Susan had chosen when Nick nixed the one in the city, was originally a small house in the woods of South Salem, and Susan was looking forward to sampling it. When they got there, the maître d' told them the Fletchers were already seated. As they walked to the table, Susan looked around. The walls were stone, and there was a roaring fire. She'd read a *New York Times* review that said it was the only Michelin-starred restaurant outside the city. A savvy investor could do well up here if she opened a fine restaurant. Many people in Westchester and Fairfield were transplanted Manhattanites, most of whom were probably dying to spend money on a good meal.

Nick saw the Fletchers and made introductions. *God*, Susan thought. Even if a person didn't know Isabella was an actress, they had to know she was someone. Who else could look like that? The husband, on the other hand, was sort of mild looking. Horn-rimmed glasses, dark-gray suit, dark hair. Isabella had that TV star look Susan knew so well: a large head designed for camera closeups, the size-double zero body for getting hired, violet eyes—perfect for crying in those sappy screen scenes—and expertly highlighted, shoulder-length, tawny hair. She wore a sleeveless Gucci little black dress that showed off her toned arms and made Susan glad hers had sleeves. Isabella was wearing the Ferragamo pumps Susan had considered buying but passed on because they were like any other pair of heels except for the price.

A waiter came over with a bottle of pricey champagne Nick had ordered for the table. *Nice champagne flutes*, Susan noted. She turned the glass over and looked for the brand name. It was from Murano, but she didn't recognize the company. She made a mental note to explore rare glassware. She was tired of seeing the same chichi crystal on the tables of most New York restaurants. Maybe she should get some hotshot hospitality executive to help her open a restaurant. Or she could do it herself. She had $12 million dollars in her brokerage account, courtesy of her husband.

Susan pretended to listen to the table conversation, then excused herself to use the bathroom. Really, she just wanted to see if it was super clean—even acclaimed eateries failed her restroom test. This one was okay. Not quite up to her standards. She would have to ask Nick to check out the men's room.

When she returned to the table, she asked Blake Fletcher what he did for a living.

"Blake was just telling us how hard it is to offer quality care to patients, with HMOs running the system," Nick said.

"You're a doctor."

Blake smiled. "A gastroenterologist."

"Which hospital?" Susan asked.

"Lenox Hill, but I have a private practice on Park Avenue."

"How nice." Susan refrained from telling him about her hemorrhoids. She probably missed some important parts of the conversation while she was in the bathroom, but she was reveling in her fantasies about life as a restauranteur. She continued to pay close attention to the waiters, décor, and food on other people's tables. "Blake," she said. "Have you found a lot more people scheduling colonoscopies ever since Audrey Hepburn?"

The doctor looked dumbfounded.

Not a trick question, Susan wanted to say. She wouldn't let him near her intestines. "You must remember. Audrey died of colon cancer ... what? Four years ago? She was only sixty-three."

He looked away from her for a second, then pretended to know all about Audrey. "I remember. Yes," he said and nodded. "People are always more responsible about their health issues when a celebrity is involved."

"That makes sense," Susan said, smiling politely. What she thought was that the "doctor" was a pompous man who needed a quasi-famous woman to make him feel like he was important. What was the term? Oh yeah, *arm candy*.

She turned to Nick. He was asking Isabella if she was still on *One Life*.

Isabella pouted. "No, they killed me off about three months ago. My character died in a Jet Ski accident. But I'm up for several parts, one on *SVU*. It's just episodic work, but I would play a murderer, which would be so challenging. Of course, there are always offers from LA. My agent thinks I should audition out there, but I couldn't leave Blake." She looked lovingly at her husband.

Yeah, right, Susan thought. Isabella, with her made-for-TV name, was full of shit. Entertainment people could be amusing, but not this one. "Ever work with Tommy Lee Jones?" Susan asked.

Isabella looked bewildered. "No."

"Because he used to be on *One Life* …?"

Isabella's face lit up. "Oh, that's right! No one ever thought he'd make it in the business, but look at him now. You know, he was on the show maybe twenty years ago. I never watched it then. I mean, I was a baby."

"I watched it then," Susan said. She lost interest in the little actress. She had ordered duck with raspberry sauce—so had Nick and Blake Fletcher—and was looking forward to seeing the presentation.

When the food came, the duck was beautifully laid out on the plate, the dark meat on one side, the light meat on the other, and the sauce spooned judiciously with individual raspberries framing the plate. Colorful grilled root vegetables were displayed on a separate plate. As they ate, Susan and the men all seemed to be loving their food, hardly talking while they ate. Isabella pushed broccolini around her plate. *Watching her calories*, Susan thought. Isabella would probably die of cancer. If Susan owned a restaurant, she wouldn't put anything on the menu for those too-skinny women. They wasted everyone's time with their special requests. Isabella probably ate a gallon of ice cream at midnight and then threw it up, leaving her husband, the gastroenterologist, clueless.

"Susan, you have a huge smile on your face. What's so amusing?" Isabella asked.

"I didn't realize I was smiling," she lied. "I was just wondering if Blake sees a lot of bulimics."

"Not really," he said. Dr. Fletcher sounded petulant.

"Of course, I don't have that problem."

"Well, thank goodness," Isabella said.

Susan eyed Nick as he scanned the rest of the room. "Look," he said. "There's Elizabeth and Danny. I'm going to say hello. Excuse me for a moment." He got up and walked to the corner where they were sitting.

"Ask Elizabeth if there's anything in particular she wants us to bring to her dinner party," Susan added as Nick walked away. "And ask her how she's feeling." She turned to Blake and Isabella. "Elizabeth used to work with Nick at *The Street*. He sold it to someone else, who renamed it and ran it into the ground. Anyway, she's a very good editor, but she has MS now."

Isabella stared at Elizabeth, then looked back at Susan. "That's very sad," she said.

Susan cringed. The actress made everything sound like she was reading from a soap script.

"Actually, researchers are making great strides with MS now," Blake said. "All sorts of new drugs."

Susan couldn't stand him any longer. "I'm sure if there's a new drug, Elizabeth is on it." She probably sounded as annoyed with him as she felt.

Susan ate more of her vegetables while Isabella talked about her new horse, a jumper, that Blake had bought her. "Her name is Lady," she said proudly.

I wonder who the tramp is? Susan thought as she finished her duck—it had been sublime. She wanted to get the recipe for her chef if she ever got one. She'd use a different fruit sauce, of course. Although, the raspberries had been brilliant. A prompt busboy expertly cleaned the table with one of those silver brush things.

Finally, Nick came back to the table. "What did Elizabeth say?" Susan asked.

"She's doing great. Looking forward to the party next week and told me to tell you not to bring anything but yourself."

As if, Susan thought, but she nodded politely.

For dessert, they ordered coffee and crème brûlée. Susan pricked through the burnt crust. Scrumptious. She was disappointed when Blake ordered after-dinner drinks for them. The liqueur was good enough, but her feet were killing her. When the check came—in a little antique box, no less—Nick graciously grabbed the bill, and the Fletchers thanked him profusely.

Before parting, Susan noticed Isabella seemed particularly formal when she kissed Nick goodnight. She'd definitely slept with him. "Let's get together again soon," Isabella said.

"Let's not," Susan said when she and Nick were alone in the car. "That woman is beyond fake."

Nick put the car in gear. "Yeah, sorry. I forgot how dumb she was."

CHAPTER SEVEN
Elizabeth

Chappaqua, New York

Elizabeth watched her husband exit his closet, wearing a pair of Levi jeans, cowboy boots, and an aqua-colored sweater. His tousled brown hair and hazel eyes still moved her. His body didn't have an ounce of fat. He made her feel lusty. "Lose the jeans," she said.

"You love me in jeans. And don't look at me like that."

"Like what?"

"Like you want me to *literally* lose the jeans and jump into bed."

She laughed. "If there were more time, believe me …. Anyway, you look great. But I specifically told everyone no jeans tonight."

"Why? We're just having some friends over."

She put her hand on her hip. "Women like to get dressed up sometimes. Me included."

Danny groaned. "I can't believe you won't let me wear jeans in my own house."

Elizabeth smiled. "Just for tonight."

Danny returned to his closet. She followed and watched him toss the jeans on the floor on top of a pile of dress shirts. The custom-made suit he'd worn to work yesterday was hanging haphazardly over his closet door. No one would call him neat. He put on charcoal flannel pants. "Okay?"

"Now the boots."

"No, the boots stay."

She grinned. "Okay, you win."

"You look beautiful," he said. "I love your hair up. Shows off your face."

Elizabeth stepped away from the closet, glancing at herself in the mirror. She liked the way she looked too. She was wearing a pink cashmere sweater set and black silk pants. Her round diamond engagement ring and sapphire wedding band were on her left hand, and she wore four studs—two diamonds and two small rubies—in her ears.

"Here." Danny took a bobby pin from her hair, tucked up a few stray strands from the nape of her neck, and re-pinned it. He kissed her earlobe. "Perfect."

"Thanks, honey."

"Tell me again why we're doing this? Aren't you tired?"

She ticked off the reasons on her fingers. "Our friends haven't met each other. I feel like having them over. A little dinner, a little conversation, some drinks, then they're out the door." She smiled, but he was frowning. "*Danny.* I'm not going to get MS exhaustion. Stop worrying."

He didn't seem convinced but took her hand anyway, and they walked downstairs. Danny headed to the bar in the living room to set up glasses and cut slices of cucumber for sake martinis. Elizabeth walked into the kitchen where Carlotta, their housekeeper-slash-nanny, was mashing potatoes with grated parmesan.

Twenty minutes later, Susan and Nick arrived. Elizabeth greeted them at the door, which was flanked by two pumpkins she, Danny, and the kids had carved into jack-o'-lanterns. Nick was dressed in black—black sweater, pants, and shoes. Susan was wearing a flattering navy blue dress with navy suede heels. Her hair was glossy. She kissed Susan and hugged Nick.

"Hey," Nick said, hugging her back.

"You both look great," Elizabeth said. Inside the house, she took Susan's mink coat and the bottle of wine she had brought. "Not necessary, Susan but thank you. Here, follow me. Danny's mixing drinks." She led them into the living room.

As Susan and Nick went to get a drink, Elizabeth hung Susan's coat in the hallway closet, wondering how many people still wore mink. She had taken hers to the local consignment shop after Anna Wintour had been assaulted by PETA protesters. Anna had a sense of humor about it, but Elizabeth felt warned.

She joined her friends at the bar. "Sake martini?" Danny asked.

Susan took one, and Nick grabbed a bottle of beer with lime.

The doorbell rang again. Brooke and Tripp stood on the front steps, shivering in a blast of night wind. "Come in, quick," Elizabeth said. "Jeez, it's gotten so cold." She kissed Brooke, then turned to Tripp and kissed him too. He was wearing dark-brown corduroy pants and a light-blue Oxford shirt. When they were inside, she saw the circles under his eyes and his hollowed-out cheeks. Impulsively, she gave him a tight hug.

Elizabeth looked at Brooke and gave her a sly smile. "Chanel?" She was appraising the cropped purple jacket Brooke was wearing over a black tee and black jeans.

"You said no jeans, but I thought the jacket would make up for it." She moved closer to Elizabeth and whispered, "I got the Chanel at a secondhand store on Madison Avenue. I heard Jackie O. used to send her unwanted clothes there. I'll take you. They have stuff with the price tags still on. You wouldn't believe how little I paid for this."

"Tell me later," Elizabeth said, walking them into the living room where Susan and Nick were drinking. She introduced the two couples while Danny made more martinis.

"Where are the kids?" Brooke asked Elizabeth. "I have books for Justin that, of course, I left at the house. And I made a little silver heart necklace for Claire," she patted her jacket pocket, "which is here."

"They're upstairs, watching TV. Claire's going to be thrilled with the necklace. She loves everything you make."

Elizabeth saw Susan's eyes wander around the living room. Nick had been to her home a few times but never with Susan.

"Tell me about this house," Susan was saying to Danny.

"It was built about a hundred years ago, and it's been restored twice. I don't know how much of the outside you saw in the dark, but it's all stone. We love it."

"*Now* we love it," Elizabeth added, joining them.

"Elizabeth hated it when the realtor first showed it to us," Danny said. "She wouldn't even come in. She sat in the car and said it reminded her of *The Addams Family*. But the price was so low, I convinced her to come in and told her we could make it a great home. We found an architect who took twice as long as he promised, and a contractor I'd recommend to no one."

Susan smiled. "I like modern houses, but this one is very homey."

Brooke was looking around too.

"You've been here before, haven't you?" Susan asked.

"Yeah, I come a lot, but I always see something new. Those photos of Justin and Claire. When were they taken?" Brooke pointed to the kids playing on a beach.

"Our family trip to Club Med last year," Danny said.

Susan walked over to the baby grand in the corner. "Who plays?" she asked.

"I used to," Elizabeth said. "Now Claire's getting lessons."

"It's been about two weeks. I'm guessing that by next month, Claire will be onto something else," Danny said. "She's eight. What do you expect?"

Nick laughed. "I remember when Kelly took up piano. How long did that last, Susan? Two months?"

"Six," Susan said.

****

Susan watched Nick trying to discreetly eye Brooke. *Here we go again*, she thought. Everyone avoided looking at Tripp, who seemed to have disappeared into an overstuffed chair.

Brooke took a sip of her martini and turned to Danny. "This is great. What's in it?"

"Vodka and sake instead of vermouth."

Susan nodded at Brooke. "I agree—it's delicious." She took the stem of her martini glass and twirled it. "I never had a cocktail with a cucumber slice. And I like the way you cut it—like a lemon slice."

"I had one at a Japanese restaurant. Just copied it."

"Well, you excel at copying," Susan said.

Brooke held up her glass. "Cheers."

Nick stood beside her, and they clinked glasses.

Brooke finished her martini and asked Danny for a refill.

While she was waiting for her drink, Susan took a hard look at Brooke. She was very pretty. And thin. Susan turned her eyes to Tripp, Brooke's husband. His skin was pasty, and he twitched a lot. He looked bored. Maybe he was taking everything in, amused by the people around him. Susan had seen those kinds of people before. Pretending not to care, then suddenly offering a sardonic comment. Why were so many attractive women with loser men? Probably so they could have the starring roles in their own homes.

Turning to Elizabeth, Susan said, "I'd love a tour."

"Sure."

Susan looked at Brooke again. "You wanna come too?"

"I've been. You'll love the rest of the house."

Elizabeth led Susan into the wood-paneled library. There was another massive fireplace, more books, and an antique Chinese rug. A black leather Chesterfield couch dominated the room. She pointed to a painting of sunflowers set against a brilliant blue sky. "Danny and I like to buy paintings when we travel. We got this one in Nice a few summers ago."

They moved from a well-used family room into a kitchen with a blue-and-white ceramic backsplash. The floor was dark wood.

Carlotta was making a salad at the granite counter. Susan followed Elizabeth to the stairs where the bedrooms were. She held on to the railing, walking slowly, and Susan followed cautiously. "Are you okay?" she asked.

"Yeah, fine. I want you to see the upstairs."

"Let's go back down," Susan said. All she needed was for Elizabeth to tumble backward. Dealing with the snake had been enough drama.

Elizabeth nodded and turned. "You're right. The kids are quiet. They don't need grownups disturbing them. I should check on dinner."

"I'm going back to the bar. I want Danny to make me another one of those martinis."

"Be careful," Elizabeth said, smiling. "They're stronger than they taste."

"Good."

Susan settled in the living room where Danny was talking to Nick, who'd just explained his interest in purchasing *Sound*. She watched them from her seat on the couch, sipping her second martini.

"You want my wife to work for you again," Danny said.

"Your wife is a magazine miracle worker."

"True. But she could use some miracles herself. All that work and stress could put her back in the hospital."

Nick shook his head. "I'd never put that kind of pressure on her."

From across the room, Susan said, "Don't you think Elizabeth should make the decision herself?"

Danny looked at Susan. "Of course she can make the decision herself."

Susan looked at her husband. "So, honey, when did you decide to buy the magazine without consulting me?"

"I would never do that."

Susan turned to Danny. "I think Elizabeth would tell you if she was too sick to work, don't you?"

"Maybe," Danny said.

Nick sat next to Susan, putting an arm around her. She shrugged him off. "Anyway, there isn't any work," Nick said to Danny, "because I haven't decided to buy it." He quickly corrected himself. "*Susan* and I haven't decided to buy it yet."

"Did you make an offer?" Tripp asked.

Nick startled. Susan could tell he'd forgotten Tripp was in the room. Now, he was sizing Tripp up, probably remembering Elizabeth had said he'd made a fortune before he was thirty. "No, not yet. The guy who owns it paid four mil. Now it's probably worth double."

"But Nick is cheap when it comes to business," Susan added. "He'll bargain it down."

"My kind of man," Tripp said, smiling weakly.

* * *

When Elizabeth walked into the kitchen, Brooke was there chatting with Carlotta who was bringing a roasted turkey out of the oven.

"Carlotta, it's beautiful," Elizabeth said, looking at the food.

"It really is," Brooke added. She picked up a mixing bowl on the counter with ingredients for making a salad dressing and began whisking together olive oil, balsamic vinegar, lemon, and herbs. "Susan seems interesting," Brooke said. "Where did you find her?"

"She comes with Nick. I've known him for like centuries. I'm surprised you never met him before. Maybe we weren't hanging out in those days."

"If I had met him before, believe me, I would have remembered. He's very cool. And sexy."

Elizabeth gave her a look. Something about Brooke calling Nick sexy made her uncomfortable. She shook it off. "We became friends after college. When I was working at *The Street*, he bought it. Then he met Susan, so she's part of the package."

Carlotta was arranging a platter of roasted vegetables.

"Carlotta, do you want me to ask Danny to carve the turkey?" Elizabeth asked.

"No, I'm an expert."

"I love this kind of dinner," Brooke said, looking at the mashed potatoes. "Nobody worries about calories or cholesterol."

"Tripp looks too thin," Elizabeth said.

"It's incredible, considering what he eats. Cap'n Crunch for a snack, an entire coffee cake before lunch, soda by the gallon. Just junk food all day. Your dinner is healthier than anything he's eaten in a year."

"You're exaggerating." Elizabeth glanced around the kitchen once more and said, "All right, it looks like everything is ready. I'll go let everyone know."

Elizabeth led her guests to the dining room. The walls were painted a dramatic red gloss. The formal table was mahogany and the chairs, Chippendale. A Persian rug was under the table, and a crystal chandelier hung above. "Brooke, you sit next to Nick, Tripp, you sit next to Susan, and I'll sit next to my husband." Danny was already at the head of the table.

"I'll sit next to him too," Brooke said.

"You sit between both of them," Elizabeth said, referring to Nick.

Carlotta brought out the salads and dressing, and they began eating.

Susan took a forkful of lettuce. "So, Tripp, I heard you were one of those millionaires under thirty that *Forbes* likes to write about. And now you don't work. What's that like?"

Elizabeth shot a glance at Nick, who glared at his wife.

Tripp seemed amused. "I work," he said. "I just do it from home."

Susan gave him a skeptical look. "Really?"

"Susan, stop," Nick said.

"It's okay," Tripp said to Nick. He was smiling.

Susan continued. "And didn't I hear you had a heart attack? Aren't you kind of young for that?"

Nick put down his fork and looked at Elizabeth apologetically before staring at his wife again. "Susan."

She ignored her husband.

Tripp just grinned and turned to Susan. "I don't remember much except the pain and Brooke calling the paramedics."

"It was a much bigger deal than that. I was terrified," Brooke said.

Elizabeth saw Brooke look away from her husband and move closer to Nick.

Carlotta appeared and cleared the salad plates.

"Thanks, Carlotta," Elizabeth said.

Danny got up to help with the turkey, and a few moments later, Carlotta reappeared with two casserole dishes of mashed potatoes. Danny held a platter of sliced turkey sitting on a bed of colorful vegetables, ringed by what looked like a forest of rosemary, still on the stem.

"Carlotta, this is beautiful," Elizabeth said.

"I watched Martha Stewart on TV. She's the one who showed me how to do it." She put the turkey, vegetables, and rosemary on individual plates.

Elizabeth passed them along the table. "I love the way it looks."

"Just gorgeous," Brooke said, agreeing.

"Creative," Susan said, nodding.

"To our friends," Danny said, raising his wineglass.

Elizabeth touched her glass to her husband's and gave him a kiss.

* * *

"What's that smell?" Tripp asked suddenly.

Susan, sitting next to him said, "Rosemary."

"It smells like a candle."

Brooke raised her voice. "It does not smell anything like a candle. It smells like great food."

Quickly, Susan plucked the rosemary from his plate, and put it in a napkin. "There. Now you have nothing to complain about."

Brooke relaxed. If she was lucky, Susan could be her husband's minder tonight.

Susan leaned into Tripp. "I guess you don't like fresh herbs."

"I do. Just not those."

"So, you don't practice law anymore?" Nick asked Brooke, shifting her nervous attention away from her husband.

"No. I loved working at Legal Aid, but I stopped after I had children. I wanted to be with them."

"Susan did the same thing."

Brooke didn't say anything.

"Do you work now?" he asked.

"Not really. My hobby is metalsmithing."

Nick looked surprised. "What's that?"

"I make jewelry from different types of metals. Gold, silver, mainly. Gemstones too. "

"What do you like about it?"

"Working with diamonds, rubies, fire, chemicals."

He raised his eyebrows. "Chemicals?"

"You need chemicals to make jewelry." She stared into his eyes. "Toxic chemicals."

He grinned. "Do I need to worry about you?"

She smiled. "No, I'm not going to burn your house down."

"Good to know." He picked up his fork and began eating one of the carrots.

"If you want to worry about me, worry that every time I use one of those chemicals, I'm taking a day off my life."

"Dangerous business you're in."

She looked around the room. The other people were talking or eating and weren't listening to her. "I love danger," she suddenly whispered, then immediately felt ashamed of her own boldness. She looked at him, and he tilted his head, waiting for her to finish. Brooke blushed. "Really, it's just something I'm good at and passionate about."

"I'd like to see your jewelry."

Brooke reached into her Chanel jacket and pulled out the small heart necklace she'd made for Elizabeth's daughter. Nick put his fork down and opened his palm. She dropped it in. He wore a simple gold wedding band. His fingers were long and tapered.

Brooke had put her engagement ring and diamond wedding band in the safe last year. Now she wore a carved silver band she had made.

Nick examined the silver heart, turning it over. "Very nice." He handed it back to her and resumed eating.

Brooke straightened and glanced over at Susan. She wondered how someone as confident, handsome, and wealthy as Nick could be married to that woman. He was well mannered. Graceful. Susan seemed to enjoy being rude and provocative. Then Brooke almost laughed at herself.

I'm *the person judging mismatched couples?*

Brooke turned her attention back to Tripp. He'd hardly touched his turkey or vegetables. Instead, he was stuffing his face with mashed potatoes.

"I don't think you should wolf down your potatoes. My trainer tells me to eat mindfully and chew slowly," Susan said.

Tripp seemed to think about it. He shrugged and smiled slyly. "I was brought up in an orphanage. It was survival of the fittest."

Tripp obviously didn't know Brooke was listening. She rolled her eyes. "He definitely was *not* brought up in an orphanage."

Tripp ignored her and spoke exclusively to Susan. "Food doesn't interest me."

"Apparently, mashed potatoes interest you," Susan said.

"Well, that's an exception. I like potatoes. And pretzels, chocolate, candy bars, cake, soda—"

"Fantastic diet. My daughter had the same taste when she was four."

Tripp laughed and caught Brooke eyeing him. "Don't worry, darling. I'm not going to die."

Brooke pretended not to hear him and turned back to her own food.

Nick's hand accidentally brushed against Brooke's arm, and she quickly glanced at him. He seemed to be ignoring the conversation between his wife and Tripp. She glanced back at Susan, who was saying, "No dying tonight, Tripp. I'm wearing a new dress, and I don't want you falling on me, crushing its perfect lines."

"Got it."

"Dessert will be served in the living room," Elizabeth said once everyone was finished. "Let's go."

Brooke stood up and put her arm around Elizabeth. "Very formal tonight, Lizzy, with all this room changing. I feel like we're in some comedy-of-manners novel."

Elizabeth groaned. "I just wanted to have a nice, grown-up dinner party."

"And you are."

"And you seem to like my friend Nick," Elizabeth said, walking toward the living room.

"Don't worry, Lizzy. It's just been a while since I've had a real conversation with a man."

Before Elizabeth could say any more on the subject, she was distracted by Carlotta, who had entered the room and needed help setting the sideboard with a coffee urn, milk, and sugar. In the middle of the table was an enormous sliced strawberry shortcake covered with whipped cream. After everyone had served themselves, they found places to sit around the fireplace.

"Best strawberry shortcake ever," Brooke said. She was trying to listen to what Nick was saying—something about his house—but Tripp was taking a second serving of cake and having trouble with his fork. His hand was shaking. "Excuse me," she said to Nick. She walked over to Tripp and gently took the fork from him. She cut him a small piece of cake and put it on his plate. "Why is your hand shaking?" she asked softly.

He looked down as it trembled. "I don't know, it's not a big deal. Sometimes it happens."

"You think it could be one of your heart meds?"

"Could be. Don't worry about me. I'm fine."

She didn't think he was fine, but she sat back down next to Nick and carefully watched Tripp. Goddamn him for making her worry. She became aware that her shoulders were clenched and released them.

Tripp was eating his cake when he stopped to blow his nose. Brooke watched him as he looked at his tissue. "Blood," he mouthed to her.

She started to get up again. She was going to suggest they leave, but he shook his head at her. *No.* She sat back down.

Her stomach was cramping with anxiety, and she felt a sudden urge to use the bathroom. She put her hand on her belly and willed herself to be calm. Tripp was unwell, but she felt as if he was doing this to *her.* Was it just another sign that he wasn't taking care of himself, and she had to do it for him? Or did he have some undiagnosed disease? She would talk to him and make a call to his cardiologist in the morning. Maybe he could refer someone. She couldn't do anything about it right now. Tripp seemed to have recovered enough to eat his cake without a problem, so she turned back to Nick. He gave no indication that he had seen her interaction with her Tripp. "Sorry I left you," Brooke said to him. "I just needed to ask Tripp a question."

He took a sip of his coffee and smiled at her. "It's fine."

Brooke took a bite of her cake. "So, Elizabeth tells me you have an amazing house."

"It's big," he admitted.

Brooke found it difficult to look away from his eyes.

"Too big," he said.

"Does this *too big* house have a name?"

Suddenly, his face became serious, and the playfulness was gone. "Ever read Edith Wharton?"

"Of course."

"*The House of Mirth?*"

"Yes."

Quietly, he said, "Mine is the House of Mirthlessness."

Brooke was surprised Nick was alluding to what she'd guessed about his home life, and she wasn't sure what to say. She looked away from him just as Tripp coughed and said he wasn't feeling well. It was clear he needed to leave. Brooke stood and brushed down her black jeans, wishing they didn't have to make such a quick exit. They said "goodbye" to the other couples. At the door, Brooke kissed Elizabeth and waved to Danny, who was still seated in the living room, talking with Nick.

CHAPTER EIGHT

D r. Katherine Waxman's office was in a converted Victorian home off the Post Road in Westport. Waxman, a psychologist specializing in family dynamics, was in her midsixties. Her short auburn hair was streaked with wiry gray strands. She had warm brown eyes and a soothing voice. Brooke felt safe with her. She sat on the comfortable paisley sofa and talked about her options. Again.

"If you want to stay with Tripp and let your marriage remain the way it is, that's your choice," Dr. Waxman said.

"I don't think I want that anymore." Brooke tilted her head, then tested an idea. "Or I can have an affair. Stay in the marriage, but at least have someone I can look forward to seeing. A lover." She thought of Nick Gallagher.

Dr. Waxman nodded. "You could do that."

"Or I could divorce Tripp and hopefully have enough confidence to live alone and be happy about it."

"Is that what you want?"

"I don't know. If I were divorced, there's also the chance I could meet someone who I would love. Fully. Have a grown-up, serious relationship." She paused. "It would be nice to have a partner who had my back." Brooke explained how Tripp's behavior at Elizabeth's party had made her cringe. "He sat alone in a chair while everyone else was talking. Then he would suddenly ask a provocative question. At dinner, he criticized the food, which was great, by the way. He talked about his heart attack like it was no big deal. It felt like he was deliberately trying to embarrass me. And he did."

Dr. Waxman nodded. "Do you think he was trying to get your attention?"

"No, he was trying to upset me, and he did. He knows his behavior was rude. Mean. Immature. And he knows I feel like it's a reflection on me." Dr. Waxman was about to interrupt, but Brooke stopped her. "I know, I know, we're separate people. What he does shouldn't embarrass me, but how is that even possible?"

"I don't think it is possible," Dr. Waxman said.

Brooke looked down at the drab, mushroom-brown carpet. "Tripp doesn't care about repairing our marriage."

"Are you sure?"

"Absolutely. And he doesn't want to take care of himself. It's not just his heart. His hands were shaking at the party. All he ate were the potatoes and cake. When he blew his nose, there was blood." Brooke looked around the room, anywhere but at her therapist. "On the drive home, I asked him about his nose, and he told me the dry air must have caused it." She stared at the framed poster of flowers on the wall. "I think he's using drugs again." Finally ... she'd *finally* said out loud what had been worrying her for months.

Dr. Waxman leaned forward. "What makes you think that?"

Brooke shrugged.

"Brooke, tell me."

"I don't have proof."

"You sound like a lawyer."

Brooke laughed, releasing some of her pent-up frustration and rage. "You're a shrink. Doesn't he sound like an addict? He's too thin. His skin is pale. He eats junk food. He's zoned out and barely communicates. It's not like when he was doing coke. He was always rushing around then in a frenzy. He's using something, but I don't know what." She stared at Dr. Waxman and asked plainly, "What do you think? What kind of drugs would make him behave that way?"

"I can't diagnosis a person I've never met. Have you asked him?"

"He wouldn't tell me the truth."

Dr. Waxman shook her head. "I'm urging you to ask him. And if he's using, is it possible he's doing it in the house with your daughters present?"

Brooke stared at the doctor. Her eyes welled up. "Oh no. I have to get Amanda and Tara out of there." Her mind was swimming.

Dr. Waxman talked about waiting until Tripp seemed clear-headed enough to bring it up. "You know that addiction is a disease, right?"

"Of course."

"Is Tripp capable of being violent?"

"He's the opposite of violent."

"Okay, because if you think there's a possibility, you need to take the kids and leave. If you want to help him, you can suggest rehab."

Rehab again, Brooke thought.

"But you can't *make* him go," Dr. Waxman said. "Do you understand me, Brooke? An addict doesn't stop using unless he wants to get better and commits to getting help. It must be Tripp's decision. No enabling."

Brooke was hearing bits and phrases of what Dr. Waxman was saying, but it was overwhelming. How did she end up here, with this man? She didn't want to do the work to try and keep her marriage alive. A giddiness was rising up from her gut. If he was using again, he had crossed a line with her, and she was out. Free. *No*, she told herself. *This isn't the time to feel free.* Now was the time to provide him with support. But she was so tired of all his issues. Supportive wife, or stop letting him drag her down and get out? Tripp was a burden, not a husband. "I'm going to make an appointment to see a divorce attorney." Her own words gave her courage. "I don't want to do any of the things you're suggesting. I want to take my kids and leave."

Dr. Waxman nodded again. "Then a divorce attorney is a good idea. And if you need to talk, I'm here."

After she left her therapist's office, Brooke drove to the Westport library and assembled a group of books on addiction. She found a table where she could be alone and started to skim them. The symptoms she'd seen Tripp exhibiting seemed to coincide with a few drugs, but when she read about heroin, she instinctively knew that was the one. She was appalled. Heroin. A street drug. In her house. No one she knew had ever used heroin. In college, it had been the one drug everyone stayed away from. She wanted to call Elizabeth and tell her, but she was too ashamed.

Her persistent anxiety that no one would love her if she left her marriage, or that she would be single for the rest of her life, evaporated. If Tripp was addicted to heroin, she was out. The mixture of worry and glee bubbled up inside her again. *No one should be happy that their partner was sick*, she chastised herself. When she thought about their life together, she realized she'd married him when she was barely an adult. The first few years had been good, but she stayed almost twenty years after he'd stopped being her friend or lover. Every time she wanted to end it, she'd think of Tara and Amanda. She didn't want them to grow up in a broken home. She had tried to convince herself that Tripp would regain his spark. Now she realized she'd been lying to herself. She was on her own.

CHAPTER NINE
Elizabeth

One of the cruelest symptoms of MS for Elizabeth was when she couldn't find her words. Sometimes, she knew what she wanted to say, but her mouth couldn't force it out. Other times, she found herself stuttering or stammering, her brain's way of buying time to connect with her tongue. The worst was when she would suddenly lose her train of thought. Her neurologist said the symptoms would get better with her new medicine, and they had for a while, but then it started again. Words had been her livelihood when she was an editor, and she fought hard to prevent the disease from taking them away.

Three days after the party, Nick called and asked her to lunch. He had suggested a diner near her home, but she wanted to go into the city. A week later, she was on the Metro-North commuter train to Grand Central Station. She had a three-seater to herself and the *New York Times* in her lap. They were meeting at Michael Jordan's Steakhouse on the mezzanine of the terminal. Nick had picked the spot so she wouldn't have to walk far. Elizabeth knew he was still thinking about buying that magazine, but she was unsure how close he was to making a deal. Years ago, they had talked about creating one together. She couldn't do that now; she didn't have the stamina, nor could she commit to the project the way she would want to.

She entered Grand Central around noon and stood in awe, as always, at the architectural beauty of the station—its high ceilings with constellations, the huge arched windows, and the iron chandeliers near the Lexington Avenue exit. Carefully, she climbed the steps to the restaurant. This morning, her legs were rigid, so she held tight to the railing as other people jogged past her. She glanced up and saw Nick wave from a table. He was the only friend she could think of who valued promptness as much as she did.

"How do you feel?" he asked as he stood up and kissed her cheek. He pulled out a chair and helped her get settled.

"I'm good."

"That was a great party, by the way. Susan and I both had a good time."

"Thanks. Your wife sent flowers the next day. Very gracious of her."

He nodded. "And you look beautiful today."

Elizabeth smiled. She felt pretty and was glad Nick noticed. She was wearing a sage Armani suit left over from her days as editor in chief of *The Street*. Underneath, she had on a white T-shirt from Petit Bateau, an expensive children's clothing brand here, but Elizabeth had bought it in Paris at Monoprix, the Parisian equivalent to Woolworths with a price to match. Her natural curls settled around her neck. Her choker, designed with smooth pieces of green sea glass, had been a gift from Brooke.

"Don't get angry," Nick said, "but I ordered for you. New York strip, creamed spinach, and home fries. You're the only woman I know who loves to eat and doesn't gain weight."

"Oh, I gain plenty of weight."

"You always look good to me."

The food arrived, and Elizabeth looked at Nick mischievously. She cut a piece of steak. "Last month, I had a flare-up, and they gave me IV steroids, so I gained five pounds. I should be watching

my calories and not eating this." She pierced a potato. "Tomorrow."
She grinned.

Nick smiled.

"So what's up? You were talking to Danny about buying a new
magazine, but he didn't tell me anything other than that."

"*Sound.* I think we can compete with *Rolling Stone* if we do a
redesign and change the editorial."

"Jann Wenner would love that," she said sarcastically, referring
to the owner of *Rolling Stone.* "And who's 'we'?"

"You and me."

Before Elizabeth could say no, Nick launched into an outline of
the magazine's readership and editorial staff, what was wrong with
the articles, and covers and ad sales, and what he'd be willing to
pay. "I want you to be the editor in chief."

Elizabeth smiled. She loved that he had faith in her. "I've never
edited a music magazine," she said. "And I have MS."

"You and I know music inside and out because we're fans,
like the readers. Besides, you know a good article when you see
one. And you're queen of covers. That's what the magazine needs.
Some good writers too. Truth? You can't do anything wrong. The
magazine is a piece of shit. Any work you put into it would only
make it better."

She made a face.

"Just look at it and tell me what you think."

"No."

"Please."

"Nick, I can't come into the city every day. The commute, the
kids, and having this frigging disease. There are no warning signals.
I have relapsing, remitting MS. You know what that means because
no one has given more money to the research than you." She blew
him a kiss. "Thank you."

"You're welcome. Your MS isn't as bad as progressive. You
could stay the way you are forever. Never get worse."

"There's no guarantee. And when I get a relapse, it's not like
a cold, where you feel it coming on and take some vitamin C or

chicken soup to try and prevent it from getting worse. One day, I'm me, and the next, I can't speak a coherent sentence."

Nick smiled tenderly at her. "Don't worry about it. You'll be the boss. You decide when you come in and what you can do. Aren't you the woman who said, 'I don't work hard, I work well'? You'll find editors and an art director. They'll find photographers and writers. It's easy for you. Besides, half the top editors we know are on sales calls or TV, talking up their magazines. I'll make sure you have a car service to get you back and forth to work."

"How generous." She shook her head. He was persuasive. And part of her did want to work again and be a successful member of the magazine world. She wanted to contribute financially to her family, be a woman her kids could be proud of. Well, they were proud of her. A woman *she* could be proud of. She wanted to be a heroine. She was imagining her script. *Sickly, young (okay, middle-aged) editor, past her prime, sidelined by a chronic disease, comes back with determined force to be a winner once again.* "Yeah, but—"

"'Yeah, but' my ass. Come on, Elizabeth. Let's do this."

She gazed at Nick, her friend for decades. Could they make magazine magic one more time? "Tell me why you want to buy it," she said. "Are you looking for a toy because you're bored?"

"Maybe," he admitted. "I hate retirement. I spend my days avoiding Susan."

"That's mean."

He shrugged. "On the other hand, I wouldn't call a multimillion-dollar investment in *Sound* a toy." He took a sip of red wine. "I don't think I'll lose a dime," he said. "If you take the job, I'll make a fortune, and so will you."

She raised her eyebrows.

"You can invest in it if you want, become a partner."

Well, that's interesting, Elizabeth thought. *Danny would certainly love the idea.* "I appreciate you thinking of me and believing that I can work again." She looked at him. It had been years since she'd noticed Nick as a man rather than her friend. He really was quite handsome—his sky-blue eyes, his lanky grace. "Give me six back issues and the circulation reports. I'll take a look and tell you what I think. But that's all," she said emphatically.

"Elizabeth …."

"That's all I can promise, Nick. Ugh! I hate you for making me think about this!" She looked up at the ceiling. "Honestly? I don't think I'm up to it, even with all your pretty promises. But maybe I can find someone who is."

They were both quiet for a few minutes as she ate her spinach. She put the fork down and asked, "Do I have any between my teeth?" She smiled so he could look.

He leaned forward and touched her cheek. "Elizabeth. I. Want. You. And no, there's nothing in your teeth. I don't know why you even eat spinach. You always ask me the same question."

She smiled broadly, showing off her clean teeth. "Because I love spinach."

"I like your friend Brooke," he said.

"Now we're talking about Brooke?"

Nick shrugged.

"I saw you two flirting at my party."

"Yes, Elizabeth," he said, as if talking to a child, "no one can fool you." He took a moment before saying, "She didn't seem particularly happy in her marriage, so we have that in common."

"Do me a favor and stay away from her. If you're not worried about your own marriage, think about me. I don't need more complications in my life, and before you say it's not going to affect me, just stop."

"I'm not going to do anything that's going to complicate your life."

"That's a lie. If you get involved with her, it's going to be very stressful for me. You know that."

"Elizabeth, nothing's happened. Besides, there's a magazine to concentrate on." He smiled at her. "I'm thinking about that."

"Good."

After coffee, Nick paid the bill and handed Elizabeth a manila envelope. "Here are the last six covers, two full magazines, and the circulation numbers."

"Because you were planning on me saying yes."

He shrugged. "I've known you a long time."

She sighed, said she would look them over, and kissed him goodbye.

They'd finished in time for her to make it back to Chappaqua before the kids came home from school. Before MS, she would have taken a taxi to the Whitney Museum to see their Biennial exhibit. Afterward, she could have met Danny at his office, two blocks away from Grand Central. But these days, she was sapped.

CHAPTER TEN
Nick

Nick drove his Porsche up the Henry Hudson and merged onto the Hutchinson River Parkway. The more he thought about his conversation with Elizabeth, the more excited he was about working with her again. He imagined the two of them collaborating on covers and headlines. Elizabeth could lead a staff of editors and writers who would add irreverence to articles but also take the subject seriously. She would commission compelling interviews, not the fluff Joe Noonan put in the magazine.

He would hire an ad staff. Susan wouldn't want to be involved with the magazine at all, thank God. She was consumed with restaurants. But his wife could certainly recommend some salespeople for the business side.

He put a Doors mixed CD in the slot and listened to "Light My Fire." Jim Morrison, now there was a guy who always sold magazines. Jann Wenner had phenomenal sales when he put the dead singer-songwriter on the cover of *Rolling Stone* in 1981: "He's hot, he's sexy, and he's dead" was a cover line everyone in the business remembered. Classic. Nick mulled over the profits and losses of *Sound*. He would offer Joe Noonan $5 million and be willing to go as high as six. That would be fair to them both.

His mind wandered to Brooke Hayworth. She was very beautiful, but there was also a sadness about her. She'd said she was a lawyer. Or was it a jewelry maker? A metalsmith, she'd called herself. He said the word aloud and liked the way it sounded. Metalsmith. That moment at the dinner party, when she'd placed the heart in the palm of his hand. Why had she done that? He wanted to see her again. He imagined Brooke with Tripp. They didn't go together. Tripp struck Nick as sly. But he was also clearly ill. It must have been terrifying for the two of them when Tripp had a heart attack. Was that why he looked so unhealthy? His skin was gray. *Didn't make sense*, Nick thought. The heart attack was years ago. Wouldn't he look healthier by now? *Not my business*, he decided.

Morrison was singing "Love Her Madly" now. Nick tapped the steering wheel along to the beat. He wondered if Danny would try to convince Elizabeth that her health had to come first and she shouldn't work at the magazine. He might, but Elizabeth was like Susan when it came to her career. She would listen, but she'd make up her own mind.

CHAPTER ELEVEN
Elizabeth

That night, after she and Danny had put the kids to bed, Elizabeth stood in her home office, contemplating the group of *Sound* covers she had placed on the floor. Her arms were crossed as she eyed each one critically.

A half hour later, Danny joined her. "I didn't know where you were," he said.

"Because you fell asleep in front of the TV." He was about to reply, but she cut him off. "I know, I know, you had a long day."

He looked at the covers with her, something he used to do when she'd been an editor.

"Covers for *Sound*, the magazine Nick wants to buy."

Danny cocked his head to the side. He picked up the January issue with Jewel on the cover. "Boring," he said as he scanned the cover lines and photo. "Jewel is beautiful. This photograph doesn't do her justice." He put it back on the floor and turned to her. "You want to go back to work?"

She pursed her lips. "I can't go to an off …" she stammered. She knew the word but couldn't say it. *Office* was in her brain, but it wouldn't reach her tongue. She looked at Danny.

He gave her an encouraging smile. "Do you want me to say it for you?" he asked gently.

She shook her head, no.

"Breathe," he said.

Office, she said to herself. *The word is* office. *Say* office. "Office!"

Danny smiled.

"Where was I?" She was momentarily confused. He didn't interrupt. "I know. I can't go to an *office* every day, but if I could help remake this magazine and work flexible hours, I think I would like it. It could be ex ... exhilarating to be part of the creative process again."

He put his arm around her. "Lizzy, is this conversation stressing you? Is that why you're having trouble with your words?"

"I don't know."

"I think maybe that's it."

She wasn't sure.

"Look, you were conflicted about your career even before you were diagnosed. I remember it, Lizzy. If you were at work, you thought you should be with the kids. If you were with the kids, you thought you should be at work."

"It's called being the mother of small children."

He shrugged. "If you think you can do it, you should. The kids love Carlotta, and we know we can trust her if anything came up on the spur of the moment. Claire and Justin think she's their second mother."

"I'm their *only* mother!" Elizabeth snapped.

"I just meant that you don't have to worry about them with Carlotta here."

"That's not what it felt like."

Danny sighed. "Whatever you decide, I'm behind you." He kissed her neck. "I'm going to bed."

After Danny went to sleep, Elizabeth wandered around the house, returned some emails, and took another look at the magazines, reading some articles this time. Nick had been right.

The photography was bland. Many of the pieces were hack jobs. With the right editorial lineup, real journalists who were serious about music, and an editorial staff who respected the reader, she could improve *Sound*. And if Nick was willing to let her make her own hours and be flexible, she could have a career again. The disease wouldn't control her life.

When she was first diagnosed with MS, Elizabeth had been relieved. Finally, the symptoms she experienced had a name. For years, she had been looking for a doctor who could explain what was happening to her. They didn't know why her arms tingled—a herniated disc in her neck?—or why she stuttered intermittently (find a speech therapist). They were puzzled by her chronic exhaustion. The occasional but searing pains in her legs confounded them. Her tests were all normal. Finally, a neurologist at NYU compared a year-old brain MRI with her new one. He showed her the lesions on her corpus callosum and made the diagnosis. Elizabeth's initial relief quickly turned to fear. Would Danny leave her?

He'd been insulted when she asked. "What kind of jerk do you think I am? And yeah, I'm still attracted to you. I'll be making love to you till the last day of my life."

"What if I end up in a wheelchair?"

"Then I'll push the wheelchair."

She'd hugged him tightly. Tears were in her eyes.

Danny was her rock, now and forever.

CHAPTER TWELVE
Brooke

Brooke moved into the guest room in the main house. She didn't want her daughters alone with Tripp. What if a dealer showed up in the middle of the night while she was in the carriage house? What if he overdosed? As for leaving, now wasn't the time. Better to stay than uproot everyone's lives.

She decided not to consult a divorce lawyer for now. Her girls knew their parents weren't sleeping together. When they'd asked her why, she was only partially honest. "When Dad decides to clean up the bedroom, I'll move back in."

"Why don't you clean it?" Amanda had asked. "Or Rosaline?"

"Why don't you, Amanda?"

"Because it's not my job! And it's disgusting."

"Exactly."

Brooke had been jarred when Tara asked her last week why she was still married to Tripp. "He's your father; we're a family," she'd said.

"You think this is a family? It's not how you grew up."

Tara had been right. Brooke didn't know what to say.

"Mom, if you're not happy, you shouldn't stay with him. Honestly? I'd feel better if you were divorced. At least we'd stop pretending. I hate living like everything is fine when it's not."

Brooke had looked away.

"Mom, when are you going to admit that staying married to Dad has nothing to do with Amanda or me? You won't leave him because you don't want to."

That had stung. "It's more complicated than that," she murmured.

The next morning, Brooke sat at her jewelers' bench in the carriage house. She picked up a six-inch piece of silver and a black felt marker. How to leave Tripp? Her left hand drew a dagger on the metal. She took out her saw and carefully inserted a long, thin blade. Putting the metal over the V in her bench, she carefully began to cut around the edges of the design. When the saw got stuck in the silver, she gently moved it out, making sure not cut herself, and rubbed the teeth with candle wax so it would cut more smoothly.

"You are married to a heroin addict," she said aloud.

She'd expected the words to free her, but they didn't. She put the silver aside, took a piece of paper out of the drawer, and sketched a choker of daggers. She transferred the picture onto the silver and continued to saw.

Brooke imagined Tripp in the big house, wearing a soiled bathrobe, eating a bag of chips, sprawled out on the couch in the den, watching his mother on television. He constantly criticized her acting. "She's over the top. All that drama, the long pauses, flashing eyes when her character is angry. Her range is limited. She'd never make it in film."

"You spend a lot of time watching her, considering how awful you think her work is," Brooke had said. He ignored her.

Brooke thought Charlotte was a fine actress, especially considering the kind of show she was on. *Oak Hill* reminded Brooke of *Dallas*—addicting and fun. Her girls adored it. They were crazy about their grandmother.

Every time Charlotte visited New York, Tripp wouldn't see her, but Brooke and the kids did. She took them to plays—always house seats—trendy new restaurants, even tea at the Plaza Hotel when the girls had been little. If Charlotte was surrounded by autograph-seekers, she would sign all the pieces of paper people pushed at her while her granddaughters beamed.

Charlotte offered the girls advice on makeup and boys and told them racy stories about Hollywood actors. Having a famous grandmother made them popular in school. In fact, the only time they had friends over was on Thursday nights when *Oak Hill* aired. Brooke watched the way Tara and Amanda behaved when Charlotte was on TV. They basked in her reflected glory.

Charlotte played a commanding, steely-eyed matriarch who oversaw the family's Big Pharma business. Brooke admired her looks. Charlotte was one of those women who looked beautiful with silver hair. It was bright, short, and stylishly cut. Her eyes were deep blue. Her cheekbones were high, and her skin was always tan but never leathery. She was tall with a regal bearing. Clothing hung gracefully on her body. She was the definition of a woman well aged.

Tripp used to tell Brooke outrageous stories about his mother. She was an alcoholic, she slept around. She lost all her money. When Brooke asked him how he knew all this—since he never talked to her—he said his father had told him. *Liars*, Brooke thought now. *He and his father were liars.*

She stretched her back and realized she was hungry. She walked across the lawn to the main house to make herself something to eat. Tripp was pulling a brownie and cream soda from the refrigerator.

Ask him, she thought. *Ask him what he's using. Have the conversation, you coward.*

"I don't remember buying that garbage," Brooke said. "Is that what you're having for lunch? Sugar and more sugar?"

"Yes."

She pulled a can from the cupboard. Her stomach was churning with nerves. "I'll make a tuna salad." Her hands were shaking so badly, she nicked her finger opening the can. She put it under the faucet to stop the blood.

Tripp didn't notice. "Enjoy the salad; I'm fine," he said. He turned his back to her and took his food into the den, where she saw him put a video cassette in the VCR and his mother come on the TV.

She couldn't continue to live like this and hate herself for it. She finished the tuna, washed her dish, and walked out. Once in the Jeep, she drove to town and looked for a pay phone.

CHAPTER THIRTEEN
Susan

On Friday, Susan rolled out of bed at nine o'clock. She'd heard Nick get up a while ago. She knew he was headed to the city, probably to meet some woman. She really didn't care. Let Nick figure out his own life. She was going to open a restaurant! The final impetus had been those little rosemary sprigs that decorated the turkey at Elizabeth's party. She loved food, but she also appreciated the way it could be presented.

She showered and selected a pair of jeans. She slipped them on. *Oh my God*, she thought, *they're a size ten and fit perfectly!* She'd gone down a size since she'd started working out regularly and eating slowly. Now she was even more motivated. She found a navy cotton shirt and bravely tucked it in. She looked at herself in the mirror and grinned. Nope. No need to cover her belly.

Susan pressed the house intercom button in her room. "Maria, please make me a cup of coffee and a scoop of cottage cheese." Jenna would be proud of her breakfast choice.

Susan sat down at her bedroom desk and took out a yellow legal pad and pen to make a list:

- Find someone who owns a restaurant and interview him about the plusses and minuses of the business.
- Find a superb executive chef and sous chef. Dessert chef too.
- Scout for a perfect location.
- Get an expert waitstaff from the city.

She put her pen down and thought. It was hard to find really good waiters in the burbs. And would a professional be willing to travel from New York City? She would have to call around. She went back to her list:

- Find out how much this business is going to cost.

She doodled on the paper. Maybe she could find some celebrity investors. It would add buzz to the place. Nick knew people. She would ask him. Susan looked over her list. Yes, opening a restaurant was the exactly right thing to do. Today, she'd start looking at locations.

She wrote down the name of some villages that seemed promising, then called Carly Leahey at Roundview Real Estate. She had been the one who found them the land where they now lived. When she picked up, Susan dove right in. "I'm looking for property to build a restaurant, want to help out?"

She imagined Carly salivating at the thought of the 6 percent broker fee she would collect. Susan had little patience for real estate people.

Carly said she would do some research, then clear the day so they could look at properties together.

Susan said, "Be at my house at one." After hanging up, she ran down the stairs and straight into her daughter, Kelly. "What are you doing home? I'm so glad to see you!" She threw her arms around her daughter.

"I wanted to surprise you and Dad. I don't have classes Monday, and I can make up the ones on Tuesday, so I thought we could have a long weekend together." Kelly smiled a little sheepishly. "I miss you guys."

"Oh honey, we miss you." Susan stood back. "Look at you, so tall and beautiful." Her eyes were damp.

"Mom, are you crying because I'm here? I didn't know I had that effect on you."

Susan pulled her into another hug.

"Where's Dad?"

"The city. He's making an offer on some magazine. But I have exciting news of my own." She put her arm around her daughter as they walked into the kitchen. Maria had a pot of coffee ready, the cottage cheese, and some late-season strawberries. Susan spotted Kelly's duffel bag on the floor and called for her housekeeper. "Maria will do your laundry, won't you, Maria?"

"Of course!" She kissed Kelly. "*Mi niñita.*"

"*Cómo está*, Maria? I'm so happy to see you. José is doing okay?"

"*Si.*" Maria picked up Kelly's bag and walked downstairs to the laundry room.

Kelly gave Susan a mock serious look. "Have you turned my room into a den yet?"

"Darling, we have enough dens, but we don't have enough daughters."

Kelly raised her eyebrows and grinned. "And I'm the best daughter you have." She poured herself a cup of coffee. "So what's your news?"

"I'm going to open a restaurant." She sat next to her daughter and sipped her coffee. "I haven't even told your father yet."

Kelly widened her eyes. "I'm shocked." Then she added, "But you seem thrilled."

"I am!"

"You look like a little kid with a big secret. And very pretty." She squinted her eyes. "Have you been losing weight?"

"A little," Susan said shyly.

"Woman, you are getting skinny."

Susan was gleeful. "I'm eating healthfully now, as you can see." She pointed to her plate of strawberries and cottage cheese. She told Kelly there were eggs and bacon in the fridge. "I think Maria bought some blueberry muffins this morning, if you want."

Kelly shook her head.

"And I work out with Jenna every Tuesday and Thursday."

"Who's Jenna?"

"Jenna Callas. She's my trainer. I'd love you to meet her. What time are you leaving on Tuesday?"

"Dawn. So next time. You really look fabulous, Mom."

"I'm going to keep losing weight." Kelly started to say something, but Susan interrupted her. "Plenty of restauranteurs are slim, Kelly." Although, she couldn't think of any at the moment. Were there any female restaurant owners who weren't already chefs? She would have to research that.

"I just don't want you looking like one of those silly X-ray women. I like my mama with some meat on the bones. When you hold me in your big arms, I feel safe."

Susan smiled warmly. "You'll always have a place in my arms, but next time you see me, expect them to be muscular." She put the leftover strawberries in the fridge. "A real estate agent is coming by the house at one to show me some properties for the restaurant. I hope you can come. I could use your advice."

"Done. I'll go upstairs and take a shower." Kelly started to walk out the door. "I saw there weren't any Halloween decorations when I was coming up the driveway. When did you stop doing that?"

"Kelly, the only people who come to trick-or-treat are parents using their kids as decoys. They just want to look inside the house."

Kelly laughed. "What about Thanksgiving?"

"We're going to see your grandparents in Bernardsville."

"I'm glad. I miss them. And Dad said something about skiing in Utah over Christmas?"

"Or we could go to that spa in Mexico."

"Spas ... Utah. Mom, I have friends at Cornell who've never seen a county outside of their own. I never realized how fortunate I was until I went to college."

"Kelly ...."

"Really. I just wanted you to know I'm thankful."

Susan watched as her daughter looked out the kitchen window at their expanse of land.

"If anything happens to either of you, I hope I'll be able to take care of you the way you take care of me."

Susan winked at her daughter. "Just remember what I told you every night when I put you to bed."

Kelly rolled her eyes and said, "I love you. Sweet dreams. Never put me in a nursing home."

CHAPTER FOURTEEN
Brooke

Brooke had left the house determined to call Nick Gallagher. It was a risky move, calling a married man at home, but she wanted to see him again. By the time she found the one remaining phone booth in town, she'd changed her mind. One night of flirting and she was ready to call him? Besides, Susan could be home, and God, that woman was intimidating.

Brooke walked out of the booth, got in her car, and thought for a few minutes. She had such a strong yearning to make a change in her life. She made a decision and drove to her hair salon. She sat in her regular chair, her stylist nodding as she described what she wanted. Ninety minutes later, she looked in the mirror and loved what she saw. Her blonde hair was highlighted and a full twelve inches shorter. Her stylist had left her bangs long in the front and angled across her forehead. She pushed the fine pieces behind her ears and reinserted her pearl studs. She looked like the woman she wanted to be. She touched her neck. It felt strong.

Back in her car, she thought again about Nick. She took out her flip phone and dialed information. Nick and Susan Gallagher's phone number was listed. If Susan picked up, Brooke could make something up. Maybe say how much she enjoyed meeting them at Elizabeth's party and suggest the four of them get together.

A few rings later, Nick's deep voice said, "Hello."

Brooke's face flushed, and she immediately hung up. *I'm acting like a desperate woman*, she thought.

***

Elizabeth wasn't surprised when Tripp had answered the phone. She asked for Brooke.

"Not here," he said.

"What are you doing?"

"Hanging."

Of course, she said to herself. *What else would you be doing?* She was quiet for a few moments, then said, "Do you ever feel sorry for yourself?"

Other than "Hello, how are you," Elizabeth hadn't had a real conversation with Tripp in many years. She was surprised at herself for blurting out such an intimate question. They weren't really friends. But Tripp was the only person Elizabeth knew who also had serious health problems at a young age. She thought he would understand how she felt.

"Sometimes."

"I don't want to be defined by my disease," she said.

"Yeah, we're supposed to find some greater meaning in all this. The day before I was released from the hospital, a social worker said to me, 'You'll see that your life will have more purpose now.' I told her my life had plenty of purpose, mainly not to have another heart attack. So is that what's worrying you? Are you worried that your life doesn't have a greater purpose? Were you reading one of those 'I have a disease but the disease doesn't have me' kind of books?"

Elizabeth laughed. She had been—until she finished the first chapter and threw it across the room.

"The idea of sick people needing to be heroic? That's bull, Elizabeth. It's a get-rich theme for self-proclaimed-expert authors. According to them, we're supposed to be role models."

Elizabeth moved the phone around and tilted her head against it.

"Get a disease, become a guru on the meaning of life," he said. "They care about their bank accounts, not us."

She had called to speak to Brooke, but now that she had him talking, Elizabeth admitted, "I feel depressed."

"You have a right."

"I wish I found that simplicity in life everyone talks about once they get a bad diagnosis."

"Elizabeth, I'm telling you, don't listen to those *experts*. They say whatever their press agents write for them." He paused. "Once the cameras are off, they're on to their next guest appearance."

"When did you become so cynical?"

He scoffed. "My mother's a television star. I know how that BS works, and so do you. Weren't you on television when you worked at that fashion magazine? You know how smooth the lies can sound." He paused again. "I'll tell you something your best friend probably doesn't know. I don't work anymore. I barely pay the bills, and I stay high. That's the way I deal with my life."

"What?" That was what Brooke had suspected, but Elizabeth was shocked Tripp was admitting it to her and not his wife. He just casually mentions he stays high, out of the blue? To *her*? Was he reaching out to her for help? *Oh God*, Elizabeth thought. *This poor man, he's falling apart.* "I'm sorry," she said and meant it. "I think you need help. Tell Brooke."

"I don't think so."

"Would it be okay if I told her?"

Silence on the other end of the phone, until finally he said, "I don't know. There's nothing she can do. And I don't need her nagging me."

"I'm going to tell her, Tripp. It's the right thing to do. And honestly? This secret isn't something I can carry around. How am I supposed to talk to her when I know what you're doing?"

"Do what you want, Elizabeth. As far as the MS goes, give yourself a pass."

Elizabeth thanked him and hung up.

CHAPTER FIFTEEN

She listened for the sounds of her kids arguing. Thankfully, it was quiet. There was so much Elizabeth loved about being a mother, but the patience she needed to arbitrate fights and take her kids to art classes, soccer, ballet, and the Hebrew school Danny had asked they attend was more than she could manage. There were times when she longed for the day when they would be in college and out of the house. Maybe working would solve that problem. Carlotta could help organize their playdates and activities. Elizabeth decided she was a wimpy mother. Work or home? The same struggle she'd had since she gave birth to Claire. What if there were a bomb scare at school or worse? She would never forgive herself if she was at the magazine when the kids needed her the most.

Elizabeth took her speech therapy handouts, wrapped herself in a chunky sweater, and went outside to the backyard patio. Sitting on a chaise lounge, she practiced her vocal exercises. "Ahhhh ...." She tried to say the sound for a full twenty seconds. It was supposed to build up strength in her vocal cords. She repeated the exercise five times.

She took another sheet her speech therapist had given her and followed the instructions. She had to read the simple sentences ten times on the page slowly and loudly, enunciating each word. "Gregory got groceries from Gary on Garland Street." Slowly and loudly, slowly and loudly. She checked the voice meter the therapist had given her and frowned. Her voice was too low.

She put the papers aside and sighed. Her feelings were all jumbled. Her speech aphasia and dysarthria were becoming more frequent. Her balance was sometimes off. She didn't tell her family, but last week, she had tripped on a rock outside and fell. There had been a few times when walking that she wasn't able to perceive both her footpath and whatever impediment was in her way at the same time. And maybe the house was too big. All those stairs, angles, and corridors. There was so much she loved about her home, but a smaller one would suit her better. Someplace with a pretty view, perhaps a one-level ranch where it would be easier to maneuver if she ever needed a wheelchair. She gazed up at the two majestic oaks, bright yellow now.

Danny was frustrated these days too. But his anxiety was always loud. He worried about work. She was consumed with her health. And sex.

She craved sex with her husband. He was the most creative, imaginative lover she'd ever been with. She never questioned Danny's fidelity. But faithful sex required compromise and consideration for your partner. She was at the mercy of her husband's desires. He decided where, when, and how they made love. If he didn't want to be intimate because he was tired or had a lousy day, she was deprived, and it felt unfair. How many times had she not been in the mood but went along, knowing that if they got started, she would enjoy it? Always. Why wouldn't he do the same for her?

Occasionally, she would find her courage and be bold. A few Saturdays ago, when the kids were spending the weekend at her parents' house, she'd planned an erotic evening that still made her horny just thinking about it.

While Danny was out on an errand, she'd soaked in a hot bath, moisturized her body, and sprayed Shalimar perfume on her neck and wrists. It was the only perfume Danny liked, and she knew why: all men his age loved Shalimar—it reminded them of the girls they'd crushed on in high school. Every time she wore it, men of a certain age would sniff around her. "What is that? It smells so good."

She put on a white La Perla thong and a matching lace demi bra. She wore a cream-colored satin robe over her lingerie and high heels. When her husband returned, she hoped he'd be excited.

As a teenager, *The Sensuous Woman* and *Cosmo* were Elizabeth's maps to sexuality. Thirty years later, she still remembered many of their helpful hints—pick your husband up at the airport wearing a mink coat and nothing else; on the way to a social engagement, tell him you forgot to put on your panties. They came in handy over the years of her marriage.

When Danny got home that day, he'd instantly responded to her, grabbing her outside their bedroom door and kissing her deeply. She untied her robe and opened it for him.

"You look so hot," he'd whispered. His hands searched her body, grabbing her ass, roughly rubbing her breasts, moving from romantic to lusty. He put his tongue in her mouth and kissed her deeply. Elizabeth was ready to have sex right then, but he made her wait. "Get into bed," he said.

She'd responded to the authority in his voice. This was how they played.

His hand had pushed aside the thong and reached between her legs, thrusting his fingers into her. She moaned.

He'd pulled back and stared down at her. "You should see yourself. You want it so badly."

"I do."

She'd smirked, and Danny tried to suppress his own smile as he watched her. "Look at you. What would all those magazine readers think if they saw Miss Editor in a thong, dying for her husband to screw her?"

"They'd be envious. Come on, Danny. I want it now."

"Say it again."

She had, but he'd just stared. She started to touch herself.

"Stop. That's my job."

She'd pretended to be contrite, and he climbed into bed fully clothed and moved against her. She unzipped his pants, and he reached behind her and took a fistful of her hair as he moved inside her.

A cool wind was blowing now, and Elizabeth hugged her sweater closer. Why couldn't it always be that way? Why didn't her husband see sex the same way she did—as a time for adults to have free, unabashed fun?

After her diagnosis, he had told her he was sometimes afraid that making love would trigger an MS attack.

"No," she had said. "No doctor, no literature has ever said that. If I feel sick, I'm not going to have sex. Don't treat me like something fragile."

He had agreed, but there was more to their dynamic than MS.

She was tired of telling Danny she felt hurt when he turned her down, and that is why she rarely initiated making love anymore. He'd said he understood her feelings and would try to be more considerate. He adored her. He was sexually attracted to her. He didn't understand himself. Elizabeth thought she knew the truth, even if he didn't. Danny liked having power—at work and in the bedroom. And if he thought his power was diminishing, he became anxious.

Last night, he'd started worrying about a stock market crash. "Tech is going to be a bubble," he'd said. "Remember that kid we met in Vail last Christmas?"

Elizabeth hadn't.

"We went to that black-tie New Year's Eve dinner at the hotel, and he was dressed in jeans and a T-shirt?"

"Oh yeah, I remember. You're worried about *him*?"

"He said he had a job in Silicon Valley where they could wear anything they wanted. That's when I knew. Those kids think they're masters of the universe. Trust me, when people show that kind of arrogance, their industry starts to crumble. This tech thing everyone is investing in? It's going to crash."

Elizabeth had acted like she was listening, but she wasn't. Crashes, no crashes, they'd be fine.

"Maybe we should move to Montana," Danny had said distractedly.

Ah, Elizabeth had thought, *it's going to be that conversation.* He was going to tell her they were going to run out of money and have to move. She was expected to play the role of the reasonable wife, but she got annoyed. "Montana, Idaho, Wyoming, it all takes money," she said by rote. "Let's not go there tonight. All the flights are probably booked."

"It's not funny, Elizabeth." He'd turned and left the room.

Later, when she'd fallen asleep in her ragged Robert Plant T-shirt, she felt him gently take off her black-frame glasses and pull the paperback from her hands. When he got into bed, he snuggled against her back. "Thanks for putting up with me," he whispered. "You're my best friend, my lover. You're my skin."

"You're lucky to have me." She was smiling.

She'd heard him chuckle.

"Danny, you were always the man I was waiting for." She'd turned around and smiled at him. "Corny, but true."

CHAPTER SIXTEEN
Nick

The phone was ringing in the Gallagher house. After the third time, Nick picked it up in his home office.

"Nick? It's Brooke Hayworth. Elizabeth's friend? We met at her party."

He was surprised. It was bold for her to call him at home—unless she wanted to talk to Susan. "Remember you? You put your heart in my hand."

She laughed. "That I did. I wanted you to know how much Tripp and I enjoyed meeting you and Susan ...."

He could practically hear her trying to work out what she wanted to say next.

"I was wondering if we could meet because—"

"You want the four of us to get together?"

"No."

"You want to get together alone?"

"Excuse me?"

"You called me, Brooke. Did you want to talk on the phone about something or get together in person?"

"That's blunt."

Now it was his turn to laugh. "Believe me, if I wanted to be blunt, you'd know it. Let's get together. I'd love to see you. Alone."

She was quiet.

Nick waited.

"I can meet you in the city if that works," she said.

"Actually, I have to be there tomorrow."

Brooke hesitated. "Tomorrow is good. I have an appointment at Barneys on Madison. A friend of a friend wants to look at my work. He's the assistant buyer for their jewelry department."

"Congrats." He was impressed the store was interested in her jewelry. "There's a French café, Deux, on Sixty-Fifth just east of Madison. You want to meet there for lunch at one?"

Brooke agreed on the location and exchanged cell phone numbers with him before hanging up.

Nick sat still for a few moments before going to his files and pulling out the legal documents regarding *Sound*. He read them, using a yellow highlighter on points he wanted to bring up with Joe Noonan. A frown began to form on his face.

At Elizabeth's dinner party, Brooke had asked him what the name of his house was. "The House of Mirthlessness," he remembered saying.

Sitting next to her that night, he'd been aware of her perfume. A woodsy scent. Her hair was thick and blonde. The Chanel jacket paired with jeans.

He put his papers in a leather portfolio and left them out so he would remember to take them in the morning. He took a pen from the drawer and wrote a note to himself. *Make res at Deux, 1:00 p.m.* He felt a tingle in his stomach. It wasn't one he'd had for a long time. He got it when he was anticipating something exciting.

* * *

The next morning, Brooke put together samples of her work to show the guy at Barneys. She considered wearing one of the necklaces she'd made, then changed her mind. That was overdoing it. She pulled a few pairs of jeans from her closet, trying to decide what to wear. She felt jittery, like she was going on a date.

After trying on several pairs, she chose dark denim and tucked in a man's tailored white shirt with French cuffs. She looked through her drawers and found turquoise cufflinks and a belt Tripp had bought for her in New Mexico years ago. They matched her eyes. She opened the top two buttons of her shirt and left her neck bare, then pulled on navy boots and a black leather jacket. She took a final look in the mirror and fluffed her hair. *Good*, she thought. *I look good.*

CHAPTER SEVENTEEN
Nick

At five after one, Nick was drinking his iced coffee when he saw Brooke walk into the restaurant. Her hair was very short, and he thought it looked sexy. With her long legs and leather jacket, she was striking. He noticed other diners looking at her too.

He gave her a light kiss on the cheek as he held a chair out for her. "I love your hair."

"Thank you."

He wanted to run his fingertips around the base of her hairline and in the small hollow of her neck. "All that turquoise. It brings out the color in your eyes." He saw her blush and changed the conversation. He didn't want to make her uncomfortable. "How did your meeting at Barneys go?"

"Well, I thought it was just going to be a meet and greet, but he actually seemed to like my pieces." She explained that Barneys was thinking about setting up a case for up-and-coming designers whose work would be priced in the hundreds rather than thousands. "He said my edgy pieces would probably do well there."

"I thought you made pretty little hearts."

"Daggers too." Nick raised his eyebrows, and Brooke smiled. "Yeah, the assistant buyer had the same reaction. No, Nick, I don't plan on killing anyone. I take all my aggression out on the metal. Girly jewelry isn't my thing. I mean, I made that heart you saw for Claire, but I like rougher stuff."

He eyed her leather jacket. Her rougher stuff was very feminine.

She pulled a box out of her tote bag and handed it to him.

He opened it and fingered the choker of daggers. It was stark. Susan wouldn't have worn it, but his daughter would have.

"I told him I was aiming for a younger market. The women who are sick of red and pink nail polish. There's a reason blues, blacks, and greens are selling. I think women who are buying those colors would like my jewelry."

"So would the readers of *Sound*."

She didn't respond. Nick looked at Brooke's fingernails as she put away the necklace. They were short, clean, and void of any color. She was wearing the same silver wedding band she'd worn when they first met. He was wearing his.

"Anyway, he gave me his card and said I should call him next week."

Nick thought about Brooke's budding career. She might be able to launch a line if she had someone to help her with sales and marketing. "What's the name of your business?" he asked.

"It's not really a business. I've just been playing."

"Selling at Barneys isn't playing. You need a name."

She shrugged. "If I'm lucky enough to get Barneys, I'll figure out a name. Now let's talk about you."

He didn't want to talk about himself. He wanted more time with her. He tapped his fingers for a few seconds. "When's the last time you were at the Met?"

She cocked her head. "Mmm, maybe last winter? I'm not exactly sure, but when I'm there, I'm usually looking for the jewelry. The ancient pieces inspire me. I have to search all over the place for rings or bracelets and necklaces because there isn't one area that says

'Jewelry Gallery.'" He watched her look up at the ceiling. "I usually visit with the kids and Charlotte. Tripp isn't big on museums."

"I want to take you to my secret place at the Met."

She smiled and glanced down at her watch. "Maybe another time. I have a train to catch."

"Come on. I'll bet you a dime that you've never been where I want to take you."

She looked doubtful.

"Let me surprise you."

She grinned. "Maybe I already know your 'secret place.'"

"Don't think so. C'mon. I'll get the check, and we can go."

"Fine."

They walked up Madison, passing galleries and shops. He watched as she lingered in front of the Ralph Lauren store, her eyes fixed on the Sale sign.

They took a left on Eighty-Second Street to Fifth Avenue and the Metropolitan Museum of Art. As they approached the museum, Nick saw people flooded on the grand steps, eating their lunch and watching musicians playing on the Avenue. Crowds were always there, never stepping inside. Maybe they were inimidated by the size of the museum. It was a shame because they didn't know what beauty there was behind those massive doors.

Nick guided Brooke through the checkpoints. Even on a weekday, the Great Hall was teeming with people. He paid the entrance fee for both of them. Instead of leading her toward the Grand Staircase, he turned right and passed Egyptian sarcophagi. The crowds began to thin out.

"Okay, where we going?" Brooke asked.

She was a few steps behind him, and he waited for her to catch up. "You'll see."

He located the elevator and pushed the button to the second floor.

They got off and took a few turns. There were just a few people in the hall. He stopped at Gallery 217.

"Here we are."

As they walked through the circular moon entrance, Nick watched Brooke catch her breath, taking it all in.

He had discovered the Astor Chinese Garden Court twelve years ago—not at a Met special-invitation-only event, but when he, Susan, and Kelly were still living in the city. After work one night he stopped at the museum before going home. He had been visiting the galleries devoted to Asian art before finding this one. Then, like now, the room was devoid of people. Over the years, he had taken Kelly here a few times, but never Susan. It wasn't an actual decision; it just worked out that way.

* * *

Brooke stood in the middle of the room. What *was* this place? She walked gingerly through a narrow, twisty passageway. There was a pagoda. Behind it was a private … what? Office? Study? The room was made of different kinds of wood. Some bamboo. There were limestone rocks that looked prehistoric. Ceramic tiles. Chinese paintings, a few benches. A skylight and windows with lattice work. It *was* a secret garden. She sat down on a bench in front of a waterfall that fed into a koi pond.

Nick was standing to her side, his arms folded in front of him, admiring the room as if for the first time. "So what do you think?" he asked without looking at her.

"I think …." She didn't finish her sentence because her eyes kept flitting around, finding another statue or banana tree or structure that made her feel awed and tranquil at the same time. The garden had harmony. How had she not known this place existed? What was it doing at the Met? How did *he* know about it? And why were they the only people in the room?

Brooke got up and stood beside him, watching the koi swimming near the water's surface. If she'd known about this gallery when her kids were young, she would have taken them here when they visited the Met. A place of peace after lugging them around to see the Monets, Tiffany glass, and pre-Columbian necklaces.

She tilted her head and smiled at Nick. "How did you find this place, and I didn't?" She was teasing him but also meant it.

Nick shrugged and walked back to the bench to sit down. "I don't think a lot of people know about it. If they did, it'd be pretty crowded. I just walked in one day."

She sat down next to him and felt his arm around her shoulders. It was comfortable. Like they were two old friends but more. Because his warm hands made her want to kiss him. She scooted a few inches closer. *This would be a great place to make out,* she thought. Who was this man? He didn't fit her notion of a media mogul, but really, what did she know about moguls? They were just people. He discovered a secret place in one of the world's most public museums, and for her, it added another dimension to who he was.

"This garden blows me away," she said as she got up to look at the plaques along the walls. She also needed to get away from his nearness. It was too much. She felt a wave of guilt being with him here. She was married. He was married. Being alone with him in the Chinese garden—his place—felt almost adulterous.

"Astor Court," she read aloud. "Recreated courtyard from Suzhou, China." Then to herself she read, "Ming Scholar Retreat."

She sat back down next to Nick, feeling him looking at her. She let out a long breath and closed her eyes. It was peaceful and calm. An intimate space. And he was sharing it with her. She turned and locked eyes with him. "So to answer your question, no, I've never been here before. I'm also a little jealous that you found it before me. Call it cultural competition."

She expected him to give her a witty comeback, but he didn't. His eyes were warm as he touched her shoulder again and pulled her toward him. She resisted the urge to kiss him, gently untangling herself and rifling through her handbag. She found her wallet and took a dime out of the coin compartment.

"Here," she said. "You won the bet."

An hour later, he was helping her out of a cab at Grand Central so she could catch the next train to Westport. When he kissed her full on the lips, she opened her mouth, and their tongues swirled together. She broke away, feeling a tinge of guilt, but that feeling was overpowered by lust. Could he tell? Her face hot, she dared to look up at him.

He smiled and nodded his head.

Oh, he knew, she realized.

Brooke turned to go when he said, "Okay. We'll see each other again. Soon."

As she entered the station, she felt his eyes on her back. *Don't look back*, she told herself.

* * *

At Joe Noonan's office, Nick signed a letter of intent.

Afterward, he walked to Central Park and wandered around the zoo. It was November, and the trees were bare now. The moody dim gray light and cooling temperature appealed to him.

On their walk to the Met, he had asked Brooke why she had called him. She said she hadn't been alone with a man other than her husband in years, but he sparked something in her. "When we talked at Elizabeth's," she'd said, "I felt something. I wanted to get to know you better." She looked away from him shyly, then said simply, "I'm drawn to you."

He'd been thinking of her too. At Elizabeth's dinner, he'd felt a bolt of attraction. What else could he call it? When she phoned him, it was his suggestion they get together. His gut told him she was genuine.

Nick walked through the zoo to see Gus, the polar bear. Gus reportedly had been depressed. He was hiding behind a boulder now, doing his best to shield himself from humans. Of course he was depressed. He was living in New York City. Nick had read an article that said an animal therapist had been sent to see him and diagnose the problem. *They want Gus to stop feeling anxious and depressed?* Nick thought. *Send him back to the Arctic!* He felt a stab of sympathy for the polar bear. He walked over to an area where the monkeys were playing.

Why had he taken Brooke to the museum? Why had he shared a place so personal to him? Maybe it was less about showing her the Astor Garden and more that he wanted her to see another side to him. He wanted to share something with her that showed he was more than a man with money looking for sex. Brooke made him feel vulnerable in a good way. She was candid about her feelings, and it allowed him to loosen up and be honest about his own.

He'd told her about his marriage and daughter. His friendship with Elizabeth and the early successes of his career. He said he was trying to persuade Elizabeth to join him at the magazine, and Brooke agreed that going back to work would be good for their friend.

He explained that owning *Sound* would give him a chance to turn around another property, and he would feel challenged to make it successful. He didn't normally discuss his feelings with anyone. Not Susan, occasionally Elizabeth. But Brooke interested him. And not just because of her arresting good looks.

When he had intimated he would be willing to help make her jewelry into a business, she didn't react. He was used to women who wanted something from him. Sex, a business introduction, maybe a personal loan.

He loved Susan. She was his wife, his family, but he was able to connect with Brooke differently. Susan was tough, something he'd always admired. But Brooke was soft, and he liked it more. The truth was, she was more captivating than his wife. Susan had shut off the romance, and Brooke reminded him he needed it. All those other affairs he'd had, they were just for sex. But now, he felt he needed more than that. The things missing from his marriage— romance, spontaneity—maybe he was letting her in to see if it could happen. It was a cliché, but she had a combination of vulnerability and strength he found alluring. Brooke wasn't tough like his wife, but she was smart. He wanted to be with her again, and that frightened him.

CHAPTER EIGHTEEN
Susan

It took only five hours for Susan to find the perfect spot for her restaurant. It was located in South Salem, off Route 35, between Katonah, New York, and Ridgefield, Connecticut, close to all the major highways. There was a deserted wreck of a motel on the property, but it sat at the edge of a serene pond. Mature weeping willows and maple trees surrounded the would-be restaurant. It would be a welcoming oasis for city people if they were looking to spend a day in the country. She wanted the restaurant to be on everyone's "must" list as a place for a romantic evening. But it had to be more than just a venue for special occasions. Her restaurant would be known for its wine list and food. Maybe she could even add a few guest rooms.

Kelly smiled. "You could make it a weekend destination place, Mom."

Carly, the realtor, came forward with her clipboard. "Six acres, the pond, views of the Berkshires—I think this could be fabulous, Susan."

Susan didn't say anything. *Never give these people an inch*, she thought. "How much?"

Carly consulted her papers. "It's really well priced, the owner is a motivated seller."

"How much?" Susan asked again.

"Seven hundred thousand."

"He's out of his mind," Susan said. "No one is going to pay seven hundred for this. Tell him five hundred and not a cent more." Susan took her daughter's arm and headed toward the car.

She looked back at Carly, who was on her cell. "He says he'll come down to six-sixty!" Carly shouted.

Susan shook her head and kept walking. She whispered to Kelly, "Trust me, it's mine. Carly's just trying to get a bigger commission. She thinks because we live in a mansion, she can bulldoze me."

"No one can bulldoze you, Mom."

"Damn right."

Carly joined them at the car. "He said six hundred and thirty. That's a good price, Susan." She held her phone in her hand. "Should I call him and say okay?"

Susan ran a timeline in her head. If she bought the land now, she could hire contractors and designers and be ready to open by the summer. "I need to talk to Nick first," she said.

"I'll call you the day after tomorrow and check in," Carly said.

Susan watched Carly get into her car and drive away, then turned and smiled at her daughter as she got behind the wheel of her silver Audi. "That place is going to be mine."

Kelly smiled back. "Yup."

"I'm so glad you're home. I'm going to cook dinner for all of us tonight."

"You know how to do that?"

"There are lots of things I can do that you don't know about."

* * *

When Nick got back from the city, his daughter opened the front door, which wiped all thoughts of Brooke from his mind. Susan had given Maria the night off and made her delicious macaroni and cheese she used to cook when they were first married. His daughter and wife were raving about the property they had seen and the restaurant Susan was planning, and he took advantage of their excitement and good moods to tell them he had signed the letter of intent to buy *Sound*. Kelly was excited. Susan didn't say anything but tilted her head back and forth, as if weighing the decision—in Susan World, that meant she approved. For a little while, they felt like a family.

Later, he took a shower and headed to bed, where Susan was already snoring softly. He looked at her and felt a pang of sadness. Nick gathered the papers he had signed with Joe and walked silently down to his office.

CHAPTER NINETEEN
Brooke

After Brooke finished working at her jewelry bench, she intended to go back to the big house, but she was in the zone now, moving silently from pickle pot—to clean the silver—to the torch so she could anneal the metal and make it soft enough to hammer. She was creating a companion bracelet for the dagger choker.

She kept thinking about the kiss she'd shared with Nick. She couldn't remember the last time she'd kissed a man on the lips. It was a wisp of romance, and she wanted more. When her cell rang, she was surprised to see it was after midnight. Her heart hammered—only bad news was delivered in the middle of the night—and then she startled to hear Nick's voice. "Why are you calling me this late?" she asked.

"Why are you whispering?"

"What if the kids or Tripp heard me?"

"That's why I'm calling you in the middle of the night."

"Well, I'm in my studio, so no one can hear me."

"Lucky us."

It's been years since a man was interested in me, she thought. It felt delicious.

"I enjoyed lunch today, Nick."

"I think we should get together again."

She took a deep breath and looked at the tools on her bench. The kiss—it had stirred her. He was so assured and elegant. Surely, he was used to younger women making themselves available to him. How many rich, successful men were also as handsome as Nick? What could he possibly want with a confused forty-four-year-old mother of two who had a drug-addicted husband? "Look, I don't know what to do in this kind of situation. I've been married a long time. I don't remember how to flirt or play hard to get."

"I just want to spend more time with you."

"You want to go to bed with me."

"I do, but that's your choice. Anyway, it's more than that. There's a connection between us. Let's get together, not just for lunch, and see where it leads."

"We're married."

"I need more than the marriage I have with Susan." He said it without emotion, simply stating a fact. "We owe it to ourselves to see if there's something better. Maybe with each other. I'm not playing with you, Brooke."

Brooke had a momentary vision of life with Nick. She wondered if she deserved him.

They agreed to see each other the following week. Maybe a walk on the beach when her kids were still in school.

After the call, Brooke carefully shut off the torches, unplugged the pickle pot, and put her tools away. She then sponged down the bench and sink before going inside. In the big house, she snuggled under the covers in the guest bedroom. Nick was stuck inside her head. Finally, she had something to look forward to.

At 7:45 a.m., Brooke was dressed and already had her coffee when she met Amanda in the kitchen. Her daughter looked horrified. "What did you do to your hair?" She'd been on an overnight class trip to Mystic and hadn't seen her mother in a few days.

Brooke fingered her ends. "Chopped it off, and I like it."

Amanda put her hand on her hip and looked at her mother critically. "I hate short hair, but it looks good on you."

"Watch out. That almost sounds like a compliment."

Amanda gave her an *oh please* look.

Brooke nodded. "Yes, I know I'm your mother, and you have to roll your eyes at me."

"Mom, I really like it." She kissed Brooke as she was walking toward the garage. "Tara is taking me to school today, so you can have another cup of coffee." She fluttered her hand behind her. "Ciao."

Once her daughters left, Brooke called Elizabeth and told her she was coming over—she needed to talk about Nick.

Forty-five minutes later, she pulled into Elizabeth's driveway and picked up the *New York Post* and *New York Times* at the front door. She rang the bell and heard Elizabeth call out, "Door's open! I'm in the kitchen."

When Brooke walked in, Elizabeth was facing away from her, making tea. "Carlotta took the kids to the bus stop, so we have the house to ourselves, thank God. My kids—I love to see them come, but I love to see them go." Elizabeth turned and looked at Brooke. "Your hair! It looks fantastic! I've never seen you with short hair. You look gorgeous. I'm not kidding." She came over to Brooke and gave her a close inspection, but Brooke was only paying partial attention, absorbed in the newspaper. "You must have chopped off ... what? A foot? I approve. Good decision for a woman who's looking for a change."

"Always start with the hair," Brooke said distractedly. She was reading a sentence from the gossip section of the *New York Post*. Brooke pointed to an item at the bottom of the page. "Did you know this?"

Elizabeth put on her glasses and followed Brooke's finger.

John Asher, 50, owner of New York's hottest hot spots, is marrying his longtime lady love, Ashley Allen Jones, 35.

The reception will take place this summer at Asher's home in East Hampton.

Brooke watched Elizabeth as she took the paper and read it. She noticed they'd spelled Jon's name wrong, but other than that, it had to be Elizabeth's old boyfriend Jon.

The phone rang. "Hey, Nick," Elizabeth said when she answered, looking at Brooke, who raised her eyebrows. "I'm sure I'm not the only person who learns her ex is getting married from the newspaper." She was silent, listening. "Yeah, he probably had his publicist place it there so his nightclubs get a few more bold-faced lines." She was quiet, shaking her head. "No, I don't think they need it."

Elizabeth nodded at the phone. She looked at Brooke and held her finger up. *One minute*, she mouthed. "He's the only person I know who would make marriage part of his business plan," she said into the phone. Elizabeth was quiet again, listening to Nick. She rolled her eyes. "No, I haven't decided about *Sound.* Listen, Brooke is here, so I gotta go. I'll call you tomorrow. We can talk about it then." Elizabeth hung up and appraised Brooke.

Brooke immediately brought up the previous subject. "Jon."

Elizabeth shrugged. "I'll call later to congratulate him."

"How do you feel about it?"

"Weird. I mean, I haven't seen him since before I met Danny. I guess I should be happy for him."

"I'm not happy for anyone who's marrying that man. He's so cold."

"But funny."

"You're the only one who thought that. I remember the first time we all went out to dinner. No one liked him."

"We all went out? Oh yeah, to the Odeon, you and Tripp. I loved him," Elizabeth said simply. "He was a self-made man, an entrepreneur. Great in bed. And brilliant." She shrugged. "He just wouldn't commit." She smiled at Brooke. "Forget about him. You wanted to talk about Nick."

Brooke nodded her head, yes.

"When he was just on the phone? When I told him you were here? He was silent. Brooke?"

Brooke looked at her.

"Nick doesn't do silent. So what's up?"

Brooke sat on a stool at the kitchen counter and told Elizabeth about yesterday's date. She noted Elizabeth's look of concern and felt the need to defend their actions. "My marriage is a sham. His is too."

"I'm not so sure."

"He told me it's been over for a long time."

"Brooke, he's not leaving her, at least not now. And I'll be honest. I don't see him running off into your arms. He might not be in love with Susan, but they've been together a long time. He hasn't left her yet. Something is keeping him there." She glanced over at Brooke, who seemed to be considering her words.

"Well, you're the one who knows him."

Elizabeth told Brooke about her conversation with Tripp, when he'd said he got high to dull his pain. Brooke felt her body tense, and she tried to relax her muscles. It was one thing to believe her husband was using drugs again, another to learn it was true. A flash of anger whipped through her. Tripp deciding to tell Elizabeth and not her was just another way for him to try and make her feel bad.

Brooke considered telling Elizabeth about the kiss but decided against it. "Yesterday, I imagined a life with Nick." She looked carefully at Elizabeth's face for a sign of judgement, but there was none. "I know, ridiculous. I'm so desperate to get away from Tripp. Or afraid of being on my own. I don't know, Elizabeth. I felt something when I was with Nick, and I want to find out what it is."

"I get it, but you have to understand that I've known Susan for a very long time. I respect her. This whole thing puts me in the middle of something I don't want any part of. Really, Brooke? Of all the guys in the world, you have to fall for one of my closest friends?"

"Oh God, the last thing I want is to upset you." Elizabeth looked like she was about to answer again, but Brooke put up her hand. "Forget about this. I'm sorry that I've put you in an awkward position. I just wanted a sounding board, but you're not the person I should be confessing to. I have a therapist; she's the one I should be talking to. Jesus, your health comes first. I'm so sorry, I'm terribly sorry." She had tears in her eyes.

Elizabeth suggested they take a walk around the reservoir down the hill from her house. As they followed the path along the water's edge, Brooke held Elizabeth's arm in case she stumbled on the uneven dirt. She did tell Elizabeth that Nick had shared his plans for the magazine and how much he wanted her to run it. "He made it sound like you would have total freedom to come and go as you chose. If I were you, Elizabeth, I'd do it. You're not made to just settle in the suburbs."

CHAPTER TWENTY
Elizabeth

After Brooke left, Elizabeth found a listing for Jon Asher's corporate offices. She was transferred to his voicemail and left a congratulatory message. A few minutes later, he returned her call. "Eliza-betsy!" Same voice, same nickname. "What a pleasure."

"I read about you in the newspaper," she said. "Congrats. Although, I'm surprised they didn't spell your name correctly."

"Yeah, I emailed Ashley and asked her who this *J-o-h-n* was."

They had the same tempo to their conversation they'd had years ago, and it made her a little giddy, but also wonder if she should get off the phone because it felt like she was being disloyal to Danny.

"You'll always be my passion," Jon said in a light voice.

That unsettled her. "Jon, I was always too much for you."

"True." He spoke for several minutes, bringing up memories, but she was uncomfortable and, after a little while, said "goodbye."

For the rest of the day, Elizabeth wondered if she should tell Danny about her phone call with Jon. Last year, a woman Danny had lived with before they met called him at home. Elizabeth was furious, but the woman had only wanted Danny's financial advice.

He spent twenty minutes on the phone with her before Elizabeth got in his face and said, "Get off the phone!" Danny was confused by her reaction. He'd thought he was just being helpful to his ex. How could he not understand it wasn't the conversation that had upset her as much as the way he'd been talking to her? That easy intimacy between two people who had once shared a life. Like she and Jon. Maybe that was why she'd called him—she wanted to test something. A woman could know a man was all wrong for her, but the familiar conversation, the private words they'd once shared ... it was scary how quickly it had come back.

Elizabeth should have asked Danny if it was okay to call Jon. He would have said yes, but there had been something about the conversation that felt private. Was this a way of sabotaging the deeper intimacy she wanted with her husband? *"Sabotaging" is such a therapist's word*, she thought. No. It was simple: she wanted to be desired by another man.

During their chat Jon had mentioned their first date. She remembered on the way to his apartment that night, she had stopped at a kids' toy store and bought a tornado maker because she wanted to impress him with something unexpected. "That was the best first date I ever had. You were the most creative woman I knew."

"Did we ever make that tornado?" she had asked.

"In a manner, yeah, we did."

You'll always be my passion ... In a manner, yeah, we did. Elizabeth regretted the whole conversation now. The glue of her marriage was strong. To the extent that she could believe anything was forever, she felt confident she and Danny would be together until one of them died.

That night, Elizabeth and Danny went to see *Beloved* at the old movie house in Bedford, and on the way home, she blurted out that she had spoken to Jon.

"You just ruined my evening," Danny said.

Elizabeth was surprised. She hadn't actually expected him to be upset. "Really?" She felt guilty. Had she really done anything wrong? She should have kept her mouth shut, but on some level, she'd wanted to know if he was jealous of her old relationships. Apparently, he was. "You're being ridiculous."

"You'll be punished later," he said, looking straight ahead at the road.

Elizabeth felt a tingle between her legs. "Can't wait."

"You'll have to wait a month."

Elizabeth said nothing. Danny had perfected the weapon she never used—withholding sex.

In the morning, Elizabeth dressed and went to her home office. She wrote down article ideas for *Sound* on three-by-five cards and pinned them to a corkboard above her desk. She kept rearranging the cards, trying to decide where she would place them in the "book." She looked at the board again, her hand above her lips. *Start with the news and gossip. Then ads. Cover story in the well of the magazine. Big interview, small interview ....*

She was slipping a Lauryn Hill CD into the stereo when Nick called. "I signed a letter of intent with Joe. Are you going to do this with me or not?"

She cocked her head at the three-by-five cards. Danny had told her he'd support whatever she decided. And Brooke had been right: Elizabeth needed more in her life. Fuck MS. She took a deep breath. "Yes."

"Yes?" He sounded incredulous, but she could hear the smile in his words. "I was expecting a 'maybe.' Yes is perfect!"

"I have conditions."

"Of course."

"I mean financial conditions."

"Aren't you the one who said, 'Do what you love, and the money will come'?"

She laughed. "I'm older now. And I won't be your EIC, but I'll make sure the magazine launches with a talented editor. Consider me an editorial director."

"Fine. Let's have a meeting at Joe Noonan's office so we can discuss."

"Next week is good for me." Before she could stop herself, she said. "So how did your date with Brooke go?" She immediately regretted the question. She'd wanted to stay out of it.

"It wasn't a date, Elizabeth. We're all married here. You saw her. What did she say?"

"That's between us."

He laughed. "I think she's dazzling."

"*Dazzling?*" This was going to be a mess.

"I think so. And she's very, uh …"

"Don't say it."

"Fuckable."

"Stop!"

"And talented. She might start selling her jewelry at some important stores."

"I asked about her, but I made a mistake. It's not my business."

"I want to see her again."

"Really, you don't need to tell me this. It's not like you're a faithful husband who is suddenly deciding to have an affair."

"What's gotten into you? I thought you'd be happy for me."

"Are you crazy?" She was angry at his stupidity. "You just met this woman, who happens to be my closest girlfriend."

She heard him exhale. "Don't worry, Lizzy. No matter what happens, no one is going to blame you."

She hung up the phone and called Danny. "Do you think Brooke is dazzling?"

"No way. Why are you asking?"

"That's how Nick described her. This thing between them is going to get everyone in trouble. There's gonna be a big …" She tried to find the word for what she wanted to say. Danny didn't say anything. "A big … a big … a big … fallout. It's making me nervous."

"Lizzy, they're adults. Nick really said she was dazzling?"

"Yeah."

"*You're* dazzling. She's a very pretty woman with a lot of style, but she certainly doesn't light up a room the way you do."

"Thanks. Do you think I should say something to her? Like, 'Stop this before it gets worse'?"

"Would she listen to you?"

"Probably not, and she's conflicted as it is."

"There's your answer."

CHAPTER TWENTY-ONE
Brooke

Brooke turned the Jeep into her driveway just as the first fat raindrops began to fall. She was anxious but also excited about the future—maybe Nick would be a part of it. If not, she would be a single woman for the first time in her adult life. She would throw her energies into making her jewelry hobby a business. If it failed, she could always go back to practicing law. She stayed in the car and looked at her house, the way it melded into the countryside. Pine trees lined the driveway. She had once loved this place, but it no longer felt like home.

Brooke let herself in the front door—Tripp hadn't bothered to lock it—and glanced at the entrance hall table, where there had once been a silver-framed picture of their family. The four of them had all been so young. The photo was gone, and she couldn't recall who had removed it.

She dropped her purse on the table and walked toward the powder room when Tripp shouted, "Don't go in there! The toilet's stuffed."

Brooke looked up. He was at the top of the stairs in a dirty tee and jeans. His hair was uncombed, and his eyes were glazed. She asked him if he'd called a plumber. "Don't have to. I know how to fix stuff."

"Well, then fix it. Please."

"Anything you say, dear." He walked down the steps into the bathroom, his sarcasm falling flat. Neither of them had the energy to fight anymore.

"Is Tara home?"

"She went to the library." Brooke heard the toilet flushing. Tripp peeked his head out of the powder room and smiled weakly. "All done."

She was about to tell him to wash his hands, but he disappeared again into the bathroom. She was relieved to hear the faucet run. He came out, wiping his hands on a towel and stared at her.

"You're high," she said.

"You've noticed."

Her stomach tightened. "Heroin."

"Yes."

Brooke let out a deep breath. They had been through so much together—college, law school, his financial success, the birth of their daughters—and now they were here. His cardiologist had warned him that if his current lifestyle continued with no exercise and a terrible diet, he wouldn't see fifty. Now heroin. A part of her wanted to hold him, but she stood still. "I want you to get help. You can call your doctor. We can find an inpatient program, if that's what you need."

"No."

"Please, Tripp. Not only for yourself, but for Tara and Amanda."

That seemed to affect him. "I'll think about it," he said quietly.

"Do you want me to make some calls?"

"No. Stop trying to control me."

She bowed her head. He was going to die soon—she knew it and felt a sad tenderness for what they had once been. But she would no longer plead with him. Taking care of Tripp hadn't worked. She looked into his eyes—they were void of emotion. Tenderly, she touched his cheek, her eyes filling with tears as she walked past him.

* * *

"News flash: my offer was accepted," Susan told Nick. They were sitting in the glassed-in porch off the living room, sharing sections of the Sunday *New York Times*. For a moment, he didn't know what she was talking about, then he remembered—the restaurant. "I'm interviewing five chefs in the city tomorrow. I want to hear their menu suggestions before I make a choice. Then I'll take them to the property, if they're interested."

That was quick, Nick thought, *but not unexpected*. When his wife was determined, she got things done.

She said she had also found two possible architects, including the one who'd designed their home.

Nick put down the paper. "Do yourself a favor, Susan: don't use him, or the place will look like a Vegas casino."

He watched her consider his comment. "You're right. I need to keep a country inn feel to the place. You haven't even seen it. Want to take a drive?"

"Sure."

Forty minutes later, they were walking the motel's property. He nodded as he walked around. The land had potential.

"I love the pond and the weeping willows," she said.

"Me too."

She asked him what she should do to the motel structure.

"Raze it and start from scratch."

"That's what I thought."

Nick realized Ridgefield, with its antique stores and cute boutiques, was only a ten-minute drive to the east, and Katonah, also a charming little village, was a short drive to the west. Susan had picked a good location.

"If I added a few rooms upstairs," she said, "people could stay over, eat lunch and dinner here, maybe shop, have a little romance.

The next day, they could hike, fish, whatever people do. I want it to be a weekend destination. What do you think?"

His mind wandered to Brooke. He imagined them in one of those bedrooms. She would be at the mirror, taking off her jewelry, and he would come up behind her, running his hands over her body. "I think you made a smart decision," he said, looking at his wife.

Susan smiled.

"Screen in a patio," he suggested, "so people can enjoy the landscape in the summer without mosquitos. Have a full bar. A fireplace. A beautiful garden. And a continental menu with big portions. None of that designer food."

They fell silent as he surveyed the land. "You did good." He saw Susan was pleased with his approval. "I think you're going to make it."

Later that night, when Nick got into bed, gently pulling the remote from his sleeping wife's hand, he shut off the television and the light. He cuddled against her, feeling the heat her body gave off. He hadn't touched Susan in a long time, but he put an arm around her belly and took in her scent—a familiar mixture of expensive shampoo and perfume. He wondered about Brooke. His desire for her unnerved him. He hugged Susan tighter.

CHAPTER TWENTY-TWO
Elizabeth

At eight o'clock the following Friday morning, Elizabeth met Nick at his house to hammer out the details of their new business. Danny had told her not to take Nick's first offer, but it was so generous, she said "yes." Aside from her salary, he would give her 10 percent of the company up front. If she wanted a bigger stake, they would agree on a price, and she could pay him back over the next five years, interest free.

Ninety minutes later, they were sitting in the reception area of *Sound*. "Does your staff know you sold the magazine?" she asked Joe Noonan once they were seated.

"There were rumors, so I held a company meeting yesterday and told them. They weren't happy. No offense, Nick."

"None taken," he said.

Elizabeth glanced at him. He definitely didn't look offended. She explained to Joe that Nick had done this before. When he bought *The Street*, the staff had panicked until they trusted Elizabeth was still in charge. "Now it's going to be two people who are new to them. They'll freak out in the beginning, but I'm going to try and make sure the most talented people stay. And in the next few weeks, if we need to, we'll find a new editor in chief," she said.

"What are you planning for today?" Joe asked.

"Meet with key members of the editorial team, try to be nonthreatening, and get a sense of what they do best."

Some people were going to be fired, but in the magazine business, that was expected. People usually got other offers once they were out the door unless they did something unforgivable. Like that one photographer she remembered, who had been taking nude pictures of underage girls in his spare time.

By four that afternoon, Elizabeth had introduced herself to most of the editorial team, including the current editor in chief, managing editor, and art director. Next week, she would talk to the support staff.

She decided Jerry Bloomfield, the current editor in chief, was an ass. She had been shocked when he said he'd chosen magazine content based on what he and his friends were interested in. "The readers follow along," he told her. His friends liked teenybopper covers? Because there were more than one of those. He made sure she knew about his Ivy League education and the underground magazines he had worked for.

She loathed him, and her feelings were shared by others on the staff. They'd had dozens of ideas for articles and covers, but he usually passed on them. The art director, especially, felt stymied by Bloomfield. He was cautiously optimistic when Elizabeth told him she welcomed new ideas.

"We should be innovative. It's a music magazine, for God's sake," he'd said.

By the time Elizabeth and Nick left the building, they both had a clearer understanding of what the magazine needed to be successful.

When he pulled the car into her driveway and unlocked her door, Elizabeth stayed seated. She wasn't looking forward to going inside. The kids would want her time, and the day had exhausted her. Her legs were still buzzing from MS nerve pain.

"The magazine is going to be a piece of cake, isn't it?" Nick asked.

"I wouldn't go that far. But it's obvious that Joe was an absentee owner. This isn't his only property, is it?"

"He owns a small paper company."

"Oh, so because he owns that, he thinks he knows magazines?" Elizabeth was irritated. "I hate when people with money come into our business with no publishing experience and think they know what they're doing. I hate their arrogance."

"He also owns some commercial real estate."

She frowned. "Even worse."

"Hey, you're going to make *Sound* a new magazine. I have complete faith in you."

"Stop trying to sell me. I've already signed on."

He looked away from her. "Have you spoken to Brooke?"

Elizabeth was irritated, but Nick had sounded almost shy. That was a new one.

"You're not going to answer me?"

"No."

"Elizabeth. Honey, look at me."

She turned her face toward him.

"You had a dinner party. You didn't set us up on a date."

She nodded.

"Why do you even care if I call her?"

She shrugged. "I care about my friends. And their spouses— including your wife."

Her legs were settling down, and she felt a little less tired. She changed subjects. "And I'm getting rid of the editor in chief. I'm not sure who I'll replace him with, but he's gone."

"What about Cicely Jackson?" Nick asked. "You worked with her at *The Street* and said she was terrific."

Elizabeth considered it. "She's a star now."

"So are you."

"Not like her. After that last magazine she created? Cicely is supernova."

"So?"

Elizabeth nodded. "I'll call her. I think she had a baby a year ago, but maybe she's ready to come back to work." She slapped Nick on his thigh. "Okay, I'm going in," she said, nodding to the front of her house. She kissed his cheek and opened the car door.

CHAPTER TWENTY-THREE
Brooke

Brooke was sitting with Tara at the kitchen table, going over her college essay when the phone rang. It was Tripp's brother. "Hi, Andrew," she said.

"I'll go get Dad," Tara said.

Brooke held up a finger and stopped her. "I don't understand. Who's in the hospital?"

Tara looked at her mother. "Tell me," she demanded.

Brooke mouthed "stop!" She listened for a minute, then said, "Okay, I'll go. No, Tripp can't. I will." She listened. "As soon as I can make a reservation. I'll see you when you get out there." She hung up.

"What happened?" Tara asked.

"Grandma Charlotte collapsed on the set. They think she had a heart attack. She's at the hospital now."

"Oh no." Tara's eyes welled up. She yelled for Amanda and Tripp to come into the kitchen.

Brooke told them what happened. Amanda ran over to her sister and held her hand. Tripp stood alone. "I'm going," Brooke told him.

"Grandma is your mom, Dad," Tara said. "You should be going."

"He doesn't talk to her, and you know that," Brooke said. "And don't argue with me."

Tripp didn't say anything.

"He certainly likes to watch her on TV," Amanda snapped. She glared at her father.

"Your mother is right," Tripp finally said. "I appreciate her volunteering to go. Charlotte will be happy to see her. And your mom is a lot better at being around sick people than me."

"That's a lame excuse," Amanda said. "If something happened to Mom *or* you, I would be on the next flight!" She was yelling now.

Brooke shushed her. "Dad and I agree. I'm the one who's going."

"What about us?" Tara asked. "We want to go too."

"I'll leave tonight," Brooke said. "Once I know how she is, maybe you can come out."

The girls started to protest, but Brooke was adamant. She took her husband's hand, presenting a united front. She knew he couldn't face his mother now, not with all the animosity he felt. And the heroin. She couldn't chance him using on the plane.

Brooke looked at Tripp and said gently, "I'm happy to do this. I'm going to make a flight reservation, and I'll call you as soon as I'm there."

"Thanks."

Her daughters followed her upstairs into the guest bedroom. Brooke called information and got the phone numbers for American and United.

"We were going to see Grandma Charlotte for Thanksgiving," Amanda said. "I was really looking forward to it."

"Is Grandma going to die?" Tara asked, her voice wobbling a little.

Brooke turned around. "I don't know."

She dialed the number for American and was told there were only two tickets available on the six o'clock, both first class. She hung up and dialed United to see if they had any open coach seats, but their flights were fully booked for the rest of the day. *Getting to California now is more important than price*, she thought. She called American back and reserved a first-class seat. Then she called her own mother, who said she would come to Westport and stay with the girls.

"Why can't we stay alone with dad?" Amanda asked.

Tara looked at her sister. "You know Dad."

"Grandma can take care of Dad too. Plus, she's fun to be with," Brooke said.

"True," Amanda said.

"I'm going to pack," Brooke said. "Everything will be fine. Andrew said I can stay at Charlotte's house. I'll call you when I get in if it's not too late."

Brooke put some clothes in a small suitcase. From the carriage house, she took a spool of sterling silver wire, a wooden cylinder, and a snipper on the off chance she would have time to weave a bracelet.

At three o'clock, a town car arrived to pick her up. As she was walking toward the driveway, she saw Tripp outside the front door of the house. He looked helpless.

"It's going to be okay," she told him.

In the car, she belted herself into the seat and closed her eyes. It was a terrible situation, but she felt relieved to be away from her family—and Nick Gallagher.

After going through security, Brooke settled into the waiting area and used her cell to call Elizabeth.

"It was on the news," Elizabeth said. "I was just about to call you."

"I'm at JFK, heading out. Tripp can't cope with this. Do me a favor? Please call Tara and Amanda during the week, just to check up. My mother will be there too. I'm sure she would love to hear from you. You have my cell."

"Of course. Listen, I love you. Stay strong. Charlotte's a tough woman. She'll make it."

On the flight across the country, Brooke thought about Tripp and his mother. He had kept her out of his life, and for what? If she died, Brooke knew all his anger would turn into guilt. She took a sleeping pill and fell asleep.

When she awoke, the pilot was announcing the plane's descent. Brooke looked out the window and saw the glittering sprawl of Los Angeles. She was glad to be three thousand miles away from home.

CHAPTER TWENTY-FOUR
Brooke

Los Angeles, California

Brooke met her limo driver outside the terminal. Forty minutes later, he was driving her through the west gates of Bel-Air, an exclusive enclave of Los Angeles where some of the entertainment industry's richest players lived. He made a turn onto a twisty private road where Charlotte lived.

Charlotte's address was A-list, but her house was not a mansion. It was a midcentury modern that jutted out over the canyon. The lush property was lit with small walkway lights. The air was fragrant with rosemary and night-blooming jasmine. Back home, it was cold and almost barren, but here, in the late evening, the air was still warm. Andrew had said Brooke could use Charlotte's car, and Brooke noted the blue Mercedes convertible outside the detached garage as she punched in the code Andrew had given her to unlock the front door.

Brooke had stayed at Charlotte's with the girls several years ago during February break. Amanda and Tara accompanied their grandmother to the set when they weren't swimming in her pool. Brooke remembered the drives to Malibu, dinners at Le Dome and

Hugo's, the laughter and backstage gossip. At home, the girls could be pouty; at Charlotte's, they seemed light.

Brooke took a moment to look around inside the house. Nothing had changed. She saw the whitewashed walls, bleached wooden floors, and open kitchen. A sunken living room with glass doors that led to a large rectangular pool and the canyon beyond. Two bedrooms and bathrooms were on the right side of the house, Charlotte's suite on the left. The home was so much airier and cleaner than her own. She loved the stark perfection of it. A lot of Bel-Air estates looked like Disneyland castles, but Charlotte's house was distinctive for its simplicity.

Brooke went into the kitchen and found that Charlotte's housekeeper, Inez, had stocked the refrigerator with fruits, cheeses, and eggs. On a pad, Inez had written down the phone numbers for the *Oak Hill* studio and Charlotte's doctor— *Mrs. Hayworth had a mild heart attack. She has been transferred to Cedars-Sinai Hospital. Andrew called. Her doctor says she's doing okay.*

Good, Brooke thought. *No need to call anyone now.* She'd go to the hospital in the morning.

She walked into the guest bedroom with the queen-size bed and private bath, stripped off her clothes, and took a hot shower. She then tied on a kimono and crossed the house into Charlotte's room. On one of the nightstands, Brooke saw a framed photograph of Andrew and Tripp when they were little boys, standing in front of a brick townhouse on Beacon Hill. She picked it up and ran her finger over Tripp's face. He had sandy hair and a big, gap-toothed smile. No hint of the diseases that were to come. She closed her eyes for a moment, then carefully replaced the photograph.

She walked across the deep-blue area rug and poked her head inside the all-white bathroom with an enormous spa bathtub. There was another door that led to Charlotte's closet. Brooke felt a little uncomfortable looking inside her mother-in-law's private space, but she switched on the light anyway. There were dark-wood built-in drawers, racks of hanging clothes, and full-length mirrors. There was also an art deco vanity and a pink silk fainting couch. The house had straight, masculine lines, but the closet was all opulent glamour.

She opened one of Charlotte's drawers. Inside were six white shirts with the same simple collar. Tissue paper divided them. On the hanging rack were ten pairs of black pants in gaberdine, silk, or cotton. Next were the black dresses, then the cream-colored pants and dresses. On another rack hung several gowns. She peeked inside the label of a sleek black column dress. Prada, size two. There were stacks of shoeboxes arranged on shelves, marked with color and designer.

Enough snooping, Brooke told herself. She might find something she didn't want to see. She walked back into the living room and sat on the curved beige sofa surrounded by walls of books. Comfortable seating, and no signs of a man. Charlotte was a woman who lived alone and well.

Brooke went back to the guest bedroom. It was two in the morning Connecticut time, and she was exhausted. She fell asleep instantly.

At seven o'clock the next morning, the phone rang. "Hello. This is Taylor. Miss Hayworth's assistant?"

Taylor sounded very young. "I'm Brooke, Charlotte's daughter-in-law."

"Yes, I'm so glad you're here. Our producer said you would be in town. I was hoping we could messenger you all the cards and gifts that have come in for her. And next week's scripts."

Brooke was about to explain that someone who'd had a heart attack the previous day wouldn't be reading scripts and memorizing lines, but she decided it wasn't worth the conversation. "No, I'll come in and pick them up."

"Let me give you directions. We're in Burbank off—"

"I know where you are. I'll be there in an hour or two."

Brooke took a shower and washed her hair, gently pulling at her bangs with her fingers. She changed into a pair of jeans and denim shirt, took her cell phone, and stuffed it into her front pocket. In the kitchen, a short dark-skinned middle-aged woman was brewing coffee. She smiled and held out her hand and Brooke took it. "I'm Inez Cortez."

"Inez, I'm Brooke. So nice to meet you. Thank you for making the house so welcoming when I got here last night."

"You're welcome. I'm sorry about Charlotte. She's a very kind woman."

"And strong," Brooke added.

Inez nodded. "She'll get better."

"I think so too."

"So," Inez said, "I come here Monday through Friday from seven to seven unless Charlotte needs something extra." She looked at Brooke. "You must be very tired and hungry. Let me make you breakfast." She handed Brooke some black coffee and pointed to the milk and sugar on the counter.

"No need. I can make myself something to eat."

"I'm cooking an omelet for myself. I'll just add a few more eggs."

Brooke thanked her, took her coffee out to the pool, and sat on the diving board. There were hibiscus flowers and a trellis heavy with bougainvillea blossoms. The air had a chill, but the sun was peeking through the clouds. Today, the temperature would be in the high seventies. *How nice to live like this*, she thought. *No icy winters or dim November afternoons.* She walked to the edge of the lawn, where there was an ivy-covered fence. She looked over and peered down. The canyon was bottomless. She heard her cell ring and quickly fished it out of her pocket.

"How is she?" Tripp asked.

He does care about his mother, she thought. "I'm not sure. I'll know more later."

"I called the hospital last night. They said they'd be transferring her from the ICU to a private room today if nothing changed."

Not just a private room, Brooke thought. She'd read an article in an entertainment magazine about the special floor for "very important people." She knew her mother-in-law. Charlotte was certainly going to get one of those VIP suites.

"So definitely a heart attack," Tripp was saying. "Seems like it runs in the family. It would have been nice of her to tell me. Maybe mine could have been prevented if I'd known it was genetic."

"Stop it! Jesus. You have no idea what you're talking about."

He quieted.

"I'll call you after I see her. Goodbye."

She was about to put the phone back into her pocket when it rang again.

Nick.

"Elizabeth told me," he said instead of hello.

She sighed. Hearing his voice relaxed her. "Yeah, my mother-in-law had a heart attack. I flew in last night," she said. "I don't think we'll be able to take that walk on the beach."

"Disagree. I'm coming out on the noon flight. I should be in LA around two thirty. We can meet later today."

Brooke was suspicious. "Why are you coming out here?"

"To see you."

"Oh please."

"Relax. *Sound* has offices in Hollywood. I need to meet the people."

Coming out for business was a lie. He really *did* want to see her. "Don't ever tell a woman to relax. And I can't guarantee I'll be able to see you."

"I apologize for the word *relax*. But c'mon, Brooke, even caregivers need time to eat. Especially caregivers. Let's see each other."

"I'll try."

"I don't mean to be rude but I'm curious, she's Tripp's mother. Why isn't he out there?"

"That's not a quick walk on the beach, Nick. That's a dinner."

"Dinner then. See you later."

"See you."

CHAPTER TWENTY-FIVE

Brooke wore a hammered silver cuff she'd made and a gold chain necklace designed with uncut emeralds. The necklace was her good luck charm. She sat behind the wheel of Charlotte's car and put the top down. The smell from the eucalyptus trees permeated the car. Brooke opened the glove compartment, found a Joni Mitchell CD, popped it into the player, and sang "California" along with Joni. She drove east along Sunset, turning north on Laurel Canyon. Joni had once lived here. So many of the rock stars Brooke had grown up listening to had houses and partied in this canyon during the '70s. Women with patchwork maxi skirts and long, loose hair, smoking joints, baking bread, and composing music. It was a canvas of macrame, and Brooke loved it.

She collected Charlotte's stuff at the studio, turned around, and drove to Cedars-Sinai in Beverly Hills, one of the best-funded hospitals in the country. The art alone was priceless. She walked along a hallway with framed Picassos, Warhols, and Hockneys.

At Patient Relations, she learned Charlotte had indeed snagged a VIP suite. When Brooke entered Charlotte's room, she found her mother-in-law being attended to by a nurse. Quietly, Brooke stepped into a space that looked like it belonged in the Four Seasons.

Charlotte smiled weakly when she saw Brooke and beckoned her over. Brooke put the cards and scripts on a bureau. The nurse offered to place the flowers by the window.

Charlotte waved her hand dismissively and told the nurse in a strained voice, "Please take them to another floor and give them to someone who doesn't have flowers." She was propped up on pillows with an IV line running into her right arm and a cannula in her nostrils. She was terribly pale, and without her makeup, she looked older but was still exquisite. Someone had brushed her hair, and instead of a hospital gown, she was dressed in creamy silk pajamas.

After the nurse left, Brooke asked, "Can I hug you?"

"No, darling. I don't want you to catch my heart attack."

Brooke walked over to the bed. "I'm going to take a risk and assume you're not contagious." She gave Charlotte a gentle embrace, then settled into an upholstered chair. Charlotte started to remove the cannula, but Brooke shook her head. "Some place you have here, Charlotte. I love the pajamas."

"I think the pajamas come with the suite. It's very nice for a hospital room. I'm not sure why everyone doesn't get this treatment."

"Probably because they'd never leave."

"Well, I can't wait to get out of here."

"That's a good attitude. You look a lot better than I was afraid you would."

"Please. I'm an old, sick woman."

"Not even close. If I ever have a heart attack, I hope I look as good as you."

Charlotte gave her a critical appraisal. "You always look beautiful. And that short haircut suits you." She closed her eyes for a second, then looked at Brooke and smiled. "It's good to see you." Charlotte's voice had a theatrical quality to it. When she spoke, Brooke was reminded of actresses in old black-and-white movies.

"You had us all so worried. How're you feeling?"

"If you haven't read my obit, apparently I'm fine."

"Stop it. Tara and Amanda couldn't stop crying when they heard." Brooke made a mental note to call them after she left the hospital.

"My girls," Charlotte said softly. She leaned back into the pillows and closed her eyes again. "I'm very tired, darling. But tell me what's happening in the family."

"Andrew is flying in. I called and told him to wait until tomorrow. And your granddaughters are coming too."

"But not Tripp."

"Charlotte ...."

"I didn't expect him," Charlotte said.

"Enough. Goddesses aren't supposed to collapse on sets. You've given the tabloids a field day. What happened?"

"I had a stomachache for days, some nausea, but I've never missed a day of work, so I drove myself to the set. And once there ... well, I woke up here."

There was a knock on the door, and a woman who was startlingly beautiful walked in. Her wavy shoulder-length hair was ebony, and she had huge dark eyes and a voluptuous body. She wore high heels, a curve-hugging black dress, and tomato-red lipstick with her white coat. "I'm Dr. Yael Haddad, Ms. Hayworth, Chief of Cardiology. I'm pleased to see you awake. You look much better than last night." She must have seen Brooke studying her clothes because she turned to Brooke and said, "I never dress like this in the hospital. Technically, I have the day off, and I need to leave in a few minutes, but I wanted to check in on Ms. Hayworth before I left."

"Thank you," Charlotte said.

"We'll be taking you down for an angiogram this afternoon, Ms. Hayworth. It will allow me to see the extent of your heart damage."

Charlotte sighed. "Fine."

The doctor glanced at Brooke, then her patient. "Would you like to talk privately?"

"Whatever you have to say, feel free to say it in front of my daughter-in-law. She's my healthcare proxy."

Brooke did a double take. They had never discussed this. "What?"

"Yes, Brooke, I trust you."

Dr. Haddad outlined the plan.

After she left, Brooke put her hands on her hips and gave Charlotte a hard look. "Healthcare proxy? When you're feeling better, we need to discuss this. What else am I in charge of?"

"They asked for a name. Andrew isn't here, so I gave them yours. Now stop asking me questions. I need rest."

"I'll go downstairs and get a bite to eat."

Brooke stood to leave, and as she was walking out the door, Charlotte said, "My house. I've willed you my house."

Brooke spun around, but Charlotte's eyes were already closed.

CHAPTER TWENTY-SIX

Brooke paid for a Cobb salad and mineral water then found a seat at an empty table by the window. Why had Charlotte willed her the house? If she didn't want to leave it to Tripp, then certainly Andrew should have it.

Brooke ate a piece of lettuce and tried to imagine Tripp as a fifteen-year-old kid taking his mother's car and crashing it on the freeway. Of course he would be furious with her for making it public. But for thirty years? Brooke thought the car accident had been an excuse to cut his mother out of his life. Tripp had been irrevocably wounded when Charlotte had left Boston for Hollywood. He was just a little boy at the time, and as a mother, Brooke understood how he must have felt. She couldn't imagine a circumstance where she would abandon her kids. Not unless their lives depended on it. Brooke had asked Tripp to seek professional help, but he never would. He'd let the scar fester and determine the rest of his life.

After eating, Brooke went back to Charlotte's room, where her mother-in-law was watching television. She looked at Brooke. "I can't bear to see myself on TV, but I do find these daytime soaps addicting. I've never seen so much Botox in my life."

"Look who's talking."

Charlotte smiled. "I mean *obvious* Botox. In prime time, we have masters who are much more artistic. They come to the studio."

The conversation was amusing, but Brooke wanted to get back to Bel-Air and see Nick. "If it's okay with you, I thought I'd drive back to your house and see you tomorrow."

"Of course."

"Charlotte, about your will … giving me your house is generous but not appropriate."

Charlotte waved her hand. "Andrew doesn't want it. I already spoke to him. He'll never leave Boston. And Tripp would rather die than take a gift from me."

"You don't know that."

"Look, Brooke, he's your husband. You'll own the house, so you can bring him and the girls out here and continue to live as one big happy family." Charlotte paused. "Unless you aren't a happy family."

Brooke felt palpitations in her chest.

Charlotte sighed. "I know how difficult my son can be. He hasn't talked to me since the car crash." She shrugged her shoulders. "He has serious emotional problems. He was fifteen. If he hasn't been able to forgive me, he's more damaged than I remember. And I don't have time for his drama. I'll always love him, but he's certainly not the first boy who's been shuffled between parents. He's not the first to have a famous parent. And believe me, he's not the first to have been scandalized in the papers."

"Not just the papers, Charlotte. Television, radio—"

"Tripp is a grown man," Charlotte interrupted. "He picks and chooses his relationships. I've always wanted him back in my life, but that's his decision." She raised her eyebrows and stared at Brooke. "How's he treating you, darling?"

"We're fine," Brooke lied. "When you're out of the hospital, we can speak about it."

A nurse came in and cut off the conversation. Brooke gave Charlotte a quick kiss. "We'll talk more tomorrow." She grinned. "Love you, movie star."

"'TV star' to you."

Back in the Mercedes, Brooke used the car phone to call Inez. After updating her about Charlotte, Brooke told her to go home. Next, she called Tripp. No answer. She left a voicemail, explaining Charlotte's current situation and asking him to have the girls call her. Then she phoned Andrew and told him Charlotte was doing well. "Call me when you land."

"Of course. And keep the house to yourself I'm going to stay at a hotel," he said.

Interesting choice of words, Brooke thought.

CHAPTER TWENTY-SEVEN
Elizabeth

New York

Nick was being an ass.

Elizabeth was angry at him and herself. She was going to *Sound*'s offices this morning to give the staff a pep talk and fire the editor, and she was frantically blow-drying her hair so she could leave on time. Nick was supposed to have gone with her. Instead, he'd called at dawn and asked if she minded him going to Los Angeles so he could meet the staff out there. She was barely awake and said, "Fine." Now she realized he had probably just wanted to be with Brooke. If this was the way it was going to be—him being irresponsible, her doing all the grunt work—she was quitting.

Her arm was starting to go numb from pulling her hair with the brush. Damn Nick and the stress he was causing her. She swallowed her morning meds and prepared to give herself an injection. It wasn't until she was about to jab the needle into her thigh that she realized she had forgotten to fill the syringe. Nice. A shot full of air. It would have been the perfect ending to a lousy morning.

She pulled a short plaid skirt from her wardrobe, a navy sweater, and some chunky platform heels. She stuck two pairs of gold studs in her ears, then walked downstairs with a portfolio of notes. Everyone had left for school and work over an hour ago. They'd been excited for her—Mom's first day at the magazine.

Elizabeth ordered a limo and charged it to Nick.

* * *

Susan poured herself a second cup of coffee. She knew all about Nick's affairs. There was an unspoken agreement between them—if she wouldn't have sex with him, he could see other women as long as he didn't embarrass her. If he had desires—gargantuan desires, from her perspective—let him fill them elsewhere. She knew none of those women would last. They were like toys that he would take out and play with. When he got bored, he put them away and was home in their bed almost every night.

Susan had never doubted her marriage was secure. Now she wasn't so sure. Nick had told her this morning he was going to California for *Sound* business and would be staying at the Bel-Air Hotel. Bullshit. Nick hated traveling for work. He was going to see a woman.

Susan got up and put some honey in her coffee. What kind of woman was worth flying three thousand miles for? And why now, just as she was starting her restaurant business? She had found an executive and sous chef who had worked together at a restaurant in Napa, where people sometimes waited months to get a reservation. Their menu suggestions were simple and hearty. When Chef came to her house, he had cooked a simple roasted chicken with braised onions, turnips, and carrots. It was sublime. Of course, she would need a dessert chef, but he happily whipped up a Grand Mariner soufflé for her to sample. Susan took a bite. Heaven. He wanted more money than she was willing to pay, but she knew that for many people, ownership trumped salary. She offered him a percentage of the business, and he took it.

She'd then hired a contractor who understood her vision for the restaurant. He knew how the town operated and could get work permits in a few weeks. He promised her they would open on time and in budget. She was going to call it Pond House. It would have been nice to get Nick's thoughts about this.

Susan pulled a vegetarian cookbook off the kitchen shelf. She'd need to have a few meatless entrees for her customers. She started to browse the recipes. All those ingredients for a fake burger. Ugh.

Then she switched on the TV. The actress from *Oak Hill* had had a heart attack. That was Tripp Hayworth's mother. She should call Elizabeth and get an update.

She thought about her childhood family dinners at the apartment she'd grown up in on West End Avenue. No vegetarian meals there. Her older brother was usually home from whatever sports team he'd been playing on. He didn't want to miss his mother's cooking. She was always experimenting with recipes from *Gourmet* or Julia Child. She was a wonderful cook, but her father was rarely home in time for dinner. It would be nine or ten o'clock at night before he returned from his fancy Midtown advertising agency.

He'd been having an affair with the receptionist. Susan's mother spent her days baking while Susan seethed about the situation. She tried talk to her brother about it, but he wasn't interested. He said all his friends' parents were having affairs. She imagined Dolores— that was the woman's name—with brassy red hair and big breasts and lots of makeup.

One day, when Susan was fourteen, she'd cut school and took a taxi to her father's office. She was going to confront them both. Her father didn't see her come in. Dolores was behind the reception desk, looking nothing like Susan had imagined. She had shoulder-length brown hair with a gold clip in it. Her eyes were soft, and she wasn't young. More like her mother's age. Susan noticed her wedding band. Suddenly, she lost the words to her prepared speech, yelling at Dolores to stay away from her father: "Or I'll tell your husband!" Before she ran out of the office, Susan looked back at the woman. She didn't look alarmed, just sad.

Her father never said anything to her about the incident, but he fell into a depression shortly after, and it lasted for months. Susan learned Dolores had taken a job in Queens, closer to her home.

She didn't feel the relief she'd thought she would after Dolores left. Instead of bringing her parents together, as she'd hoped, they both seemed miserable.

As an adult, was she more like her father or mother? What kind of sex life had they had? It couldn't have been great if her father was involved with someone else.

Years ago, Nick had urged her to see a therapist, but she'd dismissed him. When they were first dating, she had been very attracted to him. Sex had been fun and easy. Nick had wanted to have it every day, and she'd liked how much he desired her. Now, she was perfectly content to go through life without it.

Or was she?

During her teenage and college years, she'd had close girlfriends, but her closest was Jackie Spellman. They'd met in eighth grade and had sleepovers almost every weekend. The conversations never stopped. They were fixated on the boys in their school. No one they knew could compare to Cat Stevens or James Taylor. They had to lower the bar for the eighth-grade boys and say they were cute but not even close to their rock-and-roll idols. Susan remembered sitting on her single bed for hours, studying *Seventeen* and *Mademoiselle*, looking for inspiration to look cooler. Those had been good days.

One day, Jackie and Susan had decided they were hippies. They hated the war and believed peace and love were the answer to everything. Jackie even asked their parents if they could go to Woodstock. Susan pretended to be upset when they'd been told, "Absolutely not." Secretly, she was relieved. She didn't want to be around thousands of strangers who were doing drugs and having sex. She obsessed over what the lines to the bathrooms would be like and how they would smell once she got there. Jackie didn't seem too upset either when their parents refused to let them go. "I never expected them to say yes," she told Susan. Jackie was braver than Susan when it came to being away from their parents but not by much.

The girls had gone to Greenwich and the East Village, pretending to be part of a much older, hip crowd. In reality, they would hang in front of the clubs where the real hippies were and try to act like them. They never smoked pot, although they once came up with some kind of herbal concoction and wrapped it in a lettuce leaf. Susan couldn't remember where that ridiculous idea had come from. They'd tried smoking it, but Jackie burned her mouth on the lettuce, and they laughed so hard that every time one of them tried to stop, they'd look at the other and crack up again.

Sometimes they greeted each other with kisses. They held hands when they walked down Broadway. So did a lot of their girlfriends. Susan's mother once suggested she and Jackie were a little too close, and Susan got angry. "Mom, that's gross!" It was just a thing best friends did. They danced together in Jackie's room to Carly Simon's new album. And when they shared a bed, Susan would sometimes cuddle against Jackie's back.

Susan had cried for weeks when Jackie and her family moved to Chicago for her father's job. The girls tried to stay close and visited each other. Then college came. Jackie stayed in Chicago and went to Northwestern while Susan went to BU. They still considered each other best friends, but they were too cool for touching anymore.

During her first month at college, Susan had met another girl named Linda Keller, who became her new best friend. Sophomore year, they became roommates in an off-campus apartment. Sometimes Linda would say, "Girls are so much better than boys. We only need them for sex."

"Yeah," Susan had agreed.

"I wish you were a boy," Linda had said. "I mean not a boy, but that we could be together without the sex."

"I know what you mean," Susan had said, although she wasn't exactly sure what Linda had meant. "Girls are so much softer than boys. And smarter."

"They're more mature."

"Definitely."

"And they're prettier."

After her junior year, Linda had announced she was gay and moved in with her lover. Susan stayed in touch with them over the years.

Her mind switched to her trainer. Jenna Callas with the long blonde hair and beautiful body, who was inspiring Susan to improve her own looks. When she talked to Jenna, she felt like she was really being heard. Well, Jenna *was* an employee. Of course she would listen.

CHAPTER TWENTY-EIGHT
Elizabeth

Elizabeth was tense. Now that she was sitting alone in *Sound*'s conference room, she remembered what she'd hated about the magazine business. It was one thing to create those pages; it was another to manage a staff. And suddenly Manhattan seemed so far from home. What if one of her kids needed her? Danny thought Carlotta could handle any problem, but they were Elizabeth's children, and she needed to be with them. She tried to calm down, reminding herself she could make her own hours and work from home. Every day wouldn't be like this.

Joe Noonan ushered in the staff, over fifty of them finding chairs, some standing along the walls. After last week, she had thought she had a connection with many of them, but now, as a group, they were eyeing her suspiciously. Joe started the meeting by touting Elizabeth's many accomplishments, but she interrupted him. No one wanted to hear this.

She thanked him, and he left the room. "I've spent the past few weeks examining *Sound*, and there are several features that are very well written. But like most of you, I want to improve the magazine.

Of course, I don't know nearly as much about the music industry as you, but I hope to learn."

She looked around the room. No response. There were several back issues on the table. She picked up one with Brandy on the cover. "This is fantastic. Joe told me it was your bestseller. It grabs the eye because she looks sexy and dangerous, the opposite of what the reader expects Brandy to look like. And the cover lines are large and bold. It passes the supermarket test."

She saw a lot of confused faces. "Let me explain. When we're standing in line at the supermarket, we're impatient. All we want is for the person in front of us to bag up and leave. But that's the moment when we take a magazine from the rack and leaf through it. If we like what we read, we might buy it. Those covers and cover lines draw you in."

Jerry Bloomfield, the editor in chief, spoke up. "That's very interesting, Elizabeth, but cover lines aren't that important for us because we're basically a subscription magazine. We don't expect a lot of sales at the newsstand." He crossed his arms over his chest. "Or supermarket."

Moron, Elizabeth thought. "Yes, but newsstands and supermarkets are profitable. No postage, no discount. Besides, the same rule applies to subscriptions." She looked around the room again. Some people perked up. "When you get your mail at home, you sort it. The important stuff in one pile, the junk in the trash, and the magazines you intend to read in another pile. If the magazine makes it to a ... let's call it a 'have to read' pile, you probably have a subscriber who's going to renew. But if they put it in the 'read later' pile, well ... when the renewal notice arrives, they'll realize they hadn't read the magazine all year and won't renew."

More people were looking at her with interest. She was surprised they hadn't heard this theory before.

"So?" Jerry asked.

"That means we need consistently bold covers with intriguing cover lines that are going to attract the newsstand buyer and subscriber."

Jerry rolled his eyes. Elizabeth wanted to smack him. Instead, she focused on the editors who were listening to her. "I think you put out a high-quality product," she lied. "I want to give you the tools you need to make it as dynamic as it can be, and I want to try to take away any obstacles that might be stopping you from doing your best work."

A few of them were smiling at her, and she was starting to feel a little relieved. "I know that a change in ownership is tough. I've been there. I promise to respect your opinions and make this transition as smooth as possible."

As the staff was filing out, a few of them stopped Elizabeth to reintroduce themselves and wish her good luck.

"How are you going to run this magazine if you have MS?" Jerry asked loudly as he approached her so other people could hear him. He wasn't a man who wanted to make a good impression.

"Good question," Elizabeth said. "You people in the hall? Could you come back in for a moment?"

Everyone crowded around the door.

"Jerry just asked me how I'll run the magazine since I have MS. I don't plan on 'running it.' I thought you all knew that." She had expected Joe to tell them that and was angry he hadn't. She stared directly at Jerry. "I'm here to consult and support. I didn't feel the need to announce that I have MS because I believe health issues are private. But you brought it up, so I'll tell you. I have a mild case of the disease." Well, not really. "Obviously, I don't use a wheelchair. Sometimes I can get very tired, but so can you. MS has never stopped me from reading, writing, or editing. If it does, you'll be the first to know."

Jerry was chewing on his fingernail.

"Thanks, everyone. Have a good day."

She walked directly into Joe's office and demanded to know why he hadn't told the staff about her consulting position.

"I guess I forgot."

She told him how she felt about Jerry.

"He can be rude, but he's a good editor," Joe said. He got up from his desk and walked over to her.

Elizabeth stared. "I don't like rude people. His staff can't stand him, and he's a terrible editor." She gathered her papers and started to leave the room when she tripped on a chair leg. Joe immediately grabbed her arm. She gave him a look. "That was carelessness, not MS. Come with me."

"Where are you going?"

"To fire Jerry Bloomfield, and since Nick isn't here, you're going with me."

"Why?" He was reluctantly walking down the hallway behind her.

"Because if it ever goes to court—and Mr. Bloomfield strikes me as someone who would *love* to sue—I want a witness to corroborate what happened. Meaning you."

Jerry's door was open. He was standing next to a shelf, putting books in a box. "Beat you to it," he said as they walked in. "I got a job at an online magazine in San Francisco."

"I wish you the best of luck," Elizabeth said.

"Yeah, well, they're paying me a lot of money and like my writing. Online is the future. It's going to put print out of business. You should consider that." He stared at her.

She kept her face passive.

Joe glanced at Elizabeth. When she didn't give him any kind of sign, he held out his hand to Jerry. "Good luck. You've been a hell of an editor."

CHAPTER TWENTY-NINE
Brooke

Los Angeles

Brooke walked into the house and jumped when she saw Nick in the living room. "What the hell?"

He came up to her, gently kissing her on the lips.

She pulled away and threw up her hands. "You just came into the house without asking me?"

"I know, I'm sorry." He glanced over at his cup. "Inez makes a terrific cup of coffee."

"Inez wouldn't just let you in!" She was fuming. He was dismissing her feelings and his own behavior. If he'd thought he had enough charm to just waltz in and assumed she would be okay with it, he didn't know her.

Nick looked a little embarrassed. "I persuaded her I was your good friend. She left a few minutes ago."

"I can see that." She crossed her arms and stared at him. "What are you doing here?"

"I checked into the hotel and called your cell several times. It kept going to voicemail, and I was worried."

Then she remembered. She had shut off her phone in the hospital and forgotten to check her messages. "You don't just *appear* in someone's house."

He shook his head and nodded. "I was an ass. You're right. I'm sorry." He started to walk toward the pool.

She was galled. "Stop! What do you think you're doing now?"

He turned around. "I'm sorry, I thought you'd want to talk a little more."

"Why? What's the matter with you? And who says I want to go outside? You want to talk, *ask me*."

"You're right. I'm sorry. Again. Boy, I keep screwing up. Please forgive me." He smiled, but she didn't smile back. He looked down at his shoes and was quiet for a second. "I'm usually not this inconsiderate. I just want to talk to you."

She stayed still, frowning, her shoulders up by her neck, her hands clenching. She was appalled he would assume how she would feel. Or that he would just walk into Charlotte's house when she wasn't there. Did he think Brooke was some kind of wimp who would be okay with anything he did? And why was she also a little happy he was there? She released her shoulders and massaged her neck.

"Fine, let's talk," she said. He walked over to her and tried to take her hand. "Keep your hands to yourself. I'll let you know when I'm ready to be touched."

"Of course."

She led him out to the pool. He sat on one of the lounge chairs. She sighed and sat down beside him. Her body started to relax, and she realized how tired she was. The time difference, hospital visit, conversations with Charlotte and Tripp—all of it was making it hard for her to keep her eyes open.

Nick turned to her. "I'm sorry I came over without asking. But I was concerned, and I wanted to see you, just to make sure you were okay." He stood up. "My hotel is a few minutes from here. I'll pick you up at seven. We can have a light dinner—wherever you want. If you're not up to it, we can talk tomorrow."

"Fine," she said. "I'm sure I'll be hungry later."

She didn't bother to let him out, since he seemed perfectly capable of letting himself in.

Two hours later, Brooke awoke when raindrops fell on her face. The nap outside had refreshed her. She went inside and called home. Her mother assured her the family was fine, and Amanda and Tara were relieved Charlotte was improving. Tripp was sleeping. The girls promised they would pass along the news.

Next, she called Nick.

"How are you feeling?" he asked.

"Much better. I'd like to go to dinner. There's a restaurant in Santa Monica that I remember: Ivy by the Sea. I'm not sure if it's still there."

"I know it. I'll make a reservation and pick you up around six thirty."

A few minutes before Nick arrived, Brooke was finished getting ready. She wore a long light-blue handkerchief dress and a wavy gold choker she'd made from a wax mold. On her wrist was an enormous free-form brass cuff studded with different-sized gemstones. *I'm not a married woman going on a date*, she told herself. *I'm a woman who's just having dinner with a friend.*

CHAPTER THIRTY

Nick helped Brooke into his rented Corvette.

"Great car," she said.

"A 1968 red Corvette was the first car I ever bought. I love them." He smiled at her. "Nice dress. Very Lady of the Canyon."

"It reveals my inner hippie."

When they arrived at the restaurant, the maître d' led them to a small table in the garden. The air smelled of tropical flowers and sea salt. A waiter brought over a tall gas heater, and they settled in.

After their cocktails, Nick asked, "So, difficult day?"

"Very."

"Let's see. Charlotte Hayworth is in the hospital, you're fond of her, and you're afraid she'll die."

"That's about it. She's the sparkle in our lives, our very own celebrity. She's really a wonderful grandmother and mother-in-law. We lucked out with Charlotte."

Nick held her gaze. "Tell me the story of you, Charlotte, and Tripp."

She told him. "I understand how ashamed and angry he must have felt as a kid," she said. "A teenager in all the papers because he made a stupid mistake? It would be awful for any of us. Can you imagine if all the moronic things you did as a kid were made public?"

Nick smiled. "Me? You have no idea what a delinquent I was back then."

Brooke doubted he had ever been a delinquent. Probably just a sexy bad boy. "It could have been worse," she continued. "I know Charlotte threw a lot of money around to keep the story from growing. She tried every year, sometimes every month, to apologize to him. Letters, calls—he wouldn't listen. She admitted she made a mistake. Jesus, she even offered to do an on-air interview, taking responsibility for what she said about him. CBS had her booked. She was prepared to tell the world that her son had become one of the most successful computer nerds of his generation."

Nick raised his eyebrows.

Brooke rolled her eyes. "Well, she's an actress. The point is, she wanted to make amends, and he wouldn't let her. In fact, he threatened to sue her if she did the interview."

"But you're okay with her?"

"I probably seem like a disloyal wife to you, taking Charlotte's side."

"No judgment."

"I believe in forgiveness. I think Charlotte loves Tripp, and he won't let go of his anger. To me, that's foolish."

Their salads came. She waited for the server to leave after he accosted her with the pepper mill. "When did the pepper mill become a thing?"

Nick laughed.

"Really, they do this whole presentation like they're uncorking a bottle of wine. Anyway, I'm not a big fan of pepper. It makes me sneeze."

"Noted."

She ate a few leaves of lettuce, then put her fork down. "There are other things about Tripp that I find hard to understand." She wanted to share with him the details of her marriage. If it scared him away, better to know now. She hesitated. "This conversation is getting very personal. I'm sure you wouldn't want me asking about Susan."

"Ask away."

"I don't want to."

"Well, Brooke, that's the difference between us. I want to know all about you."

"Tripp has a drug problem."

"I'm sorry."

"He's addicted to heroin."

"That must be very hard for both of you."

Good response, she thought. Nick lived in a world of money and media and probably heard a lot dirtier details about other people's marriages than she did. "I want him to get help, but I don't want to be married anymore."

Nick listened without interrupting. When she stopped speaking, he stretched back in his chair. "May I say something?"

"Of course."

"I wish you weren't so embarrassed that your husband has a problem."

"Addiction."

"Addiction. You know it's a disease. I wish you wouldn't feel so ashamed. It's got nothing to do with you."

She felt uncomfortable. "Stop staring at me."

"Okay." He went back to his salad.

She was surprised he had so abruptly taken his eyes off her. She adjusted to the change in mood, and when their entrees came, they shared each other's food.

Nick brought up her jewelry. "Have you thought about a business plan?"

"When was I supposed to do that?"

"Think about it." He reached over and touched her bracelet. "You've got a lot of talent and some very sellable pieces."

"Thank you. I need more confidence. But who knows? Maybe there's a clientele beyond friends and family."

"I know a lot of people."

She gave him a flirty smile. "Of course you do. Don't worry, I'm not too proud to ask if and when I need an introduction. I promise to give my possible career all my attention once this crisis is over."

"Good."

They passed on dessert. When the server came over, Nick asked for the check.

"Let's get me home," Brooke said.

CHAPTER THIRTY-ONE

Nick took Sunset to Bel-Air. When he stopped short at a red light, his arm shot out to block Brooke from jolting forward. It was a move Brooke used to keep her kids from whiplash, and she loved how he had instinctively protected her.

At Charlotte's house, Nick asked if he could come in.

"Sure." Brooke hoped she sounded relaxed. It certainly wasn't the way she felt. She wanted him to touch her.

"I'm going to get a glass of water," he said, walking toward the kitchen.

"Get me one too." She settled into the living room couch, and he gave her the water and sat next to her, leaving a safe distance between them.

"You're very pretty," he said.

She took a sip. "Thank you." She felt her heartbeat accelerate.

"I want to kiss you."

He was giving her an opportunity to say no.

She nodded.

Nick gently took the water glass from her and put it on the cocktail table. He moved closer and put his hands in her hair. His mouth covered hers. His lips enveloped her. His tongue crossed her teeth, the roof of her mouth, then circled her tongue and the insides of her cheeks. She had never been kissed like this. His hands stroked her hair, then tugged at the short pieces. Just when she was about to pull away, he held her face with a softer touch. It went on like that. Grab, circle, move gently. She was being taken in a way she never knew she wanted. She was overwhelmed with lust. He would not let go of her mouth, and she didn't want him to. On and on and still he hadn't touched her below her face. Her clothes clung to her, but she wanted them off.

He pulled away. "Where's the bathroom?"

She pointed down the hall. He came back a moment later with two extra-large bath towels. Nick reached his hand out to her. "Come." She took his hand and followed him out to the pool. "What's past the pool?"

"The lawn, then the canyon."

He led her to the edge of the property. "This place is beautiful. Not just the land, but the house itself."

They could hear wild animals in the canyon below. The night air was cool. He spread the towels on the grass, and they sat down. He started kissing her neck. A chill ran through her. Then he ran his tongue below her hairline and kissed her ears. He pulled gently on her gold choker as he kissed her shoulders. Nick eased the top of her dress down, then lay her on her back. She felt the roughness of the terry towel beneath her. Her body was getting hot, and she struggled to keep her thighs together. He caught her and gently pushed them apart. Abruptly, he stopped kissing her, ignoring her breasts and moving down to her feet. He took off her ballet slippers one at a time, held her left foot, and very slowly ran his tongue along the inside of her ankle, her lower leg, and the back of her knee. He set her leg down and did the same to the other.

She started to pull away because the feeling was too intense, but he held on to her leg more firmly and kept kissing her. She began to moan.

She felt him staring at her and imagined what she looked like— her mouth parted, her eyes closed, her long handkerchief dress hiked up and billowing above her thighs. She grabbed his hand and pulled it between her legs. Nick's long fingers wandered over her lacy panties.

She wanted to savor her time with him. She didn't know if she would ever be able to be with him like this again, and Nick was in tune with every move of her body. She was caught up in her own pleasure and hadn't returned his touches or kisses. She opened her eyes and saw he was aroused just by watching, feeling, and smelling her. This impossibly beautiful man wanted her. Her feelings of guilt and concern for her husband were gone. Now her body was in control.

Brooke was left wanting when Nick's hands stopped moving. He took off his shirt and grabbed a handful of her dress, shoving it between her legs. Immediately, she clamped down on the fabric. He twisted the hem into a ball and used it to massage between her inner thighs. She pushed herself against it. He kept his fingers inside the cloth, so as she ground against it, she felt the strength of his hand inside the cloth. Still, he wouldn't undress her.

"You like this?" he whispered.

"Yes."

"I like it too."

He was the only man she'd ever been with who seemed exclusively interested in her pleasure. He continued to use the dress as an extension of his hand. A breeze cooled her face. She wasn't wearing a bra, and her nipples hardened. He bent over and sucked each one slowly. He released her rumpled dress and began tickling the outside of her panties while he licked her breasts. She arched against his fingers. As she moved more quickly, he moved slower. She could feel each of his fingers tapping on her, yet he had not put one of them inside of her. She couldn't take it anymore. She tightened herself around his hand, pushed his fingers inside of her, and came.

It took several minutes before her hoarse breath returned to normal.

Nick kissed her cheeks. "You love this," he whispered.

He was right. On this cool night in Bel-Air, with the wind blowing gently and the scent of flowers in the air, here in Charlotte's backyard, she loved it.

He lay next to her, and she slid under his arm, her face against his hard chest. After a few moments, she pushed up on one elbow and smiled down at him. "You're spoiling me," she said.

"That's the idea."

She moved onto her knees, giving his body soft little kisses. She started to undo his belt, but Nick took her hand away. He rolled on top of her and dug his hands under her, holding firmly, not letting her get away from him. He pulled up her dress, and pushed into her panties. The moment she moved against him, she started to come again. Up against the buckle and his erection, down, his hands digging into her ass. Up and down. She was breathing more quickly. Finally, she screamed, and Nick lightly put his hand over her mouth.

He smiled down at her. "You'll scare the neighbors."

He helped Brooke take off her dress. When she started to remove her underwear, he stopped her. "Let me," he said.

She knew she looked beautiful, wearing only that stretch of lacy white fabric. Her stomach was flat and firm. Her waist was tiny, and her breasts were small but full. He ran his hands over her again, slowly pulling down her panties. As she watched him undress her, she grinned.

Nick wasn't smiling. He was intent.

When he touched Brooke again, it was not as slowly as before. He opened her and pushed one, two, then four fingers inside of her. She gasped and began rocking against him. He grazed her neck with his teeth.

Nick held on to her as she shivered and came again. "Unzip my pants," he said.

She did, unbuckling his belt as well. She started to pull the belt through the loops, but he stopped her again. He took off the rest of his clothing, lay down, and pulled her on top of him. He guided himself into her.

She took a sharp breath.

"Rock on me," he whispered. "Glide."

She began to move self-consciously.

"Don't worry. It's sex. Have fun."

Brooke felt herself stripping away another layer of her armor. She glided.

"That's right," he said. His voice was husky.

She felt powerful, knowing she was exciting him too.

He held on to her hips and leaned up to kiss her neck, lips, and breasts.

She concentrated on them being locked together as he pushed harder, deeper. She was on the verge of coming but couldn't because he stilled himself.

"How can you keep going for so long without coming?" she asked.

He opened his eyes and grinned. "I think of basketball scores. Knicks ninety-eight, Lakers fifty."

She laughed, then closed her eyes. The sex was more urgent. She heard dogs barking in the distance, smelled the grass, felt his sweat. Gliding back and forth, rubbing against his pubic bone, his nails digging into her ass, faster and faster. His hands moved to her hair, pulling her now, not letting her direct their movements. She began to wail, and her body shuddered. She fell on top of him, continuing to breathe heavily while he rubbed her back. After a while, he made a little move inside her.

She raised her eyebrows and looked down at him.

"I'm telling you, basketball scores."

She slept lightly in his arms. When she woke up, the sky was beginning to lighten. They went back into the house, and she ran a hot bath. Nick took a shower and dressed, sitting on the edge of the tub to watch her. Brooke dunked her head in the water, her short blonde hair slicking back on her head.

"You really are beautiful," he said, handing her a towel.

She wrapped it around her body and gave him a long look. "Inez will be here in a few hours, and then I have to get to the hospital."

"No need to alarm Inez."

She walked him to the door where he kissed her deeply. "I'll talk to you later. Get some sleep."

Brooke couldn't sleep. She kept reliving the sex. It had been so long since she'd made love and never with the kind of passion Nick had ignited. She'd never had multiple orgasms before. Either he was a superstar in bed, or she just needed to be awakened. Both, she decided.

She picked up the notepad beside her bed and wrote down all the men she'd slept with. She frowned. It was a short list. Before Tripp, Brooke had had boyfriends in high school and college. A one-night stand when she was eighteen.

She'd once had a conversation with Elizabeth about this. Elizabeth had annual MRIs for her MS and said she'd spent her time in the MRI machine trying to remember all the men she'd slept with before Danny. "MS doctors like to test my memory. That's my way of testing it." Well, Elizabeth had slept with dozens of guys before she met Danny—lucky her.

Brooke put a star next to the men who'd made her come. One for Tripp, but that had been so long ago, back in the early days of their relationship. The other orgasm came from—surprise—the one-night stand.

Tripp had been tender in the early days but never exciting. They hadn't made love since … she couldn't remember. She was angry with herself. She should have been looking out for her own sex life, at least had a flirtation or two. She tried to analyze it, then gave up. It didn't matter. Sex with Nick made her feel lusty and free. She wasn't giving it up. Everything about him fascinated her. Brooke was going to spend as much time with him as she could. They'd work out the messy details.

A few hours later, she called the hospital. Charlotte's angiogram results were in. Several blood vessels were blocked, and she was going to have an angioplasty, a routine surgery with a very high success rate. Brooke wanted to drive over immediately, but Dr. Haddad told her to wait. She would call her when Charlotte was in recovery.

CHAPTER THIRTY-TWO
Susan

Connecticut

Susan was lying on the table of her Pilates machine, trying to tighten her belly when Jenna opened the door and dropped her shoulder bag next to the sink. "Impressive, Susan. Working out before we even start our session."

Susan got up and gave Jenna an impulsive peck on the cheek. "I'm motivated."

Jenna took a pitcher of water from the mini fridge and poured them each a glass.

Susan drank half. "Ready to start?"

She got back on the machine, and Jenna took her through the reps, making sure she didn't strain her neck or back. Why had she kissed Jenna? Were trainers like hair stylists? Did clients feel close to them because they spent time together in an intimate space?

Jenna led Susan to the bike. Susan was aware of her new strength and stamina and took a look at herself in the mirror. Even her thighs were slimmer now. She felt amazing, like she was actually getting back to the old Susan. If she kept it up, her body could look the way it had before she was pregnant. In less than a year. Maybe a nip or tuck would be necessary, but optimism was key for success.

"How's Nick?" Jenna asked. "I haven't seen him in a while."

"At the moment, he's in LA for a few days on business. He bought a new magazine, so he's very busy."

"That's exciting."

"And I'm building a restaurant," Susan said as she biked. Her breath was even. She glanced at Jenna. Her eyes had widened with curiosity. *Jenna is impressed with me*, Susan thought and smiled. Good.

"I had no idea you were interested in restaurants. You'll have to tell me more." Jenna nodded at the bike. "Five more minutes. You're doing well, Susan."

After Susan finished pedaling, she did the meditation thing. She was starting to enjoy it. She wasn't actually practicing mindfulness though—more like concentrating on her menu and building site.

When Jenna rang a small bell, Susan slowly opened her eyes and saw Jenna hunting through her knapsack. She took out a photo and brought it to her. "Remember when we first started working together, and you asked me to take a picture of you?"

"Yeah. I wanted to see if all the exercise was really going to make a difference in the way I looked."

"You were skeptical your body was going to change."

"Uh-huh. And you didn't want to take the picture. You said the work was about strength, not necessarily losing weight. You said muscle weighs more than fat or something like that." Susan smiled knowingly. "But *I* insisted on the photo."

"You did. Anyway, here's the Polaroid I took." She paused and looked at it before handing it over to Susan. "Even though I didn't want take it."

Susan put on her glasses. She was stunned. Had she really been that out of shape? She looked at the back of the photo. The date stamp was four months ago. "I was huge!"

"You were never huge. I'd say, hmm …"

"Fat, Jenna. I was fat."

"Well, you're not fat now. You look strong and lithe."

"Yeah, not quite, but I'm getting there." Susan wanted to look like Jenna. Not blonde or tall, but tight.

"Feel my arm," Susan said.

Jenna gently squeezed above her elbow. "Impressive."

"I used to be Jell-O."

"Not anymore. I wouldn't want to get in a fight with you."

Susan smiled. "Well, we're more evenly matched now. But I don't think we have to worry about getting in a fight."

CHAPTER THIRTY-THREE

Susan invited Jenna to stay for a cup of green tea. "I'm going upstairs to shower and change. I'll meet you in the kitchen." The hot water poured over Susan's body, and she found herself thinking about her friends. Not too damn many these days, she realized. Most of them were Nick's friends. She liked Elizabeth, but the two women weren't really close. Brooke and Elizabeth had a bond, but Susan didn't have that kind of relationship with any woman—not anymore.

Once she started working in the city, Nick was the only person who kept her interest. She loved Nick. But he was her husband. Everyone had a husband. Well, maybe not. She had never thought about it before. She bent down and scrubbed her toes with a loofah. Was she a loner? No, Susan decided. She had an active social life. Work, Nick, and her daughter were enough. It wasn't like she chose to keep people away—more like she didn't seek them out. Anyway, people always seemed to be around—Jenna was here right now. She got out of the shower, pulled her hair back in a ponytail, and carefully dressed in her new French underwear. She zipped into brown suede pants and a brown sweater. She glanced in the mirror. Perfecto.

In the kitchen, Jenna was chatting with Susan's housekeeper, Maria, over a mug of tea. "We were just talking about you," Jenna said. "Come, sit next to me. Your tea is still hot."

Susan was about to say, *I know where I'll sit, Jenna; it's my house.* But she checked herself and sat down.

Before walking out of the kitchen, Maria had placed a plate of cut bran muffins and almond butter on the table, and Susan chose the smallest piece. "You never told me how you ended up in Connecticut."

"I live in New York," Jenna corrected. "Somers, Northern Westchester."

"I know where it is. Just up the road from where my restaurant will be. You should come with me one day to take a look."

"I would love that. So why did you decide to open a restaurant? Isn't that very different from what you used to do?"

"I asked about you first."

Jenna smiled. She sipped her tea and told Susan about growing up in Del Mar, a suburb of San Diego. She had a "perfect" childhood—went surfing with her dad every morning before school and was on the tennis team, surf team, and studied ballet. She did two years at a community college and got a license in personal training. "I was basically a surf bum, making money as a trainer in a gym until I met a client who suggested I could make a lot more money if I moved east. She was from Westchester, so I followed her here."

Except for four years at BU, Susan had never lived outside the tri-state area, not that she wanted to.

Jenna hesitated. "She died."

"Sorry."

"It's okay. She was a wonderful person and a very close friend. Anyway, where did you grow up?"

Susan told her about living on the Upper West Side and her older brother, who lived in Denver. "We're not close. No issues, we just never were." She sipped her tea. "It was your basic upper-class, Jewish, New York City life."

"How so?"

Susan thought for a few minutes. "People who aren't from Manhattan don't really understand that it's not about the stores, museums, or Broadway. It's the neighborhoods. We actually live there and know each other. The Upper West Side was my hometown. It smells and tastes like my childhood."

"Tell me."

Susan smiled. She told Jenna about the newspaper stands near the Eighty-Sixth Street subway. The smell of ink and paper that had blown into the street on a windy day and swirled up a familiar musty odor. The carnation baskets in front of florist shops on Amsterdam that smelled like sharp cloves. The daily routines. Stopping at Zabar's after school for a big chocolate chip cookie or a pound of apricot rugalach. "My father went to Murray's every Sunday morning. Do you know Murray's?"

"I don't."

Susan did a dramatic double take. "You can't *begin* to know what you're missing. Murray's is an institution. That's where you go for your lox and whitefish. When my dad came home from Murray's, he'd make lox, eggs, and onions."

Susan had brief flashes of life with her parents before The Affair. Sunday mornings had meant her mother would be in bed, reading the papers. Susan and Jackie Spellman would be in the big kitchen with Susan's father, helping him make eggs. He would add his special ingredient—a dollop of scallion cream cheese, which made the eggs taste tangy. She'd carefully unwrap the lox and peel off one piece for herself and another for Jackie while her father toasted the bagels. She remembered the uniformed elevator men who had pressed the buttons for her when they rode up to the eighth floor. The pretty mirror and vase her mother had placed in the vestibule outside their apartment. The elderly ladies with their small dogs, sitting in Riverside Park, talking to each other and eating carefully sliced apples that they would pull out of their black leather pocketbooks. It was so far from the Greenwich way of life.

"And what did you do for fun?" Jenna asked.

Susan thought for a moment about her sleepovers with Jackie. "I stole soap," she said. She took another bite of her muffin.

"What?"

Susan grinned. "Really, I stole soap. My parents would take us on trips during school break. We went to DC a lot because my father's best friend was our congressman. There was the Fontainebleau in Miami Beach, that's where all their friends would go at Christmas. Or the El San Juan in Puerto Rico. Anyway, my job was to steal soap from the maids' carts."

"Your job?"

"Sort of. My mother grew up with that Depression-era mentality. If something was free, she wanted more of it. Just in case. She probably thought if there were another Holocaust, at least she'd be clean." Susan hesitated. "I'm kidding, of course."

"About the soap?"

"No. About the Holocaust. Anyway, she used to look at those carts like they had Fabergé eggs on them. She'd ask me if I could get extra for her. I really wanted to please her. It felt like we were conspiring. Just the two of us. I was happy to rob the carts. It was a game.

"Twice a day—in the morning and right before turndown service—I'd do a reconnaissance of the hallways. If I found an unattended cart, I'd grab a handful of soap and run it back to our room. We stayed at some swanky places, so the soap was pretty good stuff. Eventually, I graduated to body lotion and shampoo."

Jenna almost choked on her tea, she was laughing so hard.

Susan was laughing too. "When my mother died, I found drawers full of hotel soap."

"You still do that?"

"Are you kidding? I hate hotel soap. I think the whole thing had the opposite effect on me. I'm a luxury bath product addict. My stuff comes from France. But I get amused when I see a maid's cart in a hotel hallway. I know I could lift everything on it." Susan smiled. "So that's me."

"That's a great story. What about the restaurant?"

Susan told Jenna about the first moment she'd conceived of the restaurant, the planning, and eventual completion.

"But I thought you were in ad sales before you were a stay-at-home mom?"

"I hate that phrase."

"Stay-at-home mom?"

"Yeah. It's a cult term meant to separate women. I'm not a stay-at-home mom. I'm Susan."

"I never thought of it that way, but you're right."

"I was ad sales director at *Esquire*, and I was good at it. But the challenge of selling wore off. Food, though ...." Susan looked up at the ceiling. "If I could build a restaurant with fabulous meals and reservations that had to be booked weeks in advance ... that would be something."

Jenna nodded. "I didn't realize how goal oriented and determined you are."

Susan touched her arm. Jenna looked at the place where Susan had put her hand. Susan suddenly felt uncomfortable and withdrew her hand. It had been a spontaneous reaction. "I'm sorry. Are you someone who doesn't like to be touched?"

"I have no problem being touched."

"So why did you give me that look, like I was invading your space?"

"Susan, you know I'm gay, right?"

"No, and I don't know what that has to do with me touching your arm."

Actually, Susan was surprised Jenna was gay. Most of the gay people she knew had been fellow students from college, like Linda and her lover, or Nick's entertainment friends. Probably the chef she'd just hired. And there was that big divorce in Belle Haven. The husband was an obnoxious corporate raider who had come home one night to find his wife in bed with a famous socialite. They were still fighting over child custody.

"Did you always know?" Susan asked.

"Yes, and I was lucky to grow up in a family where no one had a problem with it."

"Ever sleep with men?"

"Yes, but I prefer women. It's been years since I had sex with a man."

Susan wondered if she was sleeping with someone now. She admired how direct Jenna was. *Like me*, she thought.

Jenna looked at her watch and said she had another appointment in forty-five minutes. She slipped her bag over her arm and walked with Susan downstairs to the gym door. "I'll see you for our session day after tomorrow."

"See you then," Susan said. After she left, Susan thought about what Jenna had said and why she was so interested in Jenna's sexuality.

CHAPTER THIRTY-FOUR
Elizabeth

When Elizabeth walked into her house after her first full day at *Sound*, she was happy to hear her kids' voices. The day had been long and stressful. That moron Jerry bringing up her MS had made her angry. He had tried to rattle her and succeeded. She shouldn't have let him get to her. He was stuck in her brain way past his expiration date. She was more than ready to be Mommy.

Claire and Justin stopped what they'd been doing and surrounded her at the door. "Tell us everything," Claire said. They followed her into the bedroom and waited while she changed into sweats. Then they jumped on the bed. She shooed them to Danny's side of the bed and got under the covers.

"So?" Claire asked.

"Did you meet any rockstars?" Justin asked.

Elizabeth hesitated. "It was fine. Harder than I thought."

Claire scrunched her face. "How was it hard?"

"I missed you guys. I'll have to take you to work with me when you have a day off from school."

Claire threw her arms around Elizabeth. Justin fiddled with a LEGO piece. He had been working on a model of the White House for the last two days and didn't want anyone's help.

"No rockstars," Elizabeth said to Justin. "Once we start publishing new issues, I think there'll be plenty of them."

"You should put Britney Spears on the cover," Claire said.

Elizabeth's children had been hearing magazine words since they were old enough to talk. "I'm not sure she's right for *Sound*, but thanks for the suggestion."

"I have another one, Mom. Why don't we make our own magazine? One for me and my friends. We can put Britney on *that* cover."

Certainly an easier staff to manage, Elizabeth thought. She nodded. "I like it. We could call it *Girls Rule*."

Claire jumped up. "I'm going to the computer and start it now."

She left the room and Justin cuddled into Elizabeth. She rubbed his head.

"You feel okay, Mom? Do you have MS today?"

"I always have MS."

"But are you MS-ing?"

That was the family term for her flare-ups. "I'm very tired."

"Then sleep. I don't want you to get sick." Her little protector.

She was feeling exhausted, and it was hard to speak. She kissed her son's cheek and continued to rub his head until she nodded off.

When she awoke, Danny was standing over their bed in a suit with his briefcase. "You're not feeling well?"

Elizabeth looked at the clock. It was 7:30 p.m. He must have just come home. Justin was gone, and she didn't remember falling asleep.

Danny kissed her and tossed his jacket on the bed. His face was etched with concern. "Did Nick at least call to see how your first day of work was? How were you feeling?"

"Yes, he called."

"Were you honest?"

"I told him he needed to come back. I said I wasn't going to run the …" And then she had no idea what she was going to say. What was the thought? What was the sentence? What?

Danny clasped her hand. "Tell me what you want to say."

She couldn't catch the idea. It had flown away, and she suddenly felt too tired to try.

"Lizzy?"

She looked at him mutely.

"You said you told him that he needed to come back. That you weren't going to run … the magazine? Is that what you meant?"

"Yes."

"Good, I'm proud of you. I'm glad you told him. Why don't you just rest for now?"

She felt terrified. "What if my thoughts and speech get worse and worse? What if I can't communicate?"

He stroked her face. "That's not going to happen."

"You don't know that."

"Lizzy, I believe it. Tell me more about your conversation with Nick."

He wanted to change the subject. *That's okay*, she thought. "I mean, he is working with the office in Los Angeles," she said. Her thoughts were smooth again. "It's not like he's just gone AWOL." She reached for Danny and nuzzled into his neck. "I'm such a burden."

"Cut it out."

Elizabeth shrugged. "Promise you'll never leave me, even if I get really sick." She'd said that when her MS flared, but she was disgusted by her insecurity.

"That again?" He sounded annoyed. "Yeah, I'm leaving you. Miss Brazil is available, and she's low maintenance. We're moving to Rio. I'll have to put you in a nursing home. Sorry, Lizzy. I'll give you a call every once in a while."

She looked down at her fingers and picked at a cuticle. "I'm having a moment."

He started to take off his tie. "I'll tell your friends and family it was for the best." He sat on the side of the bed and sighed. "You're going to get better. You always do. Besides, where am I going to go? I'm a mess without you." He gave her a quick smile. "I love you. You're more than my wife. You're my girlfriend. Now what do you want for dinner? Carlotta made lasagna."

Elizabeth wrinkled her nose. "Can you make me a grilled cheese? Cheddar?"

"You want to eat it in bed?"

She nodded.

"You got it. When you feel better, we'll talk about your day. If you're gonna work, you have to start listening to your body."

"I do listen to my body," she muttered after he left. "My body doesn't listen to *me*."

CHAPTER THIRTY-FIVE
Brooke

Los Angeles

Brooke decided to drive to the hospital. She wanted to be there when Charlotte woke up. She called Tripp from the car phone and gave him a status report on his mother. He sounded alert and said he would pass the news on to his brother. Then she called Nick. "What are you doing?" she asked.

"Thinking about when I'm going to see you again," he said.

Me too, Brooke thought. Instead, she said, "Don't you need to get back home?" She instantly regretted the comment. It was a childish thing to say. Testing him to see if he really wanted to be with her.

Nick was silent for a moment. "You can try to push me away or pretend last night didn't happen, but it did, and you loved it."

She let out a breath. "Yes."

"Are you seeing Charlotte this morning?"

"I am. She's in surgery."

"I'm sorry."

She fingered her hair. "I'm not used to this."

"To what?"

"Romantic dinners, attention, sex ...."

"You're not used to being desired. But you will be. Call me this afternoon. I'll either be at the hotel or *Sound*'s offices."

When she arrived at the hospital, Brooke took the elevator and exited on Charlotte's floor, daydreaming about living with Nick and the girls in Charlotte's house the whole time. She stopped when she saw Dr. Haddad at the nurses' station. "I know you said to wait until I heard from you, but I wanted to be here when she woke up. I'll be in the waiting area," she said, pointing to the solarium at the end of the floor. "Unless she's in recovery."

"I was actually just trying to call you," Dr. Haddad said.

"Why? What's going on?"

"Let's talk in my office."

Brooke had a bad feeling.

"Mrs. Hayworth, I'm sorry, but I have bad news."

"No."

"Sometimes a patient can be doing very well and unexpectedly take a turn for the worse."

"She was fine when I left yesterday. What are you talking about? What did you do?"

"She *was* fine when you left yesterday. I was very pleased with her progress. But ..."

"But *what*?" Brooke demanded. What was going on?

"Please, let's go to my office or the solarium."

Brooke felt a surge of adrenaline. "Tell me what happened. *Now!*"

Dr. Haddad paused. "I see how upset you are. I understand."

"Don't patronize me. Did the tests show something else? Does she have more blockage? Does she need surgery? What is it? Just say it!"

Dr. Haddad was watching her carefully. "I'm so sorry, Mrs. Hayworth. Your mother-in-law took a turn for the worse."

"What does that mean? Stop the doctor talk."

"She didn't make it. She passed away."

Brooke's face felt numb. It didn't make sense. She felt tears on her face and brushed them away, and her voice became softer. "But she was having an angioplasty. You said it was a *simple* procedure, and people had them all the time." She looked away, trying to understand what had happened.

"There was a clot. We did everything possible."

That phrase. *We did everything possible.* It was a line an actor read from a script.

The doctor was still talking. The beautiful doctor. "She went into cardiac arrest, and we couldn't save her. I'm very sorry. She passed away."

Twice she's said that, Brooke thought. Twice was the doctor's way of ensuring Brooke knew Charlotte was really dead. She wiped at her tears, but they kept coming.

Dr. Haddad gave her a tissue. "Let me take you to a private office so you can call your family."

CHAPTER THIRTY-SIX

Brooke numbly pushed buttons on a phone. First, Andrew. He said Dr. Haddad had already called, and he had spoken to Tripp. Andrew would be arriving tonight. She called her daughters, trying to soothe them as they cried. Tara passed the phone to Tripp. No, he didn't think he could accompany the girls to Los Angeles. No, not even for the memorial service. When Brooke tried to coax him, he said, "Brooke, I just can't. I'm not well."

"But Andrew said she wanted to be cremated and have her ashes spread over the Pacific. You won't be able to say goodbye."

"I have to take care of myself now and try to get better."

Now? she thought. All these years, now he wanted to get better? A wave of anger overcame her. And why was Tripp's voice so clear, even reasonable? She had been out of town a few days, and abruptly he was pulling himself together? "You sound ... normal. Did you do something?"

"I didn't use today. The doctor gave me a prescription to hold me over for a while."

"What prescription?"

"It doesn't matter. Look, I spoke to Amanda and Tara," he said. "I told them about my problem."

She was dumbfounded.

He sighed. "That I was addicted to heroin. It was a difficult conversation, probably the hardest I've ever had."

Why would he speak to them without her being present? Tara and Amanda had needed their mother when they heard his news. "I guess this is where I'm supposed to say I respect you for telling them. But why now, without me?"

"I don't know, Brooke. Obviously, Charlotte has something to do with it. The main thing is, I told them. They know."

"How did they react?"

"Exploded. Yelling, crying, blaming me for what was wrong with our family. Embarrassed that their father is an addict. I understand. But after a while, Tara said she was proud of me. I was pretty amazed."

"Proud of what?"

"Admitting I have a problem and going to get help."

"What did Amanda say?"

"Nothing. It's fine."

The family secret was out. It was probably a good thing. But where did he suddenly get the courage and mental clarity to speak? She wasn't going to ask him. It would lead to another emotional conversation, and she couldn't cope with that now.

Once again, he was leaving the hard stuff to her. *She* had to do the funeral. Then she felt something akin to relief. He belonged back East where he could heal and not complicate Charlotte's death with his own issues.

"Andrew told me about a place in Boston where there's an inpatient program," Tripp said. "Harvard doctors who've been doing research on addiction for years. I'm going to stay with my father until a room becomes available. I appreciate that you went out there, Brooke. She's not your mother. I owe you. But I don't belong there. If I don't take care of myself now, I'm going to die."

Her eyes were burning, and her head was pounding. "I just don't understand why you've suddenly done a one-eighty and decided to get treatment. Is it because your mother died?"

"I don't know."

She believed him. He didn't know anything about himself.

She cradled the phone in her neck and tapped on the desk. She kept telling herself that everything would be okay. "I understand that what you're doing isn't easy, and it's the right choice. I'm glad Tara is proud of you. I'm sure Amanda will be too, when she's had some time to think about it." She wished him well and said "goodbye." She didn't have time to process her feelings about Tripp. What now?

Call Elizabeth. "No, Lizzy. I don't want you to come out, but if you would contact our friends and tell them, that would be helpful." She repeated the conversation she'd had with Tripp. "Maybe it's the silver lining thing."

She hung up and dialed Nick.

"Let me help you," he said.

"No, Tripp's brother, Andrew, will be here tonight. There's a lot we have to work out."

"I'm so sorry, Brooke. You were just saying last night how much she meant to you. I could help with the media. News outlets are going to want to cover this. I can make a few calls."

"I'm sure *Oak Hill*'s publicity department can manage, but thank you."

"Okay, look, I'm staying here for a few more days. I can extend if you want."

"I can't think about that now."

"I understand. Do what you have to. One foot in front of the other. But, please, I'm here if you need me."

She called the producer of *Oak Hill,* who assured her they'd be handling all press questions and releases.

She called Inez, and they tried to comfort each other. "I'm going home, but if you need help at the house later, call me."

At Charlotte's house, Brooke changed into pj's and made herself a vodka tonic. She sat in front of the living room TV to watch coverage of Charlotte's death. CBS was showing dozens of photos, dating back to her early commercials in Boston, stills from the shows she had guest-starred on, and clips from *Oak Hill*. Brooke switched the channel to *Entertainment Tonight*. The host was talking about Tripp's car accident. Brooke closed her eyes and silently pleaded with *ET* not to run the footage of Charlotte castigating Tripp. Instead, they ran an old piece of her mother-in-law's reaction when she received an Emmy nomination. *One crisis avoided*, Brooke thought.

The phone rang.

It was Tripp's brother, Andrew. She said she'd meet him at his hotel in an hour.

CHAPTER THIRTY-SEVEN

Brooke walked into the bar of the Beverly Wilshire Hotel and saw Andrew sitting by himself at a cocktail table. He was a few years older than Tripp. He had the same eyes and hair as his brother, but Andrew was fit and muscular. She gave him a hug before sitting down.

"How are you?" she asked.

His eyes were wet. "Shocked. Dazed. Upset. The way we all feel."

They ordered club sodas.

"I've brought you Charlotte's papers," Andrew said. He pulled out two binders from a canvas bag and put them on the table. "This one is her will, and the other is a playbook for her funeral and memorial service."

"A *playbook?*"

Andrew shrugged. "Charlotte's words. You know how my mom was."

"Let me see." She leaned over to look at it.

"She's got everything planned, right down to the savignon blanc from that tiny winery in Napa she loves. She expects it to be served at the 'after-party.'"

Brooke laughed and shook her head. "Your mother."

He smiled. "Always the diva, but that's one of the things we love about her."

Brooke took the paper from Andrew. Cremation followed the next day with a "party" at her home. She scanned the guest list. Co-stars from *Oak Hill*, some names she didn't recognize, and an internationally renowned composer. "What's he doing on the list?" Brooke asked.

Andrew put on his glasses. "The Grammy winner?"

"Like, Hall of Fame Grammy winner. And Oscars and Tonys. The guy's a musical genius. He's been around forever."

Andrew shrugged. "Never saw him with her at any of the award shows. He's probably a friend. Or partner, although out here, that's hard to keep secret."

"Isn't he married?"

"I think widowed."

"Yeah, widowed."

"I'll call as many of them as I can. Can you call a few also?" he asked.

"Sure." She wondered how the songwriter fit into Charlotte's life.

"Now about the will," Andrew said. He started to flip through it. "It's straightforward. Half to Trip, half to me, and the house goes to you."

"Yeah, about that ...."

"Brooke, she was clear. It's yours. If you don't want it, sell it. You don't have to do anything right now, but I'm not moving from Boston, and I don't need the money."

"We'll see. Anyway, you must be exhausted."

He started to get up. "I am. I'll see you and the kids tomorrow. And I'll be at the house early on," he looked down at Charlotte's party list, "Thursday. We can invite people to come over after dinner."

"Okay." She kissed his cheek, then walked outside.

The next morning, she picked Tara and Amanda up at the airport. On the drive to the funeral home, they talked about their father. Why hadn't they been told he was a heroin addict? Did

Brooke think they couldn't handle it? Did she know how scared they were? Or how embarrassed?

"I've only known for a short time myself," Brooke said. She was merging onto the freeway and didn't feel confident she could concentrate on the traffic and conversation. "It's really hard for me to process, so I can imagine how hard it is for you."

"No, you can't," Amanda said.

Brooke sighed deeply. "You're right. I can't."

"You never had a father who was a drug addict," Amanda said.

Brooke saw Tara in the rearview mirror, nodding in agreement. Her father had been a stable, patient man whom she and her mother had loved and depended on. "I agree," Brooke said. "This is an important discussion. I have a proposal."

"What?" Tara asked.

"Why don't we table it until after the funeral and reception? That way, we can talk as long as we need without worrying about changing gears and putting on happy faces for Uncle Andrew and a houseful of people."

"Fine."

After the private family-only service, Andrew had found a spot at the edge of Malibu where they could empty Charlotte's ashes into the ocean.

"Did she want us to say a prayer or something?" Tara asked.

"No, but you can say anything you want."

"Grandma was my idol."

"Mine too," Amanda said.

"I love Charlotte," Brooke said. "I'm angry that she died."

"Mom," Tara said.

Brooke looked at her daughter. "I am. Charlotte was a role model. She lived her life the way she wanted." She threw Andrew an impish smile. "Heaven has a new star."

He looked out at the ocean. "Mom, you know I'll always love and miss you. Tripp will too. I know how proud you were of me. I hope you know I'm proud of you too." He emptied the urn into the ocean. "Hey, Mom? Remember when you told me you had a crush on Burt Lancaster? He's in your neighborhood now. Go get him."

"Who's Burt Lancaster?" Amanda asked.

"Oh Christ. Get in the car," Brooke said.

CHAPTER THIRTY-EIGHT

Charlotte's house was filled. As bottles of wine emptied, guests stood up to make speeches about her. The more they drank, the bawdier the stories became. Brooke saw the famous composer talking with Andrew on the other side of the room. She was about to walk over and introduce herself when a woman with short black-dyed hair, dressed in black leather pants and a hot-pink tee, touched her arm. "I'm Terry Cone, Charlotte's publicist from the old days. I just wanted to tell you how stunning your necklace is."

Brooke didn't know her. She'd been shaking hands with so many people she'd never met that they were starting to blur. She really wanted them to go home so she could be alone with her daughters. But she offered the woman a warm smile and touched her necklace. She was wearing a heavily enameled piece she'd made years ago. It was a dragonfly enameled in brilliant shades of blue and green. The chain was made of heavy 18-karat gold links. "Thank you."

"Where did you get it?"

"I made it."

"You made it?" Terry looked stunned. "May I look more closely?"

Brooke undid the clasp and handed it to the woman, who wore a silver skull ring on her middle finger.

"My clients would go crazy for something like this," Terry said, turning it over. "I represent a lot of musicians now. Rockstars. Large, colorful pieces are what a lot of them are wearing now. Where do you sell? Can you make more?"

"I'm not selling at the moment. And I'm sort of a one-of-a-kind designer. I don't have a line or anything." *Also, Charlotte just died, and why aren't you asking about her because this conversation is inappropriate and rude? And please leave my house. Yes, it's my house.* But she didn't say any of that.

"Perfect," Terry said.

By nine o'clock, all the guests had left. Only Andrew, Tara, and Amanda remained. Brooke was depleted. Poor Andrew was going back to the hotel and leaving for Boston in the morning.

"Oh, I forgot; tell me about the composer," Brooke said.

"Nice guy. Very unassuming in person. He said he met Charlotte years ago, and they'd remained close."

Brooke cocked her head.

"He didn't say how close, and I didn't ask him. But he gave me his cell phone number and said to call if I ever needed anything. I don't know what I would need from him."

"Probably just being polite. He looked a lot older than I remember. His hair is completely gray."

Andrew laughed. "At least he has hair."

"I mean, he's still very handsome." She walked Andrew to the door. "Thanks for everything."

"Don't thank me. You did all the work. I'll call you when I get back to Boston. And don't worry about Tripp. My dad and I are going to help him get back on his feet."

After he left, Brooke went into the guest room where the girls were lying in bed. "How are you two?"

"Sad," Tara said. Her eyes were brimming with tears.

Brooke pulled a tissue out of her pocket and gave it to her. "I'd be worried if you weren't sad." She glanced at Amanda, who was lying on top of the blanket, face to the wall.

"I miss Grandma," Tara said. "I don't want to be here, but I don't want to go home either. Dad is a drug addict. Our lives suck. Everything's a mess. And all those people who came here? It felt weird that they were walking around Grandma's house. They didn't even seem upset. Honestly, Mom? It made me sick."

Brooke nodded. "Me too." She walked over to Amanda and gently took her in her arms. "It's okay, honey. What you're feeling is normal."

"I know, Mom, but that doesn't make it better."

"It doesn't." Brooke held her until she stopped crying. "Do you want to talk about Dad?" she asked.

"Not really," Amanda said.

"I'm tired. It's too much, Mom," Tara said.

Brooke wasn't up for the conversation either. "I agree. I'll leave my bedroom door open if you want to talk or just cuddle," she said. She kissed them both goodnight. Tomorrow, she would tell her daughters about inheriting the house.

Before she went to bed, she called Elizabeth and updated her. Next she rang Nick and told him about her day.

"Sounds like a Hollywood send-off to me," he said when she described the reception.

"Yep."

"I'm glad you called. If you're able to come over tomorrow or the next day, let me know. I want to see you again."

She wanted to see him too.

After she hung up she scribbled a note to herself to call Dr. Waxman. So much had happened since their last appointment.

Tara came into her room a few moments later. "Mom, will you give me a sleeping pill? There's no way I can sleep. Amanda's out already."

"Grandma has a bottle of melatonin in the kitchen. Take two of those."

"Mom ...."

"Melatonin, Tara."

Tara was about to leave the room when she hesitated.

"What is it?" Brooke asked.

Tara shifted on her feet, looking at the floor. "You're going to get a divorce, aren't you?"

Brooke frowned. "Probably."

"Because of the heroin?"

"No. If it were just the drugs, I'd do whatever I could to help him get better. But you said it yourself, honey. We aren't really a family anymore. Dad and I haven't been on the same plane for a long time."

"You just realized that?"

"No, but I just accepted it. I haven't been honest with myself. Or you and Amanda. I kept denying what was happening. That's my fault. But we can move forward."

"I just wish you would have told us. I wish Dad didn't take this long to admit it."

"I didn't know myself until a few weeks ago. I wasn't paying attention. But I think we can all stop blaming ourselves, including your father. We need to heal. I promise, somehow, this will work out."

Tara sighed. "Okay, Mom."

"We'll talk tomorrow. I love you."

Tara walked out, and Brooke settled under the covers. It hadn't been a bad conversation. Her daughters just needed time to adjust to their new situation. Brooke glanced at the notepad next to her on the nightstand and idly wrote, *Brooke, Tara, Amanda*. It was her go-to doodle. She kept rewriting it. Cursive, block letters, all caps. *Brooke, Tara, Amanda. Brooke, Amanda, Tara. BAT. BAT GIRLS.* That was what she would call her jewelry company. She imagined Charlotte saying, "Now that's a trio with superpower." BatGirls.

CHAPTER THIRTY-NINE
Elizabeth

Connecticut

On Saturday, Elizabeth couldn't get out of bed. *Not again, not now*, she thought. The night before, Danny had to accompany her to the bathroom, and it had felt like she was peeing razor blades. They called her doctor on his cell—that was what they got for donating to his research, his cell number—and followed his instructions. Antibiotics for the bladder infection, go up on one med, down on another, and a three-day course of IV steroids. He would have a nurse come to the house and administer it.

Same old, same old, Elizabeth thought. She assumed she would recover from this relapse in a few days. But would it leave her just a little more disabled? The doctor didn't know.

Danny stayed with her until the nurse arrived and set up the IV. "I'll take the kids ice-skating at the indoor rink."

"Mom, will you be all right without us?" Claire asked.

"Of course." Elizabeth glanced at the nurse, who was preparing the IV. "I have her to watch over me."

"Mom, is it going to hurt?" Justin whispered.

"No, she's going to make sure it doesn't hurt. Her job is to help me get better. The IVs work. I'm going to be fine." She gave him a little nudge. "Go with Dad. When you come back, tell me all about your skating, and don't fall!"

"We'll bring you a burger" Claire said. "The way you like it, Mom. With lots of pickles and cheese."

"C'mon, guys," Danny said. "Skating, then Big Macs for everyone." He kissed Elizabeth. "And, you, don't get into any trouble."

"Pinky swear."

Elizabeth heard Danny's car go down the driveway. The nurse punctured her arm three times before she found a vein. "I'm usually very good at this." She was still fussing with the tube.

"Sometimes my veins roll."

"I see that. I'm sorry that I kept poking you."

Elizabeth smiled. She was a polite patient. She didn't want to be one of those people doctors and nurses dreaded seeing. She felt the cold liquid going through her veins. And she actually tasted salt water. It was the saline the nurse had put in the tube to flush it before starting the steroid drip. Elizabeth adjusted herself to a more comfortable position and closed her eyes.

When the phone rang, she asked the nurse to answer. It was Brooke. Elizabeth put the phone on speaker so she could talk without disturbing her arm.

"Uh-oh. What's going on?" Brooke asked.

"Tell me what's happening with you. I'd rather listen than talk."

"A woman who called herself a nurse answered your phone, Elizabeth. *You* go first."

"I don't feel well."

"I leave you alone for a few days, and this is what happens."

Elizabeth laughed. "Yeah, come home. I can't live without you."

"That's an understatement. C'mon. Truth. Don't play superwoman with me. It makes me feel guilty for having issues when you're the one lying in bed."

Elizabeth hesitated, trying to accurately describe her feelings. "I'm depressed, frightened, drained. Angry. I had a couple of good days at work. I was starting to get into the groove of building a magazine again, feeling confident. I realized I could do it, the muscle memory was there, and then boom. Every time I start to succeed, this disease stops me. I argue with myself. Why is this happening to me? Is it because I'm not spiritual enough, not a good enough mother or wife? Is this why the universe is punishing me with these fits of starts and stops? But you know what, Brooke? It's just fucking multiple sclerosis."

"You'll get better. You always do."

"Maybe."

"What does that mean?"

"It's bigger than me."

"I don't understand."

"The disease beats me up. It's relentless." Elizabeth paused. "I'm tired of fighting. It's all uphill, and I don't have the strength. Sometimes it's easier to just let it win."

"Lizzy, you feel that way now. Give in for a while—your body needs the rest. You'll come out on the other side."

"Honestly? I don't mind being in bed. It's the only time I give myself permission to be still."

"Yes. We're a country of workaholics who don't put enough emphasis on relaxation."

"Yeah."

"I think we should both get into bed, even when we're not sick. Watching *I Love Lucy* and lying around in pajamas, eating those English muffin pizzas we used to make in college." Brooke laughed. "I bet that cures a lot of problems."

Elizabeth agreed. She told Brooke she had to pee standing up now. "It's embarrassing. You know how little kids are—forever bursting into the bathroom while you're using the toilet? If they catch me standing, I'll have to explain it, and I don't want to."

"Lock the door."

"I usually don't have the time. I'm either rushing so I don't have an accident or standing because my bladder won't empty all the way when I sit."

"That should be the worst thing that happens to you."

"Yeah." Elizabeth was thinking about wheelchairs and feeding tubes.

She told Brooke how badly she felt about her kids seeing her this way—lying in bed with a needle in her arm. Was that what their childhood memories of her would be? A mother who was an invalid?

"No," Brooke said firmly. "It will be one memory. There are plenty of others. They know their mom is a fighter and the person who loves them most. You're their role model."

"I hope. Tell me about the funeral," Elizabeth said. She wanted to ask about the details, but at that moment, her thoughts weren't connecting to her tongue. Talking was beginning to exhaust her.

"The memorial service went well. No one was sobbing in the corner. No slobbering drunks making fools of themselves. The hard stuff starts now. Andrew went back to Boston. You know Tripp's going there, right?"

"Yes, it must be a relief. If he's serious about getting clean, he has family support, and you can figure out what you're going to do next."

"Go back to Westport, get a divorce, sell the house, and eventually move out here."

"No! You can't leave me. And a divorce? Are you sure?"

"It makes sense, Lizzy. There's nothing between us anymore. There's no animosity either though. I won't move until the school year is over. Hopefully, Tripp will be willing to do a fifty-fifty split on the sale of the house, and then the kids and I can move to LA."

"Are you going to stop the thing with Nick?"

"Definitely not. If I could see him all the time, I would. He's still here."

"Oh."

"Yeah. I'm seeing him tomorrow."

Elizabeth bit her finger and frowned.

"I can't get over the sex. When I listened to women who talked about how good some men were in bed, I thought I had an idea of what that was. I didn't. Now I do."

"I think great sex is crucial to a relationship," Elizabeth said.

"You always knew that. I was willing to sacrifice it if all the other boxes were checked. I did when I met Tripp."

Elizabeth considered. "For me, if the sex wasn't good, there was no reason to move forward. If there's no passion in the beginning, what's the point? Over the years, it ebbs and flows, but I could never marry someone I didn't want to go to bed with. When I was single, the bad boys who weren't right for me were amazing in bed, and the nice ones—the ones who checked my boxes—were never men I wanted to sleep with. Danny was the first man who was my friend and lover."

"I wonder if Nick could be that for me," Brooke said. "But there's Susan. The sex is great, but I don't really know him that well. Maybe it's just a fling for him."

Elizabeth had witnessed Nick and his flings, and this didn't sound like one.

"My life is changing quickly, Lizzy. Suddenly, it doesn't feel so daunting to make decisions."

"I can tell."

"I've made another one. After I move to Los Angeles, I'm going to start a jewelry business."

CHAPTER FORTY

Elizabeth was swirling with emotion. Steroid drips made her swing between wanting to scream and wanting to cry. Her best friend was moving to California and starting a new business while she was lying here in bed.

She thought about her sex conversation with Brooke. From the time she'd first gone to bed with a boy, she was always trying to prove something. *I can be smart and sexy. Try me, I dare you. See if you can handle me.* That was what she'd been trying to get across to the men she met.

The '70s had been like that, at least for her. Women were still expected to play hard to get. Teenage girls were called *whores* if they fooled around with anyone but their boyfriends. Of course, no one "slut-shamed" the boys. Elizabeth hated those words. *Sluts, whores, promiscuous.* Who were these people to define others with such judgmental, *ugly* words? She rebelled. Why couldn't she have sexual freedom and also be respected for her mind? That had been her quest, but it was a long road.

Even Nick had had a hard time accepting who she was in the early days of their friendship. She remembered going with him to a Rolling Stones concert at the Palladium in 1978. She had been wearing an eyelet white blouse without a bra.

"Why do you dress like that?" he'd asked. He wasn't angry; he sincerely seemed puzzled.

The comment had shamed her. Was he embarrassed to be with her? Twenty years later, it still bothered her. Why *had* she dressed like that? Because she'd wanted to make a statement—*I can be cool, sexy, and smart. I'm adventurous*. She didn't explain that to Nick, but a lightbulb had gone off. He was right—she didn't have to advertise herself.

When she met Danny, she had finally figured out who she was—a woman who supported herself. She would always have boyfriends and girlfriends. If she wanted to have a child on her own, she could afford to. She wasn't going to settle for a man who didn't see her the way she saw herself. Danny said she had a halo of confidence around her, and that was what he'd been drawn to. She hoped her daughter would never have to hide her strengths from boys as she grew up. She hoped that by now, teenage boys had shed the Madonna-whore thing. She and Danny were raising Justin to believe all girls deserved respect, and Claire to know her future was full of opportunity.

Elizabeth picked up an old issue of *Sound* that was lying on her bed. Why was there a boy band on the cover when hip-hop was so hot? The magazine needed more features about the genre. She'd make sure they did ... if she could get out of this bed.

Everything she read about multiple sclerosis said you should pace yourself, but what did that even mean? She could go for weeks feeling fine, doing her tasks, taking care of her family, and then with no warning, MS would take over. She was good at denying she had the disease. But when her legs froze, she was reminded it lived inside her. The exhaustion was hard to accept. She wasn't just tired; her whole electrical system shut down, and if she closed her eyes, she instantly fell asleep. If she was driving during a flare-up, she had to fight to stay awake. When people said she "looked great," they didn't understand how the disease could be ravaging her, no matter how good she looked.

While the nurse went to make herself a sandwich, Elizabeth took her plastic bag of pills from the bedside table and counted them out. Two tablets of citalopram, one bupropion hydrochloride, both for MS depression, another pill that wasn't FDA approved, but her doctor had sworn it helped MS. One gabapentin for her nerve pain and a milligram of clonazepam for her leg spasticity. A lorazepam for her anxiety. A modafinil to stay awake. And two aspirin for the excruciating headache she had. Why had her doctor put her on so many drugs? Were they keeping the disease at bay? Would she be worse if she wasn't on them?

Every health professional she'd talked to said she was not on too many meds. They agreed that stress made MS worse. Did her body know the difference between good stress and bad? Elizabeth would read pages from her journal to see if she had done anything especially taxing to bring on a flare-up. No—she had a normal, chaotic life.

She taught herself to stop dwelling on everyday problems, like the empty gas tank Carlotta sometimes left her with after she'd used the car. She handled the injustices of someone bullying one of her kids. She trained herself to be patient when her husband said he was coming home at six, then arrived at eight. But what about the constant fear she couldn't quell that she would be disabled?

* * *

Nick needed to go home. Spending time with *Sound*'s West Coast staff had made it clear the magazine was going to need more than a redesign. It needed to be recreated. *Sound* was catering to a young audience that wasn't satisfied with the editorial, and it was ignoring its more sophisticated readers who knew the history of rock and were curious enough to embrace new artists. The ideal reader would have an eclectic collection of CDs, from Sinatra to Puff Daddy. Nick had read the demographic reports. The younger readers thought the magazine was too serious; the thirtysomethings found *Sound* trite. The magazine was going to lose both sets of readers if something wasn't done. Nick thought about ad sales. If they wanted to attract higher-end brands, they needed higher-income readers. The other problem was most of their subscribers were men. Women loved music. Elizabeth would have to find a way to bring them in.

Yesterday, one of the editors had handed him a pair of third-row center tickets to see Elton John in Chicago next month. She said they'd done enough coverage on him, and she wasn't going to the show. Nick had done a double take. If setting aside a column for an Elton review wasn't worth her time, these people really didn't know what they were doing. He'd put the tickets in his pocket. Maybe he would take Susan. Or Brooke.

He walked out of his suite at the Bel-Air and sat down for breakfast in their outdoor garden. While waiting for his coffee, he dialed the American Heart Association to make a donation in Charlotte Hayworth's name.

He had called Brooke when he first woke up. She'd had a difficult morning. Her daughters were still mad at her for keeping their father's addiction a secret. "They're angry at both of us and trying to process it. They did ask what's going to happen next, after Tripp finishes rehab."

"And?" Nick had asked.

"I don't know." She'd sounded evasive.

"No?"

"I told the girls that Charlotte left her house to me in the will."

That had been odd. Why wouldn't Charlotte leave the house to her own sons? "That must have been a surprise," he said.

"To all of us."

"Happy surprise?"

She'd been quiet for a few seconds. "We'll see."

"You sound like you want to change the subject."

"I do."

"Okay. Can you meet me later?"

She'd said she would drive over to his hotel in the afternoon. She told him again how incredible the sex had been. She seemed to find it hard to believe it had been wonderful for him too. "You're used to this kind of thing," she said.

No, he wasn't. He had never been so turned on by just pleasing someone. Other women were usually grabbing at him before he was fully undressed. Except Susan, who was basically his roommate now. His good friend too. And a wonderful mother to their daughter. But they would never be lovers again. Neither one of them wanted to try. They would stay in a holding pattern until one of them said, *We need to talk.*

He pushed those thoughts away and called the hotel florist. He asked them to deliver a basket of flower petals to his room. He wanted to make love to Brooke on a bed of roses.

CHAPTER FORTY-ONE
Susan

S usan had decided to take a short course in restaurant management at a cooking school in lower Manhattan. Every morning at eight, she slid into the backseat of a town car and studied her notes on the way to the city.

Don't expect to have your weekends free in the beginning, she had written. She didn't care about weekends now that Kelly was at college. And it was energizing to be out of Greenwich. The town didn't suit her. The women she met split their time between shopping and golfing at their country clubs. A little Junior League here, a little tennis there. They were an army of headbanded blondes in Lilly Pulitzer dresses. She had nothing in common with them. In fact, she wished she had never asked Nick to move to the suburbs in the first place.

She liked going into the city every day, surrounded by stylish people who were energetic and curious. These were her people. Maybe one day, she'd move back after the restaurant took off. Maybe she'd open another one in the city. Her dreams were boundless. In class, Susan learned she would need to refine her business plan. She decided to run Pond House herself, though eventually, she would have to hire a professional manager. She listened as the lecturer explained how to gauge competition and make your restaurant stand out: "Create a menu that appeals to the demographic you're trying to reach with signature dishes patrons want to come back for, but make sure there is always pasta and steak." They were perennial favorites. Susan highlighted something one of the other students had said: "Know how to cook, or the chef might think he's the boss." Susan signed up for an additional course that day—basics and techniques of cooking for restaurant owners.

On the drive back to Greenwich one afternoon, she'd looked out her window at the Hudson River and started to think about Jenna. Would Jenna want to work for her part-time? *Doing what?* Susan asked herself. No. Jenna was a trainer. Susan's daughter had friends in the Hotel School at Cornell; maybe a few of them would want to wait tables during summer lunch hour at Pond House.

The driver exited the West Side Highway and made his way east to I-95.

"Jenna is gay," she said aloud.

Why did she think about touching Jenna? She had seen a doctor on television say sexuality was fluid. Susan wondered what it would be like to experiment. She liked the lemony scent of Jenna's hair and how hard her body was. She could kiss Jenna and see how it felt. What if Jenna didn't want to kiss her? Girls had to be better kissers than men. They probably knew how to navigate a woman's body better than men too. Nick was a good lover, but she'd stopped being interested in him a long time ago. Why was that? It wasn't like she thought other men were better looking or sexier than him.

Nick was back from Los Angeles. He and Elizabeth had been working on the magazine. When he was at the house, he was always polite and friendly. He seemed happier than before, and Susan felt sure it wasn't only the magazine. He had to be seeing someone. She could bring it up, and they could have a candid conversation, but she wanted to keep their marriage stable for now. She assumed Nick did too. If this other woman was important to him, he would have told her.

Susan looked at her watch. Five o'clock. Nick had said he had a meeting and wouldn't be home until late. When she walked into the house, she told Maria she could go home, then went into the kitchen and found a recipe for steak au poivre—a good menu staple. She changed her clothes and got to work. Susan was a very good cook when she was motivated. Besides, no chef was going to try and take over her restaurant.

Jenna arrived at six the next morning. Susan was working out earlier this week so she would have time to get into the city for her class. Riding the bike had become much easier. Jenna was increasing the time, adding weights to her regimen as well as sessions on the rowing machine.

"I don't have time for meditation this morning," Susan said. "Traffic is heavy—the president is at the UN, and they're closing streets."

"You better get going then. I'll see you the day after tomorrow." Susan was looking forward to it. Jenna zipped up her hoodie and left.

Later that day, Susan was excited when her instructor introduced a surprise speaker, Jack Aucoin, owner of Jack's Place. The Soho bistro still had its glow and popularity after thirty years in business. Actors, artists, and models called Jack's Place their hangout, but so did neighborhood regulars. He explained that part of the restaurant's success had to do with making everyone feel at home, including the servers. Their original customers still came back as well as their kids and grandkids, generation after generation. The food ranged from steak frites and burgers to scallops in béchamel sauce. It was consistently excellent. They also did a little thing that made them unique. As diners were leaving the restaurant, the host held out a platter of homemade pralines for anyone to take. It made customers feel like they were getting something for free. Susan had eaten at the restaurant a few times over the years. It was warm and didn't feel exclusive, even though it was. Jack's personality set the tone. When someone ate at Jack's, he was usually there to welcome them with an arm around their shoulder and a genuine "How are you?" In her notebook, Susan wrote, *Be friendlier to strangers.*

The next day, she received a call that the instructor was ill and class was canceled. Susan dialed Jenna, asking if they could push back their training session. They agreed on ten thirty.

Susan was wearing new black yoga pants and a white sports bra with a loose white T-shirt over it, and when Jenna entered, she was already sweating on the treadmill. She stopped for a moment to remove her shirt. Susan considered her breasts her best feature, and the bra showed off her cleavage.

After they finished, she invited Jenna to stay. "I'm testing my cooking skills and want to make a niçoise salad. Why don't you stay for lunch and give me your opinion?"

"Let me see if I can rearrange my appointments."

Susan went upstairs to shower and change, and when she came back down, Jenna was in the kitchen on her cell phone, talking to a client. "I'm free to stay for a while," she said when she'd hung up.

"Good, then we can have a nice leisurely meal."

"Do you want some help?"

"No, thanks. I'm doing this to experiment with some dishes for my restaurant menu."

As Susan flaked the tuna, she looked at Jenna and took in her dark-blue eyes. She felt a stirring inside of her. "You changed your appointment so you could be with me?" she asked quietly.

"I did."

"Why?"

"Why did you ask me to stay?"

Susan shrugged, turning her back to Jenna as she put eggs in boiling water. The recipe Maria had written out for her included red potatoes and string beans. There were a lot of ingredients listed to create this salad. It was a good item to have on her lunch menu, but she wasn't making it again herself. "I told you. To try out the niçoise, and to get your opinion on the salad." She glanced at Jenna.

"Okay."

"I'm getting a little exasperated making it. Too much work."

Jenna stood up and came around the counter. Silently, she scrubbed the potatoes and put them in a bowl. Then she cut the green beans on a diagonal.

"You're good at this."

Jenna put down the knife and gave Susan a look. "Some of us cook for ourselves. We even like it."

It felt like a rebuke. She grimaced. "If I've come off as entitled, I'm sorry. I'm starting this whole new venture, and I'm afraid it might fail. I don't do failure."

Jenna gave her a sympathetic smile. "We all do failure."

Susan shrugged.

Jenna patted her arm. "You'll be fine."

Susan was aware of the warmth left where Jenna had touched her. Her thoughts were jumbled. She felt an urge to kiss Jenna. Why? She was not gay. But Jenna was so beautiful. Susan was drawn to her, no matter how much she tried to stuff her feelings. She could not analyze the way she felt, but it was real. "Let me ask you something."

"Umm?"

"I want to kiss you, and I don't know how it works." Instantly, Susan's face turned red. She was horrified by her words.

Jenna threw her head back and laughed. "Yes, you do, Susan. Don't you see that you're flirting with me? This is a setup. We both know it. You invited me to stay for lunch because you wanted to try out a recipe on me? I don't think so."

Susan shut off the boiling water. "I did want you to stay for lunch."

"And a lot more," Jenna said. She leaned in and brushed her lips against Susan's. Her breath smelled familiar. Spicy cinnamon mints.

Susan kissed her back. Soft, generous lips. She tentatively touched Jenna's face. No lines under her eyes, her neck was firm. "I feel old next to you."

"Don't. I know your body. It's not old."

Susan led Jenna up to the master suite, and they continued to kiss. She let Jenna take off her clothes. There was no rush. Kissing, touching, holding—and no one trying to penetrate her. Susan let out a deep sigh. She felt like she was a young woman again, finally being made love to the way she'd always wanted.

CHAPTER FORTY-TWO

Nick had gone to Dallas for a few days to meet with the printers of *Sound*. Before he left, he'd told Susan Elizabeth was in bed, and Susan might want to check on her. *Fine,* Susan thought. *Elizabeth might know what Nick had really been doing on the West Coast.* She also wanted to show her the plans for Pond House. She gathered her tube of blueprints and drove to Chappaqua.

She was let in by a stern-looking nurse. "She's in her bedroom," the woman said. "I'll take you up."

When Susan entered the master bedroom, she thought she should have brought cookies or flowers, but Elizabeth smiled. "It's so nice of you to come," Elizabeth said when Susan kissed her cheek.

"I'm probably the only person who will tell you this, but you look lousy."

Elizabeth laughed.

"And what's with the closed curtains? Don't you need a little sunshine?" Susan began pulling back the curtains and shades but seeing the IV in Elizabeth's arm gave her a stab of sadness and fear. And how was Elizabeth going to be able to edit *Sound* if she was so sick? "I forgot to bring flowers," she said. "And I see my husband didn't send any, which isn't like him. What about your husband? I thought he was supposed to be very attentive."

"He is. We moved the lilies he bought into the kitchen."

Susan pulled a chair up to Elizabeth's bedside. "How are you feeling?"

"Improving. I was surprised when you called, but I'm glad you came over. I could use the company."

"Nick told me you were sick, but he didn't tell me how sick."

"It looks worse than it is."

"Doesn't matter. Did he tell you I'm opening a restaurant?"

"He did. Congratulations."

Susan picked up the tube of blueprints she'd laid on the floor. "I brought you the plans. I'd love your input."

"I'm flattered."

Susan unfurled them on the bed, pointing to the drawings of an old colonial house and the dormers, where there would be three guest rooms, the screened-in porch for summer dining, and the pond with its weeping willows. She watched Elizabeth as she looked carefully at the drawings, and she told Elizabeth about some menu ideas, the number of tables she planned to have, and how many seatings she was aiming for.

"This is terrific. Finally, we'll have a destination restaurant up here. I think it's brilliant."

"It's been a long time since I've done something I love."

"You were always a successful businesswoman."

"A long time ago ... but I'm coming back." She wanted to ask Elizabeth what she knew about Nick's trip to LA, but she couldn't think of an artful segue. She put the blueprints back in the tube. "Elizabeth, remember when Nick was in Los Angeles? He was there for several days, which isn't like him. He's usually in and out when it comes to work. Was he really there for *Sound* business?"

"Of course."

She took a deep breath. "I know my husband sees other women. And I know why. I don't blame him."

Elizabeth straightened herself up. "Susan, I've been sick in bed, and I'm exhausted. You should talk to Nick."

"Obviously." Susan gazed down at her hands and saw the chipped nail polish on a few of her fingers. She made a mental note to schedule an appointment with her manicurist. "I have a weird question for you."

"Ask."

"Have you ever slept with a woman?" *Oh, the look on your face*, Susan thought. That alone was worth coming over for. "You don't want to answer?"

"I'll answer. I was just surprised. No, I haven't. What about you?"

"I had sex last week with my trainer, Jenna." It felt good to say aloud. "It was much better than with Nick. Not that he isn't good in bed. Women can't seem to get enough of him. But with Jenna, everything felt familiar. And clean."

Susan watched Elizabeth carefully. She didn't seem to be judging her. Well, she had other things on her mind. That needle in her arm, for instance. Maybe she would pass the news on to Nick. Which wasn't necessarily a bad thing. "This isn't my business, Susan."

Susan ignored the comment. "I think a lot of women who are straight also have sex with other woman. Anyway, I like being with her."

Elizabeth still didn't respond.

"Nick is my husband. That's not changing. Nick has my back, and I've got his. But he doesn't tell me about his personal life outside of our marriage, and I don't need to tell him about mine," Susan said but thought, *Unless you want to tell him, then feel free.* She picked up her plans and gave Elizabeth another quick kiss before leaving. "Feel better."

* * *

The steroid drip did its job, and three days later, Elizabeth was feeling better. After a week, her gait was steady, her words came out in full sentences, and she was five pounds heavier. Her neurologist prescribed six weeks of physical therapy to strengthen her body. The drugs had given her extra energy, and she couldn't wait to get back to work. She was ready to put the relapse behind her and concentrate on *Sound*.

Cicely Jackson accepted Elizabeth's offer to become editor in chief of the magazine. She had been managing editor at *The Street* and done an exceptional job. She was creative and tough. They met at *Sound*'s office the following week. Elizabeth called a meeting in the conference room to introduce Cicely to the staff, who were eager to meet the editorial star.

After *The Street* folded, Cicely had created and become editor in chief of *You*, a lifestyle magazine that embraced multiculturalism. Until *You*, magazines had almost exclusively been geared toward a White, Black, or Brown audience. Men in the publishing world— though, not Nick—were skeptical that *You* would last, but after a year, it turned a profit. Cicely was regularly quoted in the media about the dearth of Black women in publishing. She was one of the few who had been given the chance to run a magazine, and her mission was to make publishing more reflective of the country. When she was six months pregnant, she quit and hired another young Black woman to replace her. *You* continued to make headlines with its glossy pages full of contrasting cultural lifestyles, traditions, and celebrities. Its profits stayed steady.

"Good morning," Elizabeth said to the staff when they'd gathered. "I want to introduce you to our new editor in chief, Cicely Jackson."

Cicely was nearly six feet tall. Her hair was a kaleidoscope of color from dark brown to bright blonde, running in corkscrew curls down the middle of her back. She had aqua eyes. Enormous wooden hoops hung from her ears. She wore a blue-and-yellow slip dress with a blue cardigan and silver bangles up and down her arms. On her feet were square-heeled slingbacks covered with a blue-and-gold kimono fabric. She was magnificent. If Elizabeth wanted a face to signal change at *Sound*, she couldn't find someone better than Cicely.

Elizabeth watched Cicely assess her audience. They were mesmerized, and Cicely was used to owning a room. "I'm the new girl in town, and I'm here to shake things up," she said as she looked around and put her hands on her hips. "Who wants to join me?"

When the meeting was over and everyone had filed out, Elizabeth turned to Cicely and said, "They love you."

Cicely laughed. "We'll see."

"Let's get together with the circulation and ad directors. Then I want you to meet our art director, Tate Johnson. He stays," Elizabeth said. "He's smart and, key, very flexible. His ideas are outside of the box. Really, Cic, I can't wait to see you two working together."

"Do you want to get started tonight? Both of you can come to my apartment. We can order in and go over some ideas."

Carlotta could watch the kids, and Elizabeth could meet Danny downtown afterward, which sounded lovely after four days in bed. She smiled. "Sure."

CHAPTER FORTY-THREE

Cicely lived with her husband and toddler on West Sixteenth Street in a three-bedroom apartment they had decorated with vintage prints and African masks. Tate laid out *Sound* cover photos on the dining room table while Cicely set up a buffet of Chinese takeout in the kitchen. Elizabeth grabbed a beer from the fridge but declined any food.

"Our audience is eighteen to thirty-five for advertising purposes," Elizabeth said, "but it's really twenty-five to thirty-five, and that's why those teenage boy band covers are tanking. We're eighty percent men, but we want to broaden our female readership. Women listen to music. And if we get more female buyers, we might be able to get beauty and fashion advertisers."

"Then we should put a woman on the new cover," Cicely said.

"I don't think it matters," Tate said. He was a handsome twentysomething man with mahogany skin and a shaved head. His glasses made him look serious and older.

"Let's brainstorm some artists and go from there," said Elizabeth.

Cicely started looking through the pile of past cover photos. She glanced up at Tate.

He put up a hand in protest. "I didn't pick them."

She laughed. "Good."

"I think our older readers share common musical interests," Tate said. "They'll always like the classics, like CSNY or Tina Turner."

"What about newer artists?" Cicely asked. "What about hip-hop stars? Hip-hop women? Or R&B women?"

"We need both," Elizabeth said.

They came up with a list of musicians: Lucinda Williams, Lil' Kim, Jay-Z, Queen Latifah, Marvin Gaye—

"He's dead," Tate said when they mentioned Marvin Gaye.

The two women looked at him, and Cicely dramatically said, "Death sells!"

They discussed putting several artists on a single cover, one from each decade going back to the '60s, but then decided it would look too cluttered.

"Lola," Elizabeth said.

"Why?" Tate wanted to know.

Cicely's eyes lit up. "Because she's a guaranteed seller."

Lola Stevens—now a one-named artist—was a Cuban American beauty who had begun her career as a fourteen-year-old rapper in the Little Havana neighborhood of Miami. She could have been put in a box labeled "urban," but ten years later, a talent scout saw her in a club singing Aretha Franklin's "Until You Come Back to Me." Her voice was a rare contralto that sounded like melting chocolate. He hooked her up with a manager who changed her hair, makeup, and clothing. Her curvy body and exotic face graced the covers of women's high-fashion magazines, but Lola's piano skills were as impressive as her vocal range. She performed mostly R&B now, but she never lost her rap fans. The raw emotion she put into her songs could silence a concert hall or make a stadium of fans dance. She had starred in a musical on Broadway that ran for a year, and her second film would be coming out in a few months. There were already whispers of an Oscar nomination. And she was one of the wealthiest artists on the planet.

"But how are we going to get her to say yes?" Elizabeth asked. "That woman could be on the cover of any magazine. Why *Sound*?"

"You didn't hire me just because I'm another pretty face," Cicely said. "You hired me because I also have connections." She got up and went to a phone in the kitchen.

Tate raised his eyebrows at Elizabeth.

Cicely came back ten minutes later with an *I told you so* look on her face. "If we come up with an interesting idea and time it to coincide with her new movie, her press agent says he'll ask her to do it. The movie comes out in March. If we shoot it in ..." She paused, thinking. "We have a three-month lead time, right?" She was looking at Tate.

"We need to shoot it in the next two weeks," he said.

"We have to." Cicely agreed. She gave him a pleading look.

"I'll make it happen," he said.

Cicely turned to Elizabeth. "Lola might have her own vision of how she wants to be shot. In which case, I say we consider what she wants."

Elizabeth was quiet. She didn't want celebrities telling the magazine how to do things. It would set a bad precedent. What they thought was best for themselves wasn't necessarily best for the magazine.

"C'mon, Elizabeth, it was your idea. And it's *Lola*. That kind of star doesn't come along very often," Cicely said.

"We'll see." But Elizabeth's opinion was firm. She wasn't going to let a star—no matter how big—tell her how to create a cover.

"We'll create a cover concept she can't refuse," Tate said, clearly sensing her stance.

The three of them began to exchange ideas. Lola was a cash machine, and she had a sense of humor about herself. What if they photographed her against a rain forest set, seminude, with money flying around her?

Elizabeth tilted her head. "Why rain forest? No, let's keep going."

They refined the concept. Forget the rain forest. Tate thought they should recreate Botticelli's *Birth of Venus*, with Lola stepping out of a seashell with hundred-dollar bills flying around her.

That was it.

By eight o'clock, they had decided on new monthly columns for the magazine. They wouldn't only review music but also movies, books, television, and maybe even fashion. The first issue would have a feature on the history of groupies, an argument for the return of vinyl, and a story about underrated singers. They would include service pieces.

"Like what?" Cicely asked.

"Umm ... like when to use a ticket broker, or how to get a star to play at your charity event," Elizabeth said.

Tate suggested a piece about drugs and music—was it possible some hallucinogens really did enhance the creative process?

Cicely shrugged. "Maybe."

"And I think the last page of each issue should be called 'Clef Notes,'" Elizabeth said. "A monthly Q and A with a musician about a particular song and what they were thinking about when they wrote it."

She looked over at Tate. He was drawing little treble notes on his pad.

They hammered out the ideas until Elizabeth put on her coat. She was going to be late for dinner with Danny. Tate would stay with Cicely so they could play with some designs on her computer.

When Cicely walked her to the door, Elizabeth said, "Don't tell anyone, Cic, because I don't want to jinx it, but I think the magazine is gonna work. I think *Sound* is going to be big."

CHAPTER FORTY-FOUR

Elizabeth met Danny for dinner in Greenwich village.

"You look happy," he said once they'd been seated.

"I am. We're probably getting Lola for the cover."

Danny tapped his fist to hers. "Very impressive. Get her, and you're going to sell out."

"Crossing my fingers. How was your day?"

Elizabeth listened carefully to Danny's concerns about the stock market, money, and their future. No new crises on the horizon. Danny was just venting.

Outside, the night was warm for early December. A soft rain was falling, and vapor misted the streetlights. They passed the Bitter End and decided to go in. It had been around since the early '60s. The place was filled with empty tables facing a small brick-walled stage. Later in the evening, a comic would do his stand-up. Elizabeth imagined the days when musicians like Bob Dylan had first tried out their songs in front of a rowdy, drunken audience. She followed Danny to the bar.

It was full, but he found two stools and ordered them Bombay martinis. He cocked his head and appraised her. "You look very sexy tonight."

"I look the same as I did at dinner but thank you."

He looked at her with concern. "We didn't have dinner, you must be thinking of someone else. Are you okay?"

"Danny."

"My name is Michael."

Oh, this is going to be fun, she thought. "Michael. Sorry. You look a little like my husband. I'm married."

He tapped his glass for a second, then without looking at her, he said, "Too bad. I stay away from married women." He turned back to his martini and took a sip.

"Well, it's not like I'm going home with you. We can talk."

He slowly moved his head back and forth, considering her comment. "True."

"So, Michael. What are you doing here?"

He looked her in the eyes. "And you are?"

She blinked. "Excuse me?"

"Your name. You know mine."

"Oh." She smiled. "Sorry. Suzanne." She waited a beat. "Yes, I'm Suzanne."

Danny grinned. "Suzanne. That's a pretty name." He was speaking very seductively. "Nice to meet you. I just quit my job, thought I'd have a couple of drinks and see the show later."

She nodded. "You quit your job. How does it feel?"

"Freeing."

She reached for the toothpick and olive that was lying across her drink and ate it. She watched him out of the corner of her eye. "Don't ask me if I come here often."

He shrugged. "Do you come here often?"

Elizabeth smiled. "I have to leave now." She pointed to the cocktail tables. "I'm going to sit at one of those."

"Why? Is your husband meeting you here?"

"Yes."

"You seem nervous."

"My husband can be jealous. He'll see right away that you're not just some guy I'm talking to. He'll figure out that I think you're hot. He can read me."

"Because you're squeezing your legs together?"

"There's that."

"Well, like I said, I have a rule about married women."

"I'm only a little married."

He twisted the stem of his martini glass and nodded. "Interesting."

She wanted to touch him. Stand up and dance, their bodies moving to the music, but their eyes staying focused on each other. Her silent plea: *Rip off my clothes*. His silent answer: *When I'm ready*.

"Suzanne? You keep squirming. Is it me?"

She paused. "Actually, it is."

"What can I do to make you feel more comfortable?"

"Get us a room."

"I can't, Suzanne."

"Please."

He waited a few beats. "I don't think so."

"I'm begging, Michael."

He was quiet, as if thinking. "Well, maybe I'll break my rule just this once about married women. Because you're just a *little* married." He nodded toward the back door. "Why don't we check out the alley behind the club? It's probably dark and quiet."

Maybe in my twenties, I'd do it, she thought. No, not even then. Her panties were wet. She wanted to grab him and find a place to have sex. Just not the alley. "I'd be afraid someone would see us."

"Don't be afraid, Suzanne. You've got me. You've never had sex behind a nightclub before?"

"No," she said, almost in a whisper. She didn't want to wait any longer. "Michael, I'm a hotel kind of girl."

He looked her over, slowly. "Yeah. I can see that. You're a St. Regis Hotel kind of girl." He ran his fingers along her arm.

She took his fingers and ran them over her lips. "C'mon, Danny."

He dropped his hand. "Michael, honey. I'm Michael. Why are you having trouble with that?"

She was bursting inside. She loved when Danny played with her.

He took a long pull of his drink. "Okay. Why don't you call a hotel and get us a room while I pay the bartender?"

"What about my husband?"

"Tell your husband to meet us there."

CHAPTER FORTY-FIVE

Nick

Connecticut

Nick had driven up to Ithaca for an overnight visit with Kelly at Cornell. She'd asked him to be a speaker at a business forum they were having. By the time he'd gotten home, Susan was already asleep. When he woke up, she wasn't in bed, but he heard the shower running in her bathroom. At seven in the morning, he threw on a T-shirt and sweatpants, deciding to take a shower after breakfast. He was famished. In the kitchen, fresh coffee and a frying pan full of bacon greeted him.

Maria handed him a mug of coffee. "Nice to see you, Mr. Gallagher."

"Always good to see you, Maria." He took a sip of his coffee. "Please stop calling me Mr. Gallagher. You've worked here for ten years. I'm Nick."

"Nick. What do you want for breakfast?" Maria moved efficiently from refrigerator to stove, carrying eggs, cheese, and vegetables.

"Some of those," he said, pointing to the eggs. He sat down on the upholstered banquette in the corner of the kitchen. "Did Susan eat already?"

"Yes, fruit and green tea."

When he finished his eggs, he put the plate in the dishwasher and walked up the stairs that led along a row of windows. The trees were covered with a light dusting of snow. Nick found his wife in her dressing room, blowing out her hair. It was down to her shoulders now and parted on the side. There was a moment when he was able to watch her without being seen—she looked very pretty. Her arms were bare and toned.

She shut off the blow-dryer. "Look who's here," she said when she'd seen him in the mirror. She didn't sound sarcastic, more like genuinely surprised.

He walked over and gave her a perfunctory kiss on the cheek.

"When did you get in?"

"Late last night. You were sleeping.

"Kelly is really an adult now, Susan. I was so proud of her. The way she talks, how informed she is. You should have seen her at that forum. She put together the whole thing. If I were a recruiter, I'd hire her in a minute."

Susan smiled. "We got very lucky in the daughter department."

"Not just lucky. She has confidence and a moral compass. Thanks to you."

"And you."

"I hope so." He looked at her for a long moment, then changed the subject, telling her he had negotiated a better price for printing the magazine. "And I'm considering upping the first run to three hundred thousand copies. Elizabeth agrees. That's tripling the current circulation. It's a gamble, but I think it's worth it."

"Sounds like a smart decision." Susan finished her hair and was applying eye shadow.

Nick pulled out a bench and sat next to her at the vanity table mirror. "I'm concerned about the staff in LA. We're trying to reorganize the magazine, but they're still operating like they did under Joe Noonan. It's a small place, only four writers and editors. I'm not sure they need anyone else at this point. I'll ask Elizabeth to take a trip out there and see what she thinks."

He looked at their reflections in the mirror. She had dark eyes, almost black. His were light blue. Still, he thought they resembled each other. Maybe it was their facial expressions. The way they smiled, frowned, or rolled their eyes at each other. *After a while, that happens to married couples*, he thought.

Susan turned to look at him. "Be easy with her, Nick."

"With whom?"

"Elizabeth. She might be okay now, but I don't know how much traveling she can do. The last time I saw her, she was lying in bed with a needle in her arm."

"She's better."

"Don't push her."

"Then I'll have to go to Los Angeles more often." He looked at Susan, trying to gauge her reaction, but she stayed busy with her makeup.

What about Brooke? he wondered. She'd said she would be moving into Charlotte's house permanently once the school year was over. He could be with her when he had business in Los Angeles. But he didn't want to split his life like that. It wouldn't be tenable, going from one coast to the other, married here, behaving like a single man there.

Despite his infidelity, Nick considered himself a family man, but Susan had made it impossible for him to have the kind of marriage he thought they'd have in the early years. They slipped into an easy accommodation with each other, but it was no longer enough for him. Aside from his wife and Elizabeth, Brooke was the first woman he'd allowed to touch his heart. Why? She was vulnerable and smart. Talented. He loved how he was able to awaken her sexually. Maybe there wasn't just one reason. Maybe she'd filled what was missing in his life, and he decided to let her in.

He watched Susan apply mascara. "What are you staring at?" she asked him as she continued.

"You. You look good."

She put down the mascara wand. "I'm working out. And tasting all that food for the restaurant? It's funny, but by the end of the day, I'm so full, I don't want a meal."

He smiled. "Makes perfect Susan sense."

She grinned.

He stood up and began unbuttoning his shirt. "What's on your schedule today?" he asked. He stripped off the shirt and walked toward his shower.

"Meeting with a restaurant manager. Demolition starts in a few days. If it isn't too cold, we can start building now and finish in the spring. Pond House is coming along."

She was such a fierce, strong woman. He felt a familiar stab of sadness for what they had once been and now become. Friends. "I'm happy for you, Susan."

CHAPTER FORTY-SIX

Nick finished getting dressed and called Elizabeth.

"I don't care what's going on in your personal life, Nick," Elizabeth said to him. "I mean, obviously I care, but you need to stay focused on the magazine. It could be huge. But you can't be staying in Los Angeles just to spend time with Brooke when we're about to launch *Sound*. Start acting like an owner. And not the Joe Noonan kind."

Nick let out a sigh. "I was also in Texas, Elizabeth, on *Sound* business. And I visited my daughter at college."

"You know what I mean. I need you here. Kelly, I understand. But you could have worked out the printing thing over the phone."

"I get it. You're angry."

"Don't try to *handle* me. Why buy the magazine if you don't want to be involved?"

"I am involved, Elizabeth. And as far as Brooke is concerned, you know I went to California for *Sound*. But then her mother-in-law died, and—"

"Yeah, it's the *and* part that's keeping you from being focused."

"I'm sorry."

"Nick, we need this thing to be successful."

"That's why I hired you."

"No," she said forcefully. "You said you were going to be here with me. I wasn't supposed to run the magazine by myself."

"I said I'm sorry. I'm getting in the car. I'll see you at the office at eleven."

"Finally. He decides to show up."

* * *

Elizabeth hung up the phone, still annoyed with Nick. He wasn't treating the business seriously, and she was surprised. He'd never let his personal life interfere with his professional interests before.

She closed her eyes and took some cleansing breaths. Susan was sleeping with her trainer, Nick was sleeping with Brooke, and Elizabeth was the receptacle for all their secrets. It was ridiculous. She was going to tell them to keep their romances to themselves. She couldn't afford this stress that would surely send her back to the sickbed. Her health was more important than the magazine and whatever ego goodies she thought it would offer her. Nick had an extraordinary mind, but he was going through something now. If it got in the way of his commitment to *Sound*, she and the staff would have to do it on their own. She didn't question their collective talent, just her unpredictable energy.

When he stepped into her office, she accepted his apology and introduced him to everyone he hadn't already met. Outside of Cicely's door, Elizabeth said, "If you don't think she's going to be a fantastic editor in chief, you don't know shit about magazines."

He smiled. "I know shit about magazines."

Elizabeth and Nick walked into Cicely's office. Tate Johnson was with her, and they were both hunched over a speakerphone, Tate scribbling on a piece of paper. Cicely walked them outside the office to introduce herself to Nick. "Tate's talking to some very important people," she said, looking at the art director. "For our cover shoot."

Nick nodded. "Elizabeth says you're going to make *Sound* huge. She likes the word 'huge.' I prefer 'profitable.'"

"We all are. Tate's on the phone with the photographer now."

"Because?" Elizabeth asked.

Cicely clapped her hands. "We got her. We got Lola."

"Cicely!"

"Congrats," Nick said.

"Tate, Lola's agent, and the photographer have been going back and forth all morning. Lola loves the cover concept—thank God. Music's most exacting singer wants to collaborate with us. The shoot is scheduled for next week. Tate's working out the details."

"I'd like to come to the shoot," Nick said.

"I think it would be better if you spend the week in your office, going over profits and losses," Elizabeth said. "Maybe meet with the ad director."

"Elizabeth."

She motioned him away. "Nick, you're a genius businessman, so work on the business side. Leave the creative to the three of us. After the shoot next week, we'll show you the mock-ups."

"So you're punishing me for being absent? I don't get to meet the music star because I was in LA?"

"Don't feel sorry for yourself. You can use your special Nick magic on Lola another time."

He frowned.

"I'm teasing you. Just think, we're going to surprise you with photos that will fill your heart with joy."

"Stop being sarcastic."

"Really, Nick, let us wow you."

She watched him think. He looked very cute when he was being serious. "Okay, I'm looking forward to a big fat wow."

CHAPTER FORTY-SEVEN
Nick

New York

A week before Christmas, Nick stood outdoors in the brisk morning air of Rockefeller Center. He sipped from his to-go coffee and looked up at the tree. It was stately, twinkling with colored lights. The angels along the plaza belonged in a fairy tale. The ice-skating rink was packed, the stores already opened and jammed. Tourists lined up in front of Saks Fifth Avenue to see their new holiday windows. He loved Manhattan this time of year. He was glad his office was only a few blocks away from Thirty Rock. It was the magical center of Christmas in New York. He checked his watch—still a few minutes before his meeting with Elizabeth, Cicely, and Tate. They were going to show him mock-ups from the Lola cover shoot.

Susan had planned a skiing trip to Park City, Utah. Kelly would be joining them. Nick said he would fly out in a few days to meet them—he wanted to see Brooke first. Since she'd returned to Connecticut, they'd met several times for dinner in the city, stealing nights to make love when they could. He was becoming more involved with her. Their sexual desire for each was urgent. And he respected her ability to make hard decisions. He was interested in her plans for BatGirls.

Nick was struck by how efficiently Brooke was dissolving her marriage and with minimum drama. Her daughters were beginning to accept that their parents were getting divorced. They were finally okay about moving with Brooke to California. Nick wished he could untangle his family mess as easily as she had. He hoped she wasn't ending her marriage because of him, but Brooke had insisted she and Tripp had been over for some time. She said she was ready to be on her own. He knew she wanted him to stay in her life. Her priority, though, was moving and getting settled with her kids.

He finished his coffee and walked to the office.

"We have five mock-ups," Elizabeth told him when he'd met her in the art department.

He stood next to Cicely as Tate tacked them to the wall. He put his chin in his palm and focused on each one individually. Lola was posed the same in each shot; it was just a question of which one she looked best in.

The singer had been superimposed on the Botticelli painting. She was standing in a seashell, partially nude, her waist-length, wavy brown hair covering her breasts and pubic area. The photo had blurred out the background to a soft pastel. It focused on the singer's face with her dark-brown eyes and delicately curved body. Swirling around her were hundred-dollar bills. Her lips formed a half smile. She looked amused, as if to say, *Do I shock you? Well, good.* She was in on the joke.

The logo was navy blue. The cover line next to the photo read, "Lola: Renewed, Reborn, and Raking it in."

Nick knew a good magazine cover when he saw one. This was going to be a blockbuster. He turned to Tate and Cicely. "Incredible."

"Thank you," Cicely said. "I think it will do really well."

"I love your work," he said to them both. "We're lucky to have you here."

Tate thanked him too.

Nick turned to Elizabeth. "Okay, you. I'm officially wowed."

Elizabeth walked with him down to his office, a large corner suite with a glass desk and two assistants outside the door. "So?" she asked after he'd sat down and she settled into one of the comfortable chairs.

"I told you, I think it's fantastic. Now we need to sell ads. How many pages in the book? And what are your other cover lines?"

"To be determined. But the ad director you hired is already getting yeses from advertisers. She's upped the price to fifty thousand dollars for a four-color full page. There are a hundred and fifty-two pages in the first issue. Her goal is forty percent in ad pages."

"Fifty thousand dollars? That's what *Vogue* gets."

"Not even close, but as you know, it's more than triple of what *Sound* is used to charging."

"And the advertisers aren't complaining?"

"The old ones are. But we're getting new advertisers. Basically, she's selling a new magazine to them. She told them about the Lola cover, and they're willing to place a buy. At least for that issue."

Nick sat back in his chair and crossed his feet on the desk. "Now that you have new editorial and high-priced ads coming in, what's my job around here?"

She folded her arms. "I told you. Showing up."

He shrugged. "Hey, Lizzy, I was in LA working, down in Texas with the printers. It's not like I wasn't doing anything."

She nodded. "Now we need you here."

CHAPTER FORTY-EIGHT
Brooke

March, 1998

The equitable separation of belongings was complete. The divorce was as hassle-free as a divorce could be. With the stock market soaring and home sales at a market high, the Hayworth's six-acre Westport house sold quickly. A dot-com woman and her family were looking to move back East and happily paid over $3 million for it. Tripp and Brooke split the profits. The buyer agreed to move in July 1, after Brooke and the girls had relocated to Los Angeles.

Tripp stayed in Boston. He took classes at MIT and looked for a partner to start a new tech firm. He was finally clean again. He went to the gym regularly. He hired a health coach and started to eat well. There was group therapy, NA meetings, and biweekly sessions with his therapist.

Amanda would visit him during school breaks and summer vacations. Tara said she would visit him when she wanted to. She claimed she was old enough to make that decision, and her parents didn't argue with her. The arrangement was like the one Tripp had had growing up, and the irony wasn't lost on Brooke. But her daughters were okay. No one was stealing cars or driving them off the highway. *So far, so good*, she thought.

Whenever the weather allowed, she would meet Elizabeth for a meal. They had gone to see some Broadway shows, even a Steely Dan concert, where they sang along to every word. She felt like she was sixteen again with her partner in crime. Once, Brooke and the girls had joined the Altmans for a Sunday afternoon at the Metropolitan Museum. But it was a bitter winter, and there were plenty of times Elizabeth didn't have the energy to do anything after work, so they talked on the phone. Brooke couldn't wait for July and the move to LA.

*　*　*

Sound was gaining momentum, and Elizabeth was comfortable relying on Cicely, whom she called "the miracle." The issue with Lola on the cover had hit the newsstands last week. Elizabeth said the seven-day report beat all expectations. They were seeing a 70 percent sell-through.

"What does that mean?" Brooke had asked her.

"It means that seventy percent of the copies on the newsstand have already sold. It could change, go up or down, but that's a fantastic number. Unheard of for *Sound*."

The magazine hired a PR firm. Cicely was doing television interviews about the remake of *Sound*. Lola was getting a lot of press for the cover too. Elizabeth said if the magazine continued to do as well as she thought it would, she'd reduce her time at the office and visit Brooke often once she settled in California.

Brooke saw Nick regularly. She didn't like the idea of sneaking around, but she craved him. His brother had an apartment on the Upper East Side he'd left empty for a few months while traveling in Europe, and they used it after occasional dinners to make love. The sex still left her breathless, and she lusted for his touch and what he did to her. When she saw pictures of him in newspapers or magazines, she marveled that the elegant man wearing a white shirt and French cuffs made love to *her*. He was quoted on television, appearing regularly on *CNBC* to talk about the profitability of publishing and the future of online magazines. She loved him.

But she was surprised she didn't pine for him. The idea of Nick leaving Susan for her felt abstract. She had asked Elizabeth if that made sense, but Elizabeth cut her off.

"I don't want to talk about your personal relationship with Nick," Elizabeth had said. "It makes me uncomfortable, Brooke. I work with Nick. I don't want to be the go-between. I know you don't see it that way, but that's how it feels to me. We're too old for this."

Brooke agreed and felt chastened. She knew she could talk to Elizabeth if things were dire, but so far, they weren't. She wanted to be an independent woman, not a smitten teenager.

She was relieved Nick didn't talk about Susan when they were together. In December, he had gone on vacation with his wife and daughter. When Kelly was home for January intersession, Brooke didn't see him at all. She didn't feel jealous when he was with his family. She knew he didn't sleep with his wife, and she admired his relationship with his daughter. And she understood Susan was a good mother. Susan intimidated her though. Brooke never wanted to have a confrontation with her about Nick, and she respected Susan's relationship with Kelly. Elizabeth once told Brooke that for all of Susan's flaws, Kelly always brought out the best in her.

Brooke knew Nick was uncertain about his marriage. His feelings for Susan were complex. He was also very busy now with the magazine. Even Elizabeth had been surprised by what she called "The New Nick." He was hiring people for the business side of *Sound*, meeting weekly with lawyers and accountants. There were circulation directors and subscription people—positions Brooke had never heard of before. Sometimes he accompanied *Sound*'s ad director to meetings with potential advertisers because he had star power.

When he was with Brooke, he was so animated about *Sound*. One evening, he had mentioned they were thinking about giving a few pages of each issue to fashion. If they did, he'd ask Elizabeth to include BatGirls jewelry in a spread.

"Thanks, but if I want to do that, I'll talk to Elizabeth," she'd said.

Most days, Brooke worked on her jewelry in the carriage house. She still took weekly classes at Silver Ore Gold to learn new techniques and get help on intricate designs. When Barneys called to offer her a booth in their new jewelry department, she said she would be moving to California. They agreed to set up a space for her in their Beverly Hills store starting in the summer.

* * *

Susan was driving Jenna to Pond House. She wanted Jenna to see the work she'd done. As they pulled into the muddy lot, Susan felt proud. A lot of people had dreams, but she had stuck with hers, and now it was almost a reality. The old motel had been demolished. In its place was a new structure made to look like a house from the 1880s—two stories, white clapboard, and large dark-green shutters.

They stepped outside, and Susan watched Jenna put her hands in her pockets as she looked around the property. She walked over to Jenna and gently took one her hands out of her pocket, kissing it lightly. "So, what do you think?"

"You built all this?"

"I had it built."

Jenna put her arm around Susan's shoulders. "I'm impressed."

They walked inside, where there were two dining rooms, a separate copper-topped bar, and three fireplaces. The architect had designed a small foyer, and Susan planned to add a few couches so diners could have cocktails in an intimate setting while waiting for their table.

Jenna walked over to the bar. "I could see myself coming here and having a drink after work."

"What about a dinner?"

"That would depend on the price."

"You know the owner, so you get a discount."

"Then I'd be here all the time."

Susan smiled. "We're still finalizing the most important part of the restaurant, which is the kitchen. Chef has been tinkering with the plans, but he'll be finished by the end of the week. He's decided on a galley kitchen." She looked over at Jenna to see if she knew about galley kitchens. Jenna didn't say anything.

Galley kitchens were designed so each cook had their own station. Susan also liked the term "BOH," which meant "back of the house," where the kitchen staff worked. She felt like asking, *Do you want to see where the BOH is?* But that was like showing off her new expertise, so instead, she took Jenna's hand and said, "Come, let me take you upstairs."

They walked up the steps, where three bright bedroom suites were spaced well apart, each with a large window overlooking the backyard. "We're planning a vegetable garden there," Susan said. "The bathrooms will have large clawfoot tubs and separate showers."

Jenna grinned. "And I'm sure only the finest shampoos and soaps."

"Ha-ha. Next steps are to finalize the menu, build a screened-in porch, and decorate the bedrooms. Other than the kitchen, the big stuff's been completed. My architect and designer are promising a July opening."

Jenna peered into one of the unfurnished bedrooms. She looked back at Susan. "Too bad there isn't something for us to make love on."

Susan turned her head and gave her a conspiratorial look. "Give me your jacket." Jenna watched as Susan took off her own fur-lined shearling and topped it with her down jacket. "Voilà! Just like a feather bed."

After dropping Jenna off at her condo in Somers, Susan took the back roads home. With Nick working at the magazine, she had large swathes of time to herself. She was glad to be busy with the restaurant, working out, and spending time with Jenna. On sunny days, they went on runs together. They hiked along Greenwich's public beaches and in the woods of Ward Pound Reservation. Susan's body continued to change. It was more muscular now. She'd changed her hair too. It fell in soft waves below her shoulders. When Kelly saw her over Christmas, she'd commented how much younger and happier Susan looked.

"Doesn't she, Dad?" Kelly had asked Nick.

"Your mother looks as good as she did when we first met," he'd said.

Susan knew he admired her. Nick was her family, but Jenna completed her in a way he never could. Sometimes she felt bad about it. Usually, she pushed those thoughts away. She didn't think she was in love with Jenna, but the relationship was teaching her more about her body. She understood it better and could show Nick what she liked. Eventually. Perhaps one day, she and Nick would find their way back to each other.

CHAPTER FORTY-NINE
Nick

New York

In mid-April, Cicely, Tate, and Elizabeth were sitting with Nick around the glass coffee table in his office. "What have you got for me?" he asked.

"A new cover concept for the July issue. We think it will work, but we wanted to run it by you," Cicely said.

"You make the decisions, Cic," Nick said.

"It's always good to have an extra eye."

The March cover with Lola had had a final sell-through of 70 percent. The April issue with Queen Latifah on the cover was expected to come in with a 60 percent sell-through. Nick was positive the May issue would sell out. Cicely had been able to get Leonardo DiCaprio. Nick didn't know if DiCaprio could sing a note, but *Titanic* had debuted in December and was the highest grossing movie of all time. DiCaprio also gave the magazine an opportunity to be flexible with its cover subjects. Now they didn't have to restrict themselves to music. Their interviews with film stars were getting good reviews from readers.

For June, Cicely wrangled Madonna. After the industry buzz about the Lola cover, megastars were saying yes to *Sound*. Since the March issue, subscription sales had gone up 20 percent. Nick calculated that if they continued the current trajectory, he could sell *Sound* in two years and make ten times what he'd bought it for. Or go public. He was learning about digital and was convinced that in five years, online magazines would outpace print. It would be wise to either sell soon or keep the magazine and create an online version.

"Are you ready to see what we've got?" Tate asked.

Nick nodded.

Tate laid out a concept cover on the coffee table. It was a photograph of a bar with a large oak table where music stars were playing poker. The background was sepia. Facing the camera was Aretha Franklin with a pair of cards in her hand, a bottle of Jack Daniel's whiskey next to her. There were four other seats at the table, each one taken by a female rock legend. Next to Aretha was Stevie Nicks, her cards face down in front of her. Her hair was long and curly, a silverly gown falling off her shoulder. She was leaning back from the chair, almost tipping it and not looking at the camera. Carole King was caught putting her hair up in a clip, a tall glass of something at her elbow. Next to King, Tina Turner was grabbing at the pot of poker chips, looking like the winner.

In the background, Paul McCartney was tending bar. Van Morrison was strumming a guitar on a stool, Bruce Springsteen was playing the harmonica next to him, and Stevie Wonder was tinkering on an upright piano. The cover line across the top of the magazine read, "The Legends Live On."

"What do you think?" Tate asked.

Nick looked at it closely. He stood up and took a few steps back. He grinned at Elizabeth. "I notice that you've put all the men in the background."

She straightened her back. "It was a group decision."

"It's a good one. Do me a favor, Tate? Can you put the cover in the rack?"

Nick had a magazine rack on the windowsill filled with past magazines. So did Elizabeth, Cicely, and Tate. It allowed them to see what *Sound* would look like to a potential buyer browsing at a magazine stand. He put his hands in his pocket and took a few steps forward. Then he looked at the three of them. "I think it's brilliant. What do the lawyers say?"

"Well, that will be the difference between it staying right here or going out to the reader, won't it?" Cicely said.

"Yep." Nick turned to Tate. "How did you do it?"

"All digital," Tate said.

"Digital is going to change everything," Elizabeth said. "We may never need to do a cover shoot again."

That night, Nick was driving home from the city. He followed the highways through Westchester to Connecticut. Spring had come to the southern Westchester cities of New Rochelle and Yonkers. Dogwood and magnolia trees along the roads were blooming. Susan had said the weeping willows at Pond House were bare. Her restaurant was about thirty miles north and still too cold to flower. They wouldn't bloom before May. Nick was thinking about the pond and how Susan could enhance it. Yesterday, he and Kelly had talked over the phone about the property, and his daughter suggested stocking the pond with koi fish and creating a little Japanese garden around it. Nick had made a mental note to tell Susan.

His thoughts drifted to Susan and Brooke. He hated deception. His relationship with Brooke had depth—she was his lover and friend. No matter what happened, he would never go back to having meaningless liaisons like he'd had with women before he met her. But could he really separate from Susan? She was happier, vital. Maybe she was seeing someone. It was possible, but why? She'd said she didn't like sex. Or was it just sex with Nick? They'd had that conversation for years, and she always insisted it had nothing to do with him.

After dinner last week, he had been having a glass of wine with her when he noticed a chip on the stem. "This glass has a crack," he said.

"Nick, we got those glasses as a wedding gift from your aunt. It's incredible they lasted this long."

Nick had agreed. The glass was hand-cut French crystal. He remembered the afternoon they'd spent at Tiffany's, filling out their bridal registry. Afterward, they walked over to Hamburger Heaven for dinner.

He'd looked at the glass again. "How many more of these do we have?"

"I think thirteen. Originally, there were sixteen."

Nick had thought for a moment. "We take care of our things."

"We do."

He'd smiled. He liked that about them.

His history was with Susan. He'd resisted leaving because he still loved her and didn't want to deal with the acrimony and ugliness that invariably accompanied divorce. He'd seen couples rip their families apart during divorce. Very few people were able to do it and remain friends. There was one couple he knew though. Friends from high school who had married right after college. They'd divorced but still spoke to each other regularly. They shared holidays with their kids, even took vacations together with their extended families. Neither of them had remarried, but each lived with a new partner.

"We love each other; we just can't live together," his friend had said.

That was the key. They both had to feel the same way.

The guy said it had been depressing signing the divorce papers. He and his wife felt like failures for not being able to make their marriage work, but they were determined to be a part of each other's lives and grow their relationship in a different direction.

Nick and Susan had to talk honestly. He was willing to have that conversation with her now. They had completed their time together as a married couple, but that didn't mean they had to stop being a family. He would always be there for her. He knew she would do the same for him. And he intended to keep his relationship with Kelly as it was—maybe they'd grow even closer.

He merged onto the Merritt Parkway. The leaves on the trees were beginning to grow again. A dusting of light green hung from the branches. He loved the Merritt—art deco stone bridges overhead, a simple steel guardrail dividing the north and south lanes, the grassy landscape opened. He was in the country when he hit the Merritt. Susan was sick of Greenwich, but he had grown to like it. He hated his house, but he admired the manicured lawns, stables, and polo fields of Back Country Greenwich. He liked driving on the leafy, secluded roads. It reminded him of Bernardsville, where he'd grown up.

He followed the driveway to his house at the of top of the hill. If they divorced, Susan could keep the place. He'd find something smaller on Long Island Sound. He'd get a boat so he and Kelly could sail. He'd buy a condo in the city too. He was going to be at *Sound* regularly and didn't want to commute. Maybe he'd also buy a house in Pacific Palisades, the Los Angeles neighborhood near Brooke. He was about to pull into the garage when the car phone rang.

"Hey," Susan said.

"Hey."

"I'm at the restaurant, going over kitchen designs. I should be leaving in about an hour. Are you home?"

"Just pulling in."

"Oh good. Can you do me a favor?"

"Sure."

"I have some clothes at the dry cleaner that I've been meaning to pick up all week."

"Can't Maria do it?"

"She has the day off."

"Which dry cleaner?"

"The one on Greenwich Avenue, but you need to go soon because they close in forty minutes."

"Okay. I'll see you later. Are we having dinner at home tonight?"

"Yeah, I'm bringing back a surprise that Chef made for us."

"Sounds good." Nick looked at his watch and put the car in reverse, turning onto Riversville, a pastoral road lined with large estates and horse farms. After dinner, he and Susan could sit in the den and talk about their marriage. Maybe they should do a trial separation.

Nick slowed in front of a house with a beautiful fence—white picket on top of a stone wall. His modern monstrosity had high gates in front of the driveway that made it look foreboding. When he moved out, he would never live in a house like that again. He suddenly thought to call Elizabeth—he loved the new concept cover and wanted to know if the lawyers had gotten back to her. He was pulling over to the side of the road to phone her when a deer leapt in front of the car. When he swerved to get out of its way, the Porsche careened and crashed into a telephone pole.

That was the last thing he saw.

CHAPTER FIFTY
Susan

Connecticut

Susan's hands and legs were shaking, her chest constricted. She found it hard to breathe. She held a pillow against her belly as she curled into the corner of her bed and wept until her body felt drained. The crying eventually started again in fits of tears and snot.

A half hour later, she was able to take the pillow away from her stomach and reach for some tissues. But she couldn't control her body and began to wail.

Finally exhausted, she rocked back and forth until she was able to put the pillow aside. She inhaled and exhaled deeply as her breath began to normalize. Slowly, she picked up the phone and dialed. *Be strong*, she told herself. *Be calm*. Her daughter answered on the third ring. "Hi, honey."

"Mom? What's the matter?"

Susan knew her voice had given it away. She'd gotten a handle on her crying, but her voice sounded weak, even to her—weak and broken.

"Tell me!"

"Kelly ...."

"Mom! What is it?"

Susan took a deep, fortifying breath. "Dad was in a car accident."

"I'm leaving Ithaca now. I'll be there in four hours. Which hospital?"

Susan was shaking her head. "No ... honey. He didn't survive."

"Yes, he did! *He did!*"

"Kelly, he hit a telephone pole. He died."

Kelly screamed.

Susan tried to comfort her, but it was so hard over the phone.

"I'm getting in the car now. I'm coming down," Kelly said between sobs. "You don't know that he's dead. They took him to the hospital. The doctors are still trying."

"I was at the hospital. He was dead by the time the ambulance arrived at the scene. He died instantly." Susan didn't believe that, but it didn't matter. She was patient and precise. "Kelly, you're not driving. You'll take a plane to Westchester Airport."

Kelly was wailing.

Susan tried gently hushing her. "Are you alone, honey? Where's your roommate?"

Kelly continued to cry.

"Kelly?" Susan's voice became firmer. "Kelly, right now. Is someone with you?"

"Julie, my roommate. She's here."

"Put her on the phone." Susan listened as her daughter handed off the receiver. She told Julie what had happened and asked her to pack a bag for Kelly and drive her to the airport. "Let me talk to Kelly again," she said after the girl agreed.

Kelly was still crying, but she wasn't screaming anymore.

"We're going to be okay. I promise. But first, you need to get home safely. Are you listening to me?" Susan voice was no longer weak. Her instincts as a mother trumped her grief at the moment.

"Yes." Kelly's voice, however, was wavering.

"Okay, good. Julie is going to drive you to the airport. She's going to stay with you until you get on that plane, and she's not leaving the airport until it takes off. I'm going to keep calling you, so leave your cell phone on. You call me too. Let's just get you to Greenwich. Step-by-step. We can do this."

Kelly was sniffling but not answering.

"Kelly? Tell me what I just said."

"Julie is going to drive me to the airport."

"What else?"

"That you'll be calling me, and I should leave my phone on."

"And you call me too, if you want. And Julie is not leaving the airport until the plane leaves. Remember that. If the plane is delayed, she'll still be there."

"Okay."

"Okay, good. I'll see you later. I love you." Susan would stay focused on her daughter. If she concentrated on Kelly, she would be okay.

CHAPTER FIFTY-ONE
Elizabeth

Susan called Elizabeth, and Elizabeth had to tell Brooke. There would be a service at Frank E. Campbell's Funeral Chapel on Madison Avenue and a cremation after. Susan had asked Elizabeth to call Nick's business associates and let them know the time and date. Elizabeth asked if she needed any more help, and Susan asked if Elizabeth would speak at the funeral. She and Kelly didn't have the strength. It was an honor, and one Elizabeth did not take lightly.

The day of the funeral, Danny kept checking on her. Did her legs hurt? How was her neck? She was stuttering a little, so maybe she shouldn't do this.

She knew he meant well, but he was irritating her. "Stop it. I'm okay." And he had.

At the service, she stood at the podium and told her fellow mourners about her friendship with Nick. They had been brother and sister for more than twenty years. She shared stories about their late-night talks in the city, their love of music, and his pride in being the man of honor at her wedding. She looked at Susan and Kelly in the front row and said she would miss and remember Nick every day of her life. She prayed that in time, their pain would ease. "I know his print will be on your hearts forever."

Elizabeth left the funeral in a daze. Her legs were zizzing. Her head felt like it was on fire. She could not accept that he was dead.

She called Brooke at home and tried to console her, but Brooke didn't want to be comforted. She wanted to be left alone.

Danny begged her to stay in bed and rest. She refused. For a week, she went to the office and tried to be productive. When media organizations called to ask how Nick's death would affect the future of *Sound*, she passed the calls to Cicely, who directed them to their PR firm. Every time Nick's name was mentioned, Elizabeth's arms would start to tingle.

She perked up when Cicely told her the lawyers had approved the Legends of Rock cover. Cicely thought they should double the print order; the monster was going to sell out. Elizabeth agreed. She wished she could share the news with Nick. He would have been thrilled.

Instead, she called Susan to tell her about the new cover. With Nick gone, Susan was technically her boss. "It's going to be the best-selling issue *Sound* has had yet," Elizabeth said. But Susan couldn't even fake interest.

"It's your baby. Do what you want with it," Susan said flatly.

"Susan, you're the majority owner."

"Nick was, not me. You should have it."

"Susan, I can't do the work Nick was doing. Keep the magazine. It'll be a great source of income for you."

"No. When we both feel up to it, we should meet. If you don't want it, I'll sell it."

"We'll talk," Elizabeth said and hung up the phone.

The following week, she was walking up the stairs to Justin's room so she could read him a bedtime story. She heard Danny in Claire's bedroom, asking questions about her day at school. She caught a glimpse of her daughter in pajamas, hands on hips, giving her father a dramatic rendition of a fight she'd had with her best friend. As she did, Elizabeth missed a step and fell. She flailed, trying to grab on to the railing, but she missed and landed hard on her butt. The kids surrounded her as Danny pulled her up. "I'm fine," she told them. "Just a little clumsy." She felt bruised on her elbows and knees, but that was the extent of her injuries. She walked back to the top of the stairs, turned triumphantly, but then caught the worried looks on the kids' faces.

Danny gathered them into his arms. "Don't worry. It's not Mom's MS. It could have happened to any of us." He walked back to the step where she tripped and looked closely at it, moving his shoe back and forth. "The carpet needs to be stretched. I'll call someone tomorrow to get it done. In the meantime, everyone be careful walking here until we get it fixed. Justin? Claire? Come here. See how it's buckling? Slow down when you get to this step. Walk around the spot."

Elizabeth's arms and legs were tingling when she went to bed, but the fall didn't seem to have done any other damage.

The following morning, she was admitted to NYU Hospital—her legs had stopped working again.

She stayed in the hospital for three nights. IVs, PT, and rest. She wanted to be released and recuperate at home, but her doctor urged her against it. "It wasn't just the fall," he said. It was the added stress of family, work, and grieving. "You have a nice private room here, Elizabeth. Read a book and try to relax."

They put a cot in the room so Danny could stay over the first night. He brought the kids to visit her after school. Claire stayed over the second night and took the following day off from school. A social worker came to see Elizabeth, uninvited, and asked if there was anything she could do for her. She was looking at notes on the clipboard attached to the end of Elizabeth's bed, and Elizabeth assumed there must have been a paragraph that read, *Friend just died unexpectedly. Patient fell down stairs.*

"No," Elizabeth said. "There's nothing you can do for me."

On the third day, she was able to walk to the nurses' station with a cane. When Justin climbed into her hospital bed the following night so she could help him with his homework, she told her doctor she wanted to be released. Nurses and doctors had been in her room throughout the night, checking her temperature and her blood pressure, adjusting IVs, switching catheters, and taking blood. It was not relaxing. She had a better chance of recovering in her own bed.

At home, the MS flare continued to dissipate, but she couldn't get out of her funk. Cicely didn't need her except when she wanted to bounce around some magazine ideas, which they did on the phone. Other than that, Elizabeth thought mostly about Nick. Brooke was her best friend since childhood, but Elizabeth's friendship with Nick had provided her with something else. Maybe because he was a man. Sometimes she got the feeling Brooke was jealous of her marriage to Danny. But Nick had always been happy for her, even if his relationship with Susan was difficult.

A month after Nick died, she'd been shopping in the mall when she smelled a whiff of cologne—it took her back to 1980 when Nick wore the same one. Driving to pick up the kids from Hebrew school, she heard Jackson Browne on the radio sing "Running on Empty" and remembered the day she'd bought the album at a record store near Bloomingdales. She and Nick talked over dinner that night, wondering if it was Jackson's best album. It was 1977. That was the summer of the great New York City blackout, when she had been alone in her three-floor walk-up. He came to her door, his car parked in front of her building, and drove her to his parents' beach house on the Jersey shore where they'd spent the week.

In the summer of 1981, they'd joined an eight-person share house in Southampton. At night, they danced at the discos, one of them sometimes bringing back a person they barely recognized in the morning. During the days, they lay together on the beach, talking about their dreams. Nick wanted to be a millionaire, and she wanted to be a freelance journalist, traveling to El Salvador where she could cover the war. What neither of them expected was to die young.

With Nick gone, Elizabeth noticed death everywhere. She'd pick up the newspaper and read about children killed in drive-by shootings. A man murdered on Park Avenue. The woman sitting next to her at the nail salon had told her about a two-year-old who'd drowned in his family's pool. His parents had been right there. Maybe they'd turned away, and in the blink of an eye, their baby was dead.

The world started to frighten Elizabeth. She had to convince herself to get out of bed. Once she forced herself into the shower, she would begin to feel better. But as she dressed, her mind would obsess with situations she couldn't control. What if there were a house fire, and her kids couldn't get out in time? What if she were driving on the highway, and a truck rear-ended her? What if? What if?

Danny talked to her about the difference between possibilities and probabilities. It was possible someone could cross the street and get hit by a car, but it wasn't probable. His words didn't convince her. He gave her space to grieve, and he was patient. If she woke up in the middle of the night from a bad dream about Nick, Danny would hold her. He was open and attentive when she'd tell him a funny story about Nick. He respected her boundaries and didn't pry about their past.

To cheer her up, he took her to see James Taylor performing at a private supper club. When Taylor began to sing "Fire and Rain," Elizabeth abruptly wanted to go home. The lyrics made her weep.

Cicely called and asked what Elizabeth thought of running a roundup piece, asking music, film, and political celebrities to name their favorite albums and why. Elizabeth thought it was a great idea. After she hung up, she searched through her own personal memorabilia—notes of her children's first years, mementoes from early dates with Danny, tearful diary entries from college. In one pile, she found what she'd been looking for: pages from a winter night in 1980, when she and Nick had written down their ten favorite albums. They'd shared the lists with each other and explained why they'd picked the albums they did.

Elizabeth had included *The Last Waltz*; *The Wild, The Innocent and the E Street Shuffle*; and *Madman Across the Water*. Nick also had a Bruce album, *Greetings from Asbury Park*. She smiled sadly as she examined his handwriting. It was very precise, as if at some point in his life, he'd tried to perfect it. Nick had a seemingly natural, smooth elegance to him, but it didn't come without work. He tried hard at everything. She read some of his other picks: *Eat a Peach* by the Allman Brothers, *Some Girls* by the Stones, *Physical Graffiti* by Led Zeppelin.

When Nick had asked her to be the editor of *Sound*, she'd said she didn't know anything about music, but that wasn't true. Like Nick, music was in her bones. It had been one of their deepest bonds.

CHAPTER FIFTY-TWO
Susan

There were only a few more weeks in the semester for Kelly, but she was able to cut them short. Cornell allowed her to take her finals early and come home. She'd applied to Columbia for the following year and had been accepted—she wanted to stay near her mother.

Two weeks after Nick died, Susan, with the help of Jenna and Kelly, had gathered up his belongings and given them to a local men's shelter. Missing him took up residence in her body as a terrible ache in her gut. All those mornings when they'd gotten up and barely acknowledged each other—what if she had made an effort to kiss him? When had she begun taking him for granted? What if they had both tried harder to keep romance in their marriage?

She kept photo albums, video tapes of special occasions, and romantic notes he'd written her over the years and put aside two of his watches—a Patek Philippe for herself and an engraved Rolex Kelly never took off. Susan put his wedding band on a chain and wore it around her neck.

She spent the following days talking to lawyers, accountants, and hedge fund managers to learn the details of the estate she and

Kelly were inheriting. They were a lot wealthier than she'd thought. Neither of them would ever have to work again, but work was the one thing keeping Susan sane and giving her purpose—the restaurant was opening in the summer.

It took only five days to sell the house in Greenwich. With Nick gone, she hadn't wanted to spend another day in that town. She purchased a co-op on West Seventy-Fourth Street, overlooking the park. It was a five-minute walk to the apartment she had grown up in. She also bought a fifteen-acre estate in Bedford, New York, twenty minutes from Pond House. It was the exact opposite of her home in Greenwich, built before the revolutionary war. When her daughter saw it, she'd fallen in love. Susan lived in the main house, a white colonial with black shutters. The previous owners had rewired the home, rebuilt the kitchen, replaced the floors, and refurbished the three stone fireplaces. It had a wraparound veranda and a new pool near a spring-fed lake in the woods. It was the kind of place Nick would have loved.

There were two smaller houses on the property. Maria and José lived in the largest. Susan had asked Jenna if she wanted to move into the other. "You've made enough changes already, and you're grieving," Jenna said. She was right, but that didn't mean Susan had to like it.

In the early years of their marriage, before they became wealthy, Susan and Nick had taken walks across the Brooklyn Bridge. They would spend weekends at the historic Mohonk Mountain House and hike or snowshoe. One weekend, he taught her to ski in Vermont. It was easy being with him. She didn't understand why she had pushed him away. Maybe she should have tried harder to be his lover. But her body had stopped being turned on. She understood now she was attracted to a person—man or woman— and that person hadn't been Nick for quite some time.

Kelly stayed with Susan at the Bedford house. She'd brought home her little black cat with green eyes she'd adopted in Ithaca. His name was Timothy, and he quickly shifted his allegiance from Kelly to Susan. Susan wasn't a cat person, but she found herself liking him. Her supposed allergies never acted up. When no one was around, she stroked him behind his ears and let him sit on her lap and purr. Kelly thought Susan should keep him in Bedford. He would be alone all day in the city while Kelly was in class.

"I thought cats like to be alone," Susan said. But the truth was, she enjoyed having Timothy around. She liked talking to him—he was a pretty good listener until she started to complain. Then, he would jump off her lap and find something more interesting to do.

Kelly didn't want to be alone after Nick had died, but she agreed to move into their city apartment when classes began in August. Until then, she continued to stay with Susan. They took care of each other. She accompanied her mother to the restaurant and offered suggestions on the menu and property. Kelly said she and Nick had talked about putting fish in the pond and building a garden around it.

Susan looked away. "No," she said, almost to herself. "I'm not good at keeping things alive."

CHAPTER FIFTY-THREE
Brooke

Nick's death had stunned Brooke. Everyone who was important to him could mourn aloud, publicly. They attended his funeral and shared their grief.

She loved him and had to keep it to herself. Elizabeth had reached out, but Brooke wasn't ready to talk. She was devastated. Every morning, she forced herself into the shower. The hot water focused her, so she could think and organize her day. Toweling off, she would look in the mirror and see a pale, sad face. She pushed herself to get to the jewelers' bench, pay her bills, and take care of her daughters, but it was all she could manage. Her weight dropped to a point where her ribs were beginning to show. That was when she finally made an appointment to see Dr. Waxman.

"Brooke, you've been through so much in such a short period of time. Your husband's addiction, your mother-in-law's death, divorce, selling your house, your upcoming move to California, and now your lover has died. Any one of those things is a major life event. You should be proud of yourself. You're resilient."

Brooke thought about it. She *was* resilient.

"When a loved one has been sick for a long time, his death often feels like a relief. At least initially. This is different."

"Because he died suddenly. We were just beginning. He gave me confidence. He saw me as a desirable woman. I craved sex with him."

Dr. Waxman nodded. "Therapists call it the 'grief no one talks about.' Sexual bereavement. You're not alone. Many people grieve the loss of sex with their partner. You're just self-aware enough to bring it up."

"I miss all of him," Brooke said. "I miss our conversations, our dinners, our walks. He was interested in everything I did and said. I'm lonely. I can't talk about him with anyone other than Elizabeth, and I don't want to talk to her about it now. She's grieving her friendship with him, and her health is fragile. We're mourning the same man but for different reasons. I was in love with Nick, but she was the only one who knew."

Dr. Waxman pursed her lips. "You were in a relationship that society traditionally doesn't know how to react to. You're experiencing grief isolation, and that's very hard. But you're living your own life, Brooke, not society's."

"I know."

"I'll tell you the same thing I tell anyone who's grieving the loss of a loved one," Dr. Waxman said. "Mourn as long as you need to. Take care of yourself. You must eat. You're too thin. Do things that give you pleasure. Know that grief is going to come in waves, sometimes when you least expect. When you're ready to share your feelings with Elizabeth, or anyone else, you will."

"I'm moving with the kids to Los Angeles as soon as school is out."

"How do you feel about that?"

"Hopeful. I wish I could move tomorrow. And once I'm there, I'm going to commit to BatGirls, my jewelry line. Nick was my biggest supporter."

"Are you doing it for him?"

Brooke considered her feelings. "No," she said. "I'm doing it because he made me realize I could."

"I know you're hurting, Brooke. You've had so many challenges to deal with, and you've met all of them. Remember, there might be days when the grief feels overwhelming, but that's normal. Grief is usually two steps forward, one step back. You might want to investigate a bereavement support group when you're out there. I'll ask some colleagues if they know of a good one."

Brooke nodded, but she wasn't ready to join a group. Dr. Waxman peered at Brooke, seeming to consider what to say. She then turned around and opened her desk drawer. "I have something I want to give you. I think it will help, at least for now." She pulled out a CD and read the title before handing it to Brooke. "It's a guided meditation," she said. "I listen to it at the end of every day."

Brooke put her hands up in protest. "Oh, no, I don't want to take yours."

Dr. Waxman smiled. "I have several copies at home. Take it."

Brooke accepted the CD and thanked Dr. Waxman.

"Remember, I'm always here if you want to talk. Pick up the phone whenever you want to speak."

"I will."

At home, Brooke popped the CD into a player beside her bed. She stretched herself on top of her comforter, listening to a woman's soothing voice. She closed her eyes as the voice told her to imagine a gold-colored liquid seeping into all spaces of her body where she felt pain. She was guided to her neck, and she imagined a fluid that looked like sunshine, swirling through her tendons. Her neck began to ease. The voice told her to concentrate on her shoulders, and the flowing gold caused her shoulders to relax. The voice continued, and the tightness in Brooke's stomach and legs went away. She became drowsy. Over the coming months, she'd listen to the CD every day—the reliable woman on the player whom Brooke could trust to make her feel better.

CHAPTER FIFTY-FOUR

In June, Brooke and her girls moved into Charlotte's house. They decided not to change a thing except the master bedroom, which Brooke had bought furniture for that was more in keeping with the lines of the house, including removing the pink fainting couch from the dressing room.

Later in the week, after it was dark, she walked outside, past the pool, to the place where she and Nick had first made love. She got on her knees and smoothed the grass with her hands, silently promising to always remember him and the confidence he had given her to believe she was worthy of being loved. She doubted she would ever meet someone who would excite her the way he had. But hopefully, she had a long life ahead of her, and he wouldn't be her last lover.

She and the girls spent a few weeks looking for a dog. "We'll see what's out there," Brooke said. "No promises."

Tara laughed.

"What's so funny?" Brooke asked.

"You're going to see what's out there? No one who loves dogs sees a puppy and says, 'We'll see.' You'll be bringing that baby home."

That comment made Brooke put it off.

The day her daughters brought home a twelve-week-old male golden retriever, she cuddled and kissed him and refused to put him down.

"Let him feel the floor, Mom. He needs to know he can walk," Amanda said.

Brooke was reluctant. When she did, he promptly peed on the tile.

"Okay," Tara said, scooping him up. "I'm the one who's training him. I bought a book. Goldens are smart; it won't take long. Now for the fun part—what are we going to name him?"

They decided on Crosby.

"Like Crosby, Stills, and Nash," Brooke said. Most nights, Crosby slept next to her. He made missing Nick a little easier.

The three of them—with Crosby at their heels—worked together to design a studio for BatGirls in the detached garage. Now that Amanda and Tara had their initials on the company name, they were enthusiastic about making it a success.

In August, Tara would start her first semester at Chapman University in Orange, about an hour from their house. Amanda was enrolled at a private school a few miles away.

Brooke hired a builder for the studio. She was used to working on a jewelers' bench three feet wide with one cabinet for her supplies. Now she had a sleek wooden counter that went along the length of the entire garage. Large windows and a skylight added natural light. There was a white tiled work area with a backsplash for her hot connections and two acetylene gas tanks for soldering. She bought fire extinguishers and installed a special ventilation system to keep the chemical fumes out. The floor was covered with industrial carpet so she could easily vacuum up any stray pieces of metal. She had a cabinet built for her spools of silver, copper, and gold wire. She bought another at the hardware store for her hammers, tweezers, and rulers. She purchased a new jewelers' kiln and a collection of enamels in brilliant colors.

She also bought silver and copper disks, a "guillotine machine" to cut lengths of precious metal sheet, punches, and cutouts. There were three drawers dedicated to green and purple wax and the tools she needed to carve it. She could make jewelry molds from the wax, creating as many copies as she wanted if she ever chose to develop a line. Then there were her gems. She kept them in little pouches with labels for type, carat, and quality. She also had an array of semiprecious beads and stringing supplies.

She bought a few emeralds, sapphires, rubies, and diamonds and kept them in a safe.

On the day the studio was complete, Brooke and her daughters did a walk-through, with Crosby trotting behind them, taking in the vast, meticulously clean workshop. Each tool had its own place. It was pristine.

"Mom, it's beautiful," Tara said, looking around.

Brooke put her arms around both her girls and grinned. "We did it together."

"Give me a sec," Amanda said. She walked out of the studio and came back a few minutes later. "Close your eyes."

Brooke scrunched them tight.

"Now open."

Amanda handed her a heavy tissue-wrapped package.

"It's from both of us," Tara said.

Brooke carefully unwrapped the paper. Inside was a tiled sign.

"We had it custom made for you," Tara said.

BatGirls Studio was written in cobalt blue across a white-painted terra-cotta tile. Little cobalt-colored bats were flying above the letters.

Brooke's eyes filled with tears.

"Mom?" Amanda asked.

Brooke kissed her daughter's cheek. "They're happy tears." She wiped her face and smiled. "This means so much to me, that you honor my work. It's perfect. Thank you, girls."

Amanda got a hammer and nail from one of the drawers and hung the sign on the outside door. "You're a professional jeweler now, Mom."

Brooke grinned. "I am."

Tara nodded her approval. "So, time to get to work."

A week later, Brooke had her first order. Out of the blue, Terry Cone, the music publicist Brooke had met at Charlotte's memorial party, called to say she'd heard Brooke was living here now. She had a suggestion. The night before the Grammys, there was a charity gala called MusicCares. "Everyone in the industry comes," Terry said. "They have a silent auction to benefit musicians who need emergency help for either health or financial reasons. It's a good charity. Why don't you auction off one of your pieces? It will get your name out there."

Brooke felt butterflies flying inside her belly. "What kind of piece?"

"The kind a rockstar would wear. I'll give your number to the woman who runs the event. She's always looking for more stuff they can auction off. One-of-a-kind jewelry is a favorite. And something else—if you're willing, I have a stylist I want you to meet. She works with my new client, Laurie Rollins. Maybe she would consider your jewelry for Laurie."

The butterflies in Brooke's belly began swooping in circles. An incredible possibility was being dropped in her lap. "That's unbelievably generous of you."

"I suggest you make another piece—something large and interesting like you wore at Charlotte's. If the stylist likes it, who knows? Maybe Laurie Rollins would consider wearing it to the Grammys."

Laurie Rollins had released this year's number one pop single. Her bluesy voice and sultry songs were getting great reviews. God, if Laurie wore one of Brooke's pieces ....

Brooke was petrified. What if the pieces didn't come out well? What if no one bid on the necklace she'd made? She was already imagining a necklace for the auction. What if Laurie hated the jeweled cross Brooke thought of creating for her? Brooke shut off the noise in her head. Always say yes to an opportunity, Nick had told her.

"I would love to do it," Brooke told Terry.

"Good. We'll stay in touch. I'll call the people at MusicCares after we hang up. They're good about getting back to people, so you should get a call or email from them within a day or two. How soon before you can get a piece ready for the stylist?"

"Can I call her? That way, I'll have an idea of what she likes."

"Let me speak to her and Laurie, and I'll get back to you."

"Okay. And thank you so much for thinking of me, Terry. I'm excited to do this."

Brooke looked around her studio and thought, *Just don't fuck it up*.

CHAPTER FIFTY-FIVE

"You're designing a piece for Laurie Rollins? Congratulations!" Elizabeth said when Brooke had called with the news while rearranging books on the shelf in her home office. "You're going to be a star!"

Brooke laughed a little. "I'm going to design it. That doesn't mean she'll wear it."

"What are you thinking of making?"

"I'm going to fabricate—"

"'Fabricate' sounds like sewing."

"I know; it's just jewelry-speak for 'handmade.' Anyway, I was thinking of a cross, but that feels a little too Madonna-ish. Then I had an idea that's really out of the box."

"Tell me."

"I've been thinking about the elephant in the room. My life has been an elephant in the room. Tripp's drug addiction was an elephant in the room. My relationship with Nick was the elephant in the room. You see what I mean?"

"It's the thing none of us talk about but affects our choices and actions."

"Right. So I thought, 'What if I do a large enamel piece?' A big elephant in a room with a bunch of people trying to ignore him."

"You can do that? Because if you can, a lot more people than Laurie Rollins will love it—you can get news coverage on a piece like that. I'm sure *Sound* would do a story about it."

"You are?"

"I'll ask Cicely if she can devote a spread to it with a sidebar about you. It's a brilliant idea. Everyone has an elephant in the room. You'd make it into a necklace?"

"A big, heavy necklace. Her publicist—the one I told you about? She said Laurie was looking for a big conspicuous piece."

"What about MusicCares?" Elizabeth asked.

"For that, I'm thinking of something smaller, maybe a ring. Not enamel because it's so fragile. Maybe something a little funky, like a spinnie ring with some gems."

"Price it high. If you don't, the stars will think it's a cheap piece of jewelry."

"That didn't occur to me, but it makes sense. Thanks for the tip," Brooke said.

Elizabeth said she would come out for the MusicCares event and the Grammys, if she felt well enough to travel.

"You have to stay with me," Brooke insisted.

"Of course." Elizabeth was silent for a few seconds. "I want to tell you about a conversation I had with Susan."

Brooke took a sharp intake of breath. "Go ahead."

"She wants to sell the magazine to me."

Brooke felt her face muscles ease. "Will you buy it?"

"I don't think so. I love what we've done with it and how well it's doing. Our instincts were right, and Cicely is a magazine magician. I like being involved—it ... reminds me of Nick. One of our bonds was music." Elizabeth hesitated. "Brooke, about Nick—"

"I don't want to talk about him."

"Brooke. We all miss him. You, me, Susan. Have you thought about joining a bereavement group?"

"My therapist mentioned it, but I haven't yet. Have you?"

"Well, I have Danny," Elizabeth said, and based on her pause, Brooke could tell she instantly regretted it. It had come out as cruel, a way to point out that Brooke was alone, and that had obviously not been her intention.

Nevertheless, it stung. "Yeah, you do."

"I'm sorry. I didn't mean to sound insensitive. I just meant the group could be a place to share your feelings."

Brooke hesitated. "When I'm ready to share my feelings, it will be with you. Anyway, I have to go, but you're coming out here, right?"

"I don't think I'll wait till the Grammys. I need my Brooke fix. How's the middle of the month?"

"Can't wait. I love you."

"Love you too."

CHAPTER FIFTY-SIX

Brooke's days started falling into a satisfying rhythm. Most mornings, she and Crosby jogged through the streets of Bel-Air. Occasionally, she drove to the UCLA campus and ran a few laps around the track. After breakfast, she changed into old jeans and a T-shirt to work in her studio. She usually left the door open so Crosby could come and visit, and she'd installed an electric fence so he wouldn't run away or, God forbid, get run over. *No more death*, she begged the universe. When it was hot, she swam laps in the pool. Dinners were usually with Tara and Amanda unless the girls were out. It only took a few weeks for them to make friends. One cute boy was coming to visit Tara regularly. Brooke didn't ask questions about him. She'd watched them flirt with each other, holding hands and giving each other knowing looks. She doubted they had something serious going on. She was just happy her daughters were adjusting to their new lives.

But it was Brooke's work that engaged her the most. Making the spinnie ring for MusicCares had been easy. She soldered and hammered an 18-karat gold ring, then fashioned a simple gold band with three small diamonds on it. The band fit over the wide ring and spun. She decided to charge $1,800 for the piece because eighteen represented luck in Judaism.

The Elephant in the Room was a challenge. She researched how the concept could be executed. On a piece of paper, she drew a picture of three people sitting on a couch, oblivious to a large elephant in front of them. She sketched out the scene, then transferred it to a sheet of silver. She was taking out her enamels so she could color-test them in the kiln when someone knocked on the open studio door.

Standing there was the famous composer Brooke had first seen at Charlotte's funeral. "Hi, I'm David Hines. You must be Brooke."

Brooke stared at him. He was wearing a USC T-shirt, white shorts, and flip-flops. His tanned face was lined. He had curly gray hair and alert blue eyes. He was trim, muscular, and much older than he appeared on those early album covers but still handsome. "Of course, you're David Hines. Please come in."

She showed him to a swivel chair at her bench. Bel-Air certainly wasn't Westport—one day, the pool guy was at the door, the next, it was David Biggest-Songerwriter-Ever Hines. "I wish I had something comfier to offer you, but a jeweler's studio isn't meant for entertaining. Unless you want to go inside the house?" She gave herself a light slap on the forehead. "Sorry for my manners. Let's go inside."

"No, no. I like it in here." He looked around, taking in her bench, cabinets, and skylight, then sniffed. "It smells like creativity."

She smiled. "What can I do for you, David Hines?"

"I'm sorry I didn't call first, but it was a spur-of-the-moment thing. I thought I'd take a shot and see if you were in."

"Here I am."

"Do you have a little time? I don't want to interrupt your work schedule. I hate when people do that to me."

She looked at her watch. David Hines was worried about *her* work schedule? "I have fifteen minutes before I have to get back to my piece."

"What are you working on?"

"A necklace for Laurie Rollins. Hopefully, she'll wear it to the Grammys.

"Congrats on Laurie. I think she's going to take home an award next year. Anyway, I stopped by to see how you're doing after Charlotte's death."

"I'm fine, thank you," Brooke said. She was getting tired of people asking her how she was. She took a rag and cleaned off the tip of one of her files. "I miss Charlotte; we all do. I'm very grateful that she gave me this house. It's allowed us a chance to begin again."

"From what?"

"Charlotte's son, Tripp. He was my husband. We've divorced."

"I'm sorry."

"Don't be."

David folded his arms and looked away. "Charlotte was my closest friend. We met at a party years ago. At the time, I was married, so we kept our friendship a secret."

"So, more than a friendship."

"Yes. And then my wife passed away, but we stayed close."

"Not to be rude, but why are you telling me this?"

"Charlotte and I, we didn't really try to hide from the public. We just lived our lives, separately but together. You understand what I mean?"

"You kept your own places but were still partners."

"Something like that. Anyway, Charlotte liked to talk about her grandchildren. She loved them, and she was very fond of you. And I thought it ... I don't know. I thought it would be nice to get to know each other."

"You're lonely?"

He laughed outright. "Well, yeah, I'm lonely."

She waited a few moments. "Sometimes I'm lonely." There was an awkward silence she finally broke. "Would you like to see what I'm working on?"

"I'd love to."

"It's called The Elephant in the Room." She smiled at him. "And don't write a song with the same title. I've heard people out here like to steal each other's ideas." She looked at his face for a moment. "You know I'm kidding, right?"

"Yes, Brooke. I've yet to meet a composer who would steal an idea from a jeweler."

She laughed. "Anyway, David. There seems to be an elephant in your room."

"No elephant. I know a lot of people, too many, but Charlotte was the one who I was happiest with."

Brooke nodded.

"I thought since you loved her, and I loved her, it would be nice to get together from time to time."

"That's it?"

"That's it. Would you like to do something tomorrow?"

"I get up early and jog in the morning, but if you want to come by around nine thirty, I can make something for us to eat." She picked up a pencil on her bench and twirled it. She looked at him coyly. "We could see if we have friend chemistry."

David grinned. "Friend chemistry sounds good. I hike in the morning, sometimes play tennis in the afternoon, not far from here. The Bel-Air Country Club."

"Fancy, fancy."

"Very."

"When do you get time to work?"

"It comes in spurts. When I'm writing music, my days are a lot more regimented. At the moment, I'm in a music desert. So, how do you feel about taking a hike with me tomorrow morning instead of jogging? Or I could jog if you'd prefer. The truth is, I'm not very good at it. Bad knees. Hiking is easier for me."

Brooke thought about it.

"Mixing up your workout schedule is good for the body, right?" he said.

"Okay, you sold me."

"Is eight too early for you?"

"No, I'm awake."

"Good." He stood up. "Coming here was hard for me, Brooke. This house holds a lot of memories. I'm having a difficult time without Charlotte. Thank you for saying yes." He shook her hand at the door. "See you tomorrow."

After he left, Brooke called Elizabeth. "You're never going to believe this, but guess who wants to be my friend?"

"Who?"

"David friggin' Hines."

"What?"

"Yeah, he and Charlotte had a thing, and he misses her, so he wants to get to know me."

"David Hines?"

"Right? But, Lizzy, I think he's being honest. It's like you and me. We both loved Nick. At some point, we're both going to want to talk about him."

"Yeah."

"I just wanted to tell you. I'll see you in a few weeks."

"Enjoy Hollywood. It seems like you're doing very well out there."

CHAPTER FIFTY-SEVEN
Susan

ize six. Oh. My. God, Susan thought. "Kelly!" she yelled.
"Kelly, I'm a size six!"

Maria came into the large closet where Susan was zipping and unzipping her jeans.

"Look at me, Maria! My jeans are too big. I weigh the same as I did before I got pregnant!"

"Good for you." Maria wasn't taking Susan's size drop as seriously as Susan would have liked. A drum roll would have been nice.

"Where's Kelly?" Susan asked. Timothy the cat was rubbing up against her legs. Clearly, he was happy for her.

"She's outside."

Susan zipped up her jeans, pulling her belt tight, then went and found her daughter in a rocking chair on the veranda, reading a book.

"I'm thinking of taking riding lessons," Kelly said when she spotted her mom. "I mean, I'm here in horse country, I may as well."

"Fine. But look at me, Kelly. My jeans are too big. Do you know what that means?!"

"Time to buy new jeans?"

"Yes! Come with. I'll get you a pair too."

"I don't know why you're making such a big deal about your weight." Kelly picked up her book and followed her mother toward the car.

Susan stopped and looked at her daughter. "This is the body I want," she said softly. "I worked hard for it. I like the way I look."

Kelly kissed her cheek and smiled. "You're right. I'm proud that you met your goals. But you almost always do."

Susan bought three pairs of jeans in different washes, a few sleeveless tanks to show off her newly muscular arms, and a bikini. She was hesitant about the bathing suit. She was leaning toward a tankini, but Kelly said she should go for it. "Time to show off your body, Mom."

At home, she dropped the bags of new clothing on her bed and called Jenna. "I bought a bikini, and Kelly says I look great in it," she said. "Come over and let me show you."

"I have one more appointment early this evening. After that, I'll stop by."

"I wish you could spend the night."

"That's up to you, Susan."

She wasn't sure. "I'm not ready to tell Kelly about us yet. We're still grieving Nick."

"I understand. Whenever you're ready. But I'm looking forward to seeing you in that bikini."

Susan hung up. The bathing suit was covered in tissue paper. She carefully unwrapped it. The ruched black bra top was a size large. The black bottom had white edging she could pull up to cover her belly button or push down around her hips. She looked at the label inside and ran her fingers over the size small label. Slowly, she got herself into it, making sure the straps were comfortable, arranging her breasts so a little cleavage showed. She let one side of the bikini bottom ride up on her right hip and kept the left side below. Standing in front of her full-length mirror, Susan noted she didn't need to suck in her stomach. She turned around and looked over her shoulder at her butt and thighs. She searched through her shoeboxes for a pair of wedge sandals and slipped her feet in. She took another look at herself. Kelly had been right. Susan looked beautiful.

* * *

Sound's success energized the staff. Cicely urged them to think boldly. It gave them confidence to present her with new ideas. The July issue would be released in late June, and Elizabeth was confident it would be one of their bestsellers. She loved her job, but she knew she couldn't continue. Cicely didn't need her, and at some point, Elizabeth's body would turn against her. The first step was to figure out what to do with the magazine, so she called Susan.

They met for dinner at a small Italian bistro in Ridgefield, Connecticut, Elizabeth arriving first and asking the hostess to seat her in a small booth. When Susan arrived five minutes later, she did a double take. Susan looked slimmer than she had in all the time Elizabeth had known her. Her chestnut hair was pulled back in a chignon, and she was wearing a body-hugging black dress with a yellow-and-black Hermès scarf draped over her shoulders.

"You look wonderful," Elizabeth said, kissing Susan's cheek.

"Mourning agrees with me," Susan said

Elizabeth smiled sadly. "And how's Kelly doing?"

"With Nick gone, she's become a Mommy's girl. I'm so glad to have her around—we're comforting each other. She starts classes at Columbia in August, but obviously, we'll still see each other a lot."

"And you're still with Jenna?" Elizabeth asked carefully. It wasn't her business, but she wanted to let Susan know she did care how she was doing.

"I am. She and Kelly have become my saviors since Nick died."

"I'm happy you have them."

Susan put on a pair of neon-blue reading glasses and studied the menu. "I'm always looking for new dishes that I can copy or reinterpret for the restaurant. They have caprese salad, which is a staple, but I like the semolina bread for sandwiches. I think we should include it in our breadbasket." She went through her bag and took out a pad and an Elsa Peretti silver pen. "I'm writing that down so I don't forget."

Elizabeth knew the pen well, and it made her miss Nick all over again. He had bought her the same one for Christmas last year. On the gift card, he'd written, *Every editor needs a silver pen for their silvery ideas.*

The waiter came to their table, and Elizabeth shut off the memory.

After he took their orders, Susan looked at her for a moment. "Elizabeth, I don't want the magazine. I think you should buy it. Nick would have liked that."

"I already own a percentage."

"So why not own the whole thing?"

Elizabeth moved her head from side to side, thinking. "It's worth a lot more money than Nick paid, and I don't have that kind of cash."

The waiter returned with their salads.

Susan said, "I think he brought our dishes out too quickly. Servers should give diners time to get settled before they rush the meal over."

Elizabeth looked back at the waiter. "I wouldn't have noticed if you hadn't pointed it out, but you're right."

"About the magazine. I'd sell it to you for what Nick paid. I told you before, I don't need the money, and I don't want to keep track of another property. I don't have the time or interest to focus on anything but Pond House."

Elizabeth had already decided not be involved with the magazine. And she didn't think she had the skillset to actually own it. But could she say no to the offer? *That would be stupid*, she thought. She would always regret not giving it a try. And if she really hated being an owner, she could sell it. She waited a few seconds. "I'd have to talk to Danny first."

"Of course. I'm prepared to give you excellent terms. Pay me over the next five years. Look, Elizabeth, it's better that *you* own it than someone who doesn't know the magazine or have the passion for it that you do."

"I'll seriously consider it, but regardless, thank you."

"Good," Susan said. "Speak to Danny. My accountant can go over the books with you and then have your attorney call my attorney." She wrote his name and number on a piece of paper and handed it to Elizabeth. "What else can I tell you?"

"Tell me about your restaurant."

Susan looked at her watch. "There's still enough daylight for you to see it. Let me pay the bill, and you can follow me over there."

Elizabeth offered to pay for dinner, but Susan said, "Absolutely not."

"Come on, Susan, then let's at least split it. You're offering me a magazine. The least I can do is pay for my salad."

"I'm offering to *sell* you a magazine. Although at a very good price."

When Elizabeth got home a few hours later, Danny was sitting in the family room reading the *New York Times*. "So how was Susan?" he asked.

"Good as she can be. She misses Nick, but she's got her daughter and friend, Jenna, who's her personal trainer and lover."

Danny put down the newspaper and gave her a quizzical look.

Elizabeth ignored it. "But, honey, you should see her restaurant. It's not like anything you'd expect from Susan. Remember that awful house she and Nick lived in? This is elegant, stately, and the property is beautiful. Mature trees, a pond. She showed me the menu. It'll be seasonal, a mixture of old-fashioned American and some new creations. Great desserts and wines. We'd want to go there even if we didn't know her."

"Good for her," Danny said. He went back to reading the paper.

Elizabeth sat down next to him. "And she wants to sell the magazine to me."

Danny put the paper down.

She had his full attention as she explained the terms. "What do you think?" she asked when she was done.

"I think it's a great deal. You'd be an owner, and you wouldn't have to be involved in the day-to-day."

She nodded. "I'm pulling back anyway."

"And if you want to keep Cicely incentivized, you can give her a percentage. Tate too."

"I think I will," Elizabeth said.

"Congrats, honey. You're about to be seriously in debt." He smiled and hugged her tightly.

"We, Danny. *We* will be seriously in debt."

"I'd be in debt with you anytime." He took her face in his hands. "Let's go to bed. I always wanted to make love to a tycoon."

CHAPTER FIFTY-EIGHT

At the end of June, *Sound*'s July issue was published with "Legends of Rock & Roll" on the cover. Cicely went on a press tour, touting the cover and solidifying *Sound*'s reputation as a magazine that delivered readers in-depth, behind-the-scenes articles about the entertainment industry. Sales were steady, advertisers were competing for page placement, and Cicely was a regular contributor to *Today* and *CNN*. Tate was teaching an evening class in magazine design at the School of Visual Arts.

When Elizabeth gave them shares in the magazine, they'd each signed five-year contracts. Cicely was already in talks with two networks about creating a *Sound* television show, and they hired an editor to begin creating an online version of the magazine. Elizabeth said she would come to the office once a month for meetings and be available by phone.

During the week, Elizabeth's kids were in day camp. On weekends, she and Danny took them to the beach, hiking, sailing, or got in the car to for day trips. Sometimes she and Claire worked on their *Girls Rule* magazine. She did PT three days a week, read, and wondered if she should write a book. Susan had the restaurant, and Brooke had her jewelry. Elizabeth knew she had to find something to engage her because she was still spending too much time mourning Nick Gallagher. She booked a four-day trip to visit Brooke the following week.

When Brooke met her at LAX, Brooke noticed the pained look on Elizabeth's face. "Why are you using a cane?"

"Because I'm traveling."

"Is that the only reason?" Brooke held the door for her when Elizabeth got in the car.

"I've had a couple of falls. It's safer this way."

"Then I'm canceling our hike on Thursday."

"We were going hiking?"

"You, David Hines, and me."

"I want to go!"

"And have you fall someplace where we can't get an EMT right away? a) Danny would kill me, and b) the answer is no."

"Well, you at least owe me a blow-by-blow about you and David Hines."

"We're friends, Elizabeth. As in, 'just good.' And that's how we both want it."

"I still want to hear about it."

"I'll tell you everything. And tomorrow morning, I want you to look at my Elephant in the Room. I need your merciless critique."

Elizabeth heard the dog barking before Brooke opened the door. When she did, a beautiful golden retriever puppy bounded toward her. "We have a new member of the family," Brooke said. "Meet Crosby, the world's greatest dog."

Elizabeth put her cane against the wall and picked him up. He began licking her neck. "Oh my God! I want him, Brooke."

Brooke took him from her. "Get one of your own," she said, smiling.

"As soon as I'm home."

Brooke put the puppy back on the floor, where he ran in circles, chasing his tail.

Elizabeth walked through the foyer and into the living room. She could see why her friend had fallen in love with the house.

The midcentury rooms were white with splashes of color. "I would never want to leave here either."

Tara and Amanda met her in the kitchen. "Lizzie! Don't you love it here?" Tara asked.

"I do. All this sunshine—no wonder you two look so healthy."

Amanda took her hand and led her toward the bedrooms. "You can sleep in my room. I'll stay with Tara."

"Thank you." Elizabeth put down her bags and opened the windows to let in the fragrant air. That night, she slept dreamlessly for the first time since Nick died.

In the morning, she used her cane as she followed Brooke to the studio. *What a space*, Elizabeth thought. *Airy, light, calming.*

"Come, see my elephant," Brooke said. "I want you to be brutally honest." She opened a cigar box where she'd placed the pendant. "I played with the execution," she said, looking down at it.

"Can I pick it up?"

"Yes, just be careful. Enamel cracks easily."

Elizabeth gently took the pendant from its box. It was four inches in diameter, enameled black. Brooke had used enamel paint to create a bright blue-and-green couch. A man and women—drawn with wispy white strokes of enamel—were seated, engaged in conversation, and oblivious to the gray elephant in the foreground. He was adorned with an emerald-and-ruby collar. His eyes were made of aquamarine.

Elizabeth examined the piece more carefully. "I don't even know what to say."

"Do you like it?"

"I love it. Honestly, I like everything you make, but this is in a class of its own. I've never seen anything like it. If Laurie Rollins is stupid enough not to wear it, I'll take out a loan and buy it myself."

Brooke smiled. "I love it too."

Elizabeth replaced the piece in the cigar box. "What about the chain?"

"I was going to leave that up to Laurie. She's coming here next week to see it. With her stylist." Brooke rolled her eyes.

"Stylists are part of the community, Brooke. Get used to it. After this piece, you're going to be working with a lot more of them."

"I hope so. I'm proud of this." Brooke looked down at the enamel. "When I started working on it, I kept thinking it was going to be a failure, I had no business being a jeweler, everyone is going to hate it, the usual. But I kept going. And now I think it's a very good piece."

"It is. Everyone has doubts when they take a risk."

"Not Nick."

Elizabeth considered that. "Nick took chances, but he had doubts about his abilities. He just didn't give in to them."

The following day, Elizabeth brainstormed with Brooke about a line of jewelry.

"I'm thinking of doing one-of-a-kind pieces for certain customers and a regular line for Barneys," Brooke said. "But it needs to be distinctive."

"What about the bat theme?" Elizabeth asked.

"I don't know how to make it work."

"Why not little flying black bat studs? The more expensive ones could have jeweled eyes. You could make bat charms for bracelets and silver or gold necklaces with bats hanging from them."

"Upside down! Don't bats hang upside down?"

"Yep."

"I could even do bat rings. Stack rings. Maybe make a few with just the wings on it."

Elizabeth nodded. "Yes, I love that."

Brooke started sketching the rings on a piece of paper. "Do you think I should have a variety of colors?"

"Just black for now. The differences should be in the length of the necklaces, the metal for the chains, and the sizes of the studs."

"I like it. See? I need you out here."

At dinner, Amanda said she wanted her mother to teach her how to carve a bat out of wax so she could help make a production line. Tara wanted to create a simple bracelet she could sell at the university to raise money for the famine in Sudan.

"It looks like all the 'bats' are working for the company now," Elizabeth said.

"Yes, we have our very own bat cave," Amanda answered, grinning.

After dinner, Brooke and Elizabeth took a bottle of merlot out to the pool. Brooke asked how Susan was doing, and Elizabeth told her, leaving out her affair with Jenna. Eventually, of course, they got around to talking about Nick.

"The thing is this, Elizabeth. You're the only person I can talk to about my feelings for Nick. I understand why you didn't want to hear about it before, but I need you to let me cry to you now. Not this minute, but over the next few months—years, even."

Elizabeth hugged her. "Brooke, I will always be here for you. I love you."

CHAPTER FIFTY-NINE
Brooke

Los Angeles

Terry Cone, Laurie Rollins's PR person, arrived ten minutes before the singer and her crew. Terry spent a few minutes looking carefully at The Elephant in the Room. Then she turned back to Brooke. "I'm blown away. The stylist is going to love it. Although don't expect her to fawn. She's not that kind of person. All business."

Brooke felt like rays of light were running through her body. Someone outside her circle of friends was validating her work. "Really?"

"If Laurie doesn't like it, I'll have another musician wearing it by Saturday. How much are you planning to charge her?"

"Three thousand."

Terry looked horrified. "No, Brooke. Girl, you need your own PR person."

"I'm honored that she's even considering it. I don't want to overcharge."

"That's not how it works here. Make it six thousand. And that's still a deal."

"*Six?*" Brooke was shocked.

"How much time did you spend on it?"

Brooke shrugged a little. "Weeks, but—"

"Then make it eight thousand. She's getting a steal, and she'll know it."

"Okay. All right. You know better than me." Brooke gave a single nod. Eight thousand dollars kept reverberating in her mind. She trusted Terry's advice. Eight thousand dollars. She was already thinking of how much gold she could buy to incorporate in her next pieces. A lot.

Laurie arrived with an entourage and looked at the pendant for a few minutes before she picked it up. "This is incredible," she said, looking at Brooke.

"Laurie, can I see it?" her stylist asked. She'd been staring over Laurie's shoulder, but when she picked it up she did a thorough inspection, turning it over, putting it up against the singer's chest.

"Can you make the chain with heavy, silver links?" Laurie asked.

"I don't think it should be silver," her stylist said.

"Definitely not silver," someone in the group said.

"Gold," said her manager.

Terry stood next to Brooke and whispered in her ear, "Look at them. You'd think they were negotiating an arms agreement."

A laugh bubbled out of Brooke, and they all turned to her. She waved them off. "Sorry. Just had a thought that made me laugh."

"What do you think we should do?" Laurie asked. "You're the jeweler."

"Stay away from metals. It detracts from the piece. I think we should use a very thick clear cord that will be practically invisible. You want the pendant to look like it's floating."

"The cord can't break," the stylist said. "What kind of cord will hold a piece this heavy?"

"Monofilament," Brooke answered. "It's used for fishing. If you can catch a seventy-pound tuna using monofilament, it can easily hold the enamel."

The stylist regarded the piece again, then looked back at Brooke, nodding. "Good idea."

"How much is the necklace?" the manager asked.

"Eight thousand," Brooke said. She was proud her voice hadn't squeaked.

He nodded. "That's reasonable. I'll have Laurie's business manager cut you a check."

"When can we have the finished necklace?" the stylist asked.

"Next week, if we're agreed on the monofilament."

"Fine. Give Terry a call, and we'll come back with Laurie to make sure it hangs right."

"I'll bring the dress I'm going to wear. Will you be able to adjust the length for it?" Laurie asked.

"Of course."

The moment they were gone, Brooke called Elizabeth. "She's going to wear it to the Grammys. I'm still in shock."

"Don't be. You're a professional now. Cicely will be coming out next week. I gave her pictures of the necklace, but she wants it professionally photographed, and she's going to do the interview with you."

* * *

Every Tuesday and Thursday, David Hines met Brooke and Crosby at Charlotte's—now Brooke's—house. They usually drove to Bronson Canyon in Griffith Park and hiked there. Bronson Cave was Brooke's favorite—a short tunnel that was once part of a quarry. It had been used as a set for many TV shows and movies, including the entrance to the Batcave for the *Batman* series—she considered it a lucky sign.

Brooke liked David. He helped her appreciate the differences between New York and LA. She was impatient with the slower pace of life in Los Angeles, especially when it came to walking.

One afternoon a few weeks before, they had been window-shopping in Sunset Plaza, one of the few places Brooke could actually stroll. She saw a store across the street she wanted to go into and told David. The sign said, DON'T WALK, but there were no cars coming in either direction. She quickly crossed the street and was confused to see David still on the other side of the road. When the light changed, he joined her.

"Why did you wait?" she'd asked.

He'd laughed and put his arm loosely around her shoulder. "Classic mistake, honey. You're trying to graft your East Coast instincts onto California. This isn't New York."

"I know."

"But it has a lot to offer." He'd turned around and pointed to the Santa Monica mountains to the north. "Look up," he said.

She had. They were magnificent.

He'd turned west. "A few miles down the road is the Pacific Ocean. You don't have that in Connecticut or Manhattan."

Or the weather, she'd thought. *Or the sweet, juicy oranges.*

David had been right. When she stopped trying to force her East Coast ways onto Los Angeles, she was able to appreciate it more.

And when she was no longer intimidated by his celebrity, she found David easy to be with.

"So, David Music Man Hines," she would say, "how are you today?"

"*Meza meza*, Brooke Jeweler to the Stars Hayworth," he usually answered.

He told her about his wife. They'd met in high school and stayed together until the last day of her life, but Charlotte had his heart. His words, not hers. She told him about Tripp and the girls and shared her own stories about Charlotte. One day, she finally told him about Nick.

The day her line launched at Barneys, he was standing in the store, watching from a distance as she stood behind her jewelry counter, taking out her pieces and showing them to customers and a photographer from *Los Angeles* magazine. "I think you're going to develop a loyal customer base. BatGirls collectors," he said.

"We'll see," Brooke said. But she was starting to believe it.

He was going to accompany her to the MusicCares event, and though Cicely had said Brooke could be her date to the Grammys, Brooke told her, "Use your plus-one for someone else. David Hines is taking me."

CHAPTER SIXTY
Elizabeth

New York

Elizabeth was giving herself an injection of glatiramer acetate one morning and hurt herself when she'd stuck the needle in her belly. She hated the medicine, but it was the only one that seemed to help her multiple sclerosis from flaring. The wound stung, then it swelled. She must have hit a blood vessel. Her body was turning into a map of the disease—entire areas of her hips, thighs, and arms were pocked with hideous necrotic lumps and bumps. She put an ice pack on her stomach.

She gathered some notes and walked into her study to work on the new magazine she and Claire were creating—*Girls Rule*. Her daughter was full of ideas. She wanted to include articles about best friends, getting good grades, babysitting, keeping secrets, and arguing with your parents so they would listen! The list went on. Elizabeth was impressed with Claire's creativity and work ethic. They had decided to present the magazine to Claire's teacher once school started and see what happened next. "Maybe you can come to school, Mom, and we could show everyone how to make a magazine."

"That's an excellent idea," Elizabeth had said.

She put her notes aside to read the editor's October issue of *Sound*. Cicely had sent it to her for a final look before it went to the printer. Elizabeth was starting to read, but when she saw the mailman at her box, she decided to go down her driveway to check it. She opened her front door, and the heat hit her in a hot, muggy blast. New York in July—it was like walking around with a wet washcloth on your face.

When she opened her mailbox, bills, bank statements, and an invitation addressed to the Altman family greeted her—the writing on the invitation was thick black calligraphy. The return address said *Pond House*. Elizabeth slid it open.

Please join Susan and Kelly Gallagher for the
grand opening of Pond House
Saturday, July 25, 1998
Seven o'clock, party attire
Kindly RSVP by July 18

She called Susan at home. "We just got our invite. Congrats! Of course, we'll be there."

Susan said she'd already received thirty phone calls from people RSVP'ing "yes."

"I know it's going to be a success, Susan. I can't wait to see you then."

On the day of the event, Danny and Elizabeth put the kids into the backseat of the car for the twenty-minute drive north to South Salem. After a week of thundershowers, the skies had cleared, and the night was warm and dry, and for now, the mosquitos seemed uninterested in human flesh.

Before they got out of the car, Elizabeth gave her children a final speech about manners, handshakes, and not saying "ugh" when they were offered food. "There won't be any chicken fingers or pizzas, so you're going to have to force your taste buds to go on a culinary adventure."

"*Culinary* means food, Justin," Claire said. "And, Mom, we're not rude."

Elizabeth laughed a little and opened the door for them. "True, and you look very handsome, Justin. Claire, beautiful." She kissed each of their cheeks.

Danny came up behind her and whispered, "Okay, here's the deal. Hello, eat, everything looks great, goodbye, good luck, and we're out in an hour."

He's such a guy. "We'll see."

They were walking toward a crowd of people when the kids veered off toward the pond. "You go without me. I'll watch them," Elizabeth said.

Danny gave her a look.

"What? Go. I'll meet you in a minute."

She caught up with her children. There were pathway lights around a Japanese garden, and the pond had an aerator and koi fish swimming along the top.

"It's pretty," Claire said.

"We'll come back before we leave. I promise," Elizabeth said.

The kids walked cautiously in front of her as she immersed herself in the crowd. A jazz quartet was playing in the background, and waiters were passing out hors d'oeuvres. Elizabeth chose a bacon-wrapped date and a spear of endive stuffed with crab. Delish. She looked for familiar faces and spotted a movie star who lived in Bedford and a couple who were the parents of a child at Claire and Justin's school. She found Danny talking to someone whom he introduced as a banker he'd once worked with at Merrill Lynch.

Kelly came over with a kiss and swooped the kids up. "We have a room for anyone under twelve," she told them.

I must be getting old, Elizabeth thought. The last time she'd seen Kelly, she was just a little girl. The young woman before her had Susan's chestnut hair but Nick's height—and those sky-blue eyes.

Kelly winked at Elizabeth. "Pizza and Nintendo."

When Justin gave his mother a thumbs-up and assured they were taken care of, she turned around, and there was Susan. "Pond House is *magnifique*," Elizabeth said after she'd exchanged hugs with her. "And, Susan, look at you—you're glowing."

Susan was wearing a fitted animal-print dress and her hair hung near her shoulders in long waves. "Thank you. Come, look around. Where's that perfect husband of yours? I want to give you both a tour."

Elizabeth walked back to Danny. "Susan wants to show us the restaurant. And I want you to meet Jenna."

He followed her inside. There were three rooms with comfy banquettes and tables, framed photos of movie stars from the '30s on the walls, and modern lighting. Everywhere Elizabeth looked, there was an element of surprise.

The woman behind the long copper bar was mixing drinks alongside two other bartenders.

"She's a mixologist," Susan said. "Try her mojito. To die for."

Danny grabbed one for himself and Elizabeth. The stir stick was a sugarcane stalk.

Susan led them to a tall blonde with a curvy body. "This is my friend Jenna Callas. She's been my rock since Nick died. Kelly too."

Danny shook her hand. "Pleasure to meet you, Jenna."

Elizabeth was amused, watching Danny trying to pretend he didn't find Jenna arresting. "Careful, Danny," she said, teasing. "Jenna's a trainer. If you act inappropriately, she can cream you."

"Me? I would never act inappropriately."

Jenna smiled. "Let me give you a tour of the upstairs."

She showed them the three bedrooms, each decorated in a different theme—beachy, country chic, and Park Avenue sophisticated.

"So if I ever want to take my wife to the shore, I don't have to deal with the traffic," Danny said, grinning.

"Book now. Reservations are filling," Jenna said.

Her pride in the endeavor—in Susan—was clear, and it made Elizabeth feel a little warmth in her chest. It was nice to see someone who so clearly cared about Susan. She needed that.

Jenna told them she and Susan were considering adding a small gym for workout classes in the fall, maybe even a yoga studio.

"She's gone from restaurant owner to innkeeper to restaurant, innkeeper, and yoga studio," Elizabeth said, laughing.

"I think it *could* be all three," Jenna said.

"With Susan as boss? Definitely."

"Let me take you to the food area. If you don't love what you eat, I'll be very surprised," Jenna said. She led them to the screened porch. "Find yourself a seat. I'll be back in a moment."

They found a two-person booth in a corner of the room, where Danny had the blackened sea bass with a special pecan and sweet potato mash. Elizabeth had pistachio-crusted salmon, her plate decorated with lemongrass and pistachios.

Elizabeth stared at her husband after they were done and patted her stomach dramatically. "She's going to do very well here."

"I think so too. Look at those desserts." He pointed with his chin at another table where people were sharing an English trifle.

Jenna came over. "You like?"

They both nodded.

"Everything is wonderful," Elizabeth said.

A waiter brought them a plate of dessert samples. "In a few minutes, Kelly is going to make a speech outside, so if you want to join us, you can always come back here for the dessert afterward," Jenna said.

"We'll be there." Elizabeth took a forkful of the trifle, then looked at Jenna, her eyes wide. "I just died and went to heaven."

"I'm so glad," Jenna said.

"Where'd Susan go?"

"She's probably out there somewhere." She waved to the outside at the front of the restaurant and took her leave.

They finished their dessert quickly and wandered outside. Justin and Claire came out of the back room with Kelly, who walked to a makeshift podium and adjusted the microphone. Next to her was a trolley table laden with an enormous white cake, with the likeness of Pond House on it. "As you know, our family has gone through a terrible tragedy," she began.

"I still don't see Susan," Elizabeth whispered to Danny.

"She's here. It's her opening. Where's she going to go?"

"Every day, we miss my father," Kelly continued. "It's been hard for us, but my mom has shown me how to keep going. It's cliché but true—grit and determination. Pond House is her passion project. Susan Gallagher isn't a woman who feels sorry for herself. She immersed herself in her dream, and this is it. As for the food, my mother told me to tell you, 'You better like it because if you don't, the servers *will* spit on it when you're not looking.'" Laughter burst from the crowd. "And she told me to tell you not to laugh. Food poisoning isn't always an accident." Elizabeth heard some concerned murmuring around her. "I'm kidding, guys! The food is fantastic. Go for it, and thanks for coming."

Elizabeth watched Kelly as the crowd clapped for her. She put down the microphone and smiled warmly when people came up to congratulate her.

"That was a beautiful speech, Kelly. But I didn't see your mom. Do you know where she is?" Elizabeth asked.

"I just saw her, maybe over there." Kelly pointed toward the pond.

Elizabeth followed the stone path down to the pond. Susan was kneeling next to it, feeding the fish little pieces of food.

Elizabeth knelt beside her.

"You shouldn't do that, Elizabeth. I don't want you falling into my pond and having to drag you out. It wouldn't be a good look for my opening night."

"Ha-ha."

Susan stood up and gave her a hand. "Here, let me help you."

"Thanks."

"So, what do you think?"

"Amazing. The food, the cocktails, and my God, Susan, the desserts! Danny had two. I'd be surprised if you weren't fully booked in a week."

"There're a few restaurant critics here tonight. They won't write anything up until they've had a proper meal when the restaurant is officially opened to the public."

"I'm not worried about the reviews. They'll be excellent."

Susan grinned. "I think so too." Her face suddenly slackened, though, and her gaze went distant. "I miss Nick. Our marriage wasn't like yours—you probably know that. But it was solid. We loved each other. I took him for granted. I thought he'd always be here. The restaurant has kept me busy, but I think of him at the strangest times. I start to get teary, then I stop myself and go back to work. I guess that's how I deal with grief."

"And you have Kelly. And Jenna."

"Thank God," Susan said.

"So, Kelly told me a little story about the pond that I found interesting. She said that it was her and Nick's idea to put a garden around it and stock it with koi. She said you didn't want to do it."

Susan looked at the water and didn't say anything as she took the few remaining fish pellets from her pocket and dropped them in the water, watching the koi surround the food and eat. "I have a black thumb, Elizabeth. Plants die on my watch. I never had any pets until Kelly dropped her cat in my lap. Then Nick died ... so I felt sure I couldn't keep anything alive."

It was an unusually honest and vulnerable thing for Susan to say, and it squeezed Elizabeth's heart a little. "Oh Susan."

She turned to Elizabeth. "It's true."

Elizabeth cocked her head a little. "What changed?"

Susan looked toward the restaurant and the people who were walking around the grounds with their food and drinks. A wry smile curved her lips. "Well, Elizabeth, even I, the invincible Susan Gallagher, can be wrong."

EPILOGUE
Susan

Susan and Jenna were lounging in the backyard of the inn and wellness center they had purchased in Nantucket, Massachusetts. Susan had ended her romance with Jenna a year after Nick died, but they were still business partners. They spent the fall and early spring in New York, managing and working at Pond House. In the winter, Susan traveled the world, vacationing and seeking inspiration to improve her properties. May through September, they lived and worked in Nantucket.

A few months after Nick had died, Susan began to see Jenna more like a daughter than a lover. The age difference between them had become a problem for her. If Susan was going to share her life with someone, she wanted them to be in the same age category. She needed a person with the same cultural references and worldview. Someone more like Nick. She didn't want to be anyone's "older woman."

But she was also deeply grateful to Jenna. Their relationship had allowed Susan to understand her body and sexual fluidity better. And Jenna had been there for Susan in those awful few months after Nick had died.

Jenna was soon seeing other women, and Susan was dating mostly men. Her relationship with Jenna had taught her how to have better sex with them. She knew what she wanted in bed now and how to achieve it. Their businesses thrived.

Susan was looking forward to the coming weekend. Elizabeth, Danny, and their kids were arriving. They had rented a summer house at the end of the island, a small wind-beaten "shack" two blocks from the beach. The Altmans had moved to the exurbs of Denver two years ago. Susan still kept in touch with them, talking via phone or email at least once a week. Colorado had been Danny's idea. He thought the housing market was going to bust, and he wanted to leave Wall Street before the world melted down. Elizabeth told Susan she was a little anxious about leaving the northeast, but the mountain weather agreed with her, and the MS was stable for now. She'd sold her shares in *Sound* and found a part-time job teaching journalism at a local community college.

But the person Susan was most excited to see was her old friend from the Upper West Side, Jackie Spellman. Jackie was married with children, still living in Chicago. Six months after Nick died, Susan had called Jackie. They picked up where they'd left off as teenagers. The conversation was that easy. Since then, they talked and saw each other all the time. Jackie would be coming up the following week and stay at the inn, alone. Susan was already planning walks along Cisco beach, showing Jackie the beauty of Nantucket. Talking into the night with her oldest friend.

Susan glanced over at Jenna, who was lying back against the chair, her eyes closed, letting the sun on her face. She seemed content. Susan stood up and walked inside to the front desk. She wanted to check the reservations for the weekend. The month of June could be iffy. Tourists didn't start flooding the island till the Fourth of July, but their Seashell Inn was sold out. She'd thought that name was corny at first—Jenna had suggested it—until she found a perfectly shaped scallop shell on the beach and took it as a sign of good luck.

Susan went back outside to the front porch. The blue hydrangeas blossomed in their window boxes. The newly mown grass was fragrant, and the roses were blooming along the trellises. She returned to the same thought she'd had since they first found the inn: *Nick would have loved this.* He would have cheered her on as she expanded her business, helped her, been proud of her accomplishments. If he had lived, she thought he might even have come to accept her relationship with Jenna. Susan knew that no matter how far they drifted from each other and how many turns their relationship would take, Nick would have always loved her. She picked one of the roses from the trellis and inhaled its fragrance deeply. There were tears in her eyes, but they were happy tears. Her marriage had been imperfect. She wished she had known then what she knew now, about her needs, her body, her sexuality. She had perserveved after Nick died, creating a new life for herself. But he never really left her. Sometimes, she would even speak aloud to him. She'd tell him how Kelly was doing, or share her newest plans, asking for his advice. The truth was, no matter how long he had been gone, Nick would always be a part of her life.

ACKNOWLEDGMENTS

In the early 1990s, the late literary agent Loretta Barrett urged me to write a book. By 2001, I had completed the manuscript. She loved the story and believed in it. In the intervening years, a lot changed for both of us. I put the book away and moved on to other projects. Sadly, Loretta died in 2014, though her agency Loretta Barrett Books, Inc. lives on.

A few years ago, I moved from New York to Florida, where my old college roommate Janixx Parisi invited me to join the Wave Writers. They encouraged me to dust off my pages, read them aloud, and begin the process of rewriting. These writers are supportive of each other, talented, and dedicated to their craft. I thank them all. Especially Janixx, Angela Page, Deborah Banerjee, Carolyn Davis, Diane Jellen, Ronni Sandroff, and LA Justice, who said after my first reading, "Now that's a writer!"

Early editors of this book include Joelle Sander, LA Justice, and Gretchen Stelter. Their comments and suggestions immensely improved my manuscript.

Karli Jackson is a stealth editor. Her feedback, criticism, and willingness to go back and forth with me over plot and characters was a gift. Our conversations made me think deeper and improve this story.

The team at Warren Publishing has been remarkable. As a small, independent, women-owned-and-operated publishing house, they proved to be a great fit for me. Professional, generous, and enthusiastic, each of them has been there when I needed them. Special thanks to Mindy Kuhn, Amy Ashby, Melissa Long, and Lacey Cope.

Corrine Pritchett at Books Forward sees the micro and macro of publicity. She is dedicated to getting this novel into the hands of as many readers as possible. Entertainment lawyer George Sheanshang always has my back.

Early readers of *Friends with Issues* include Pamela Shore and Seena Brown. Yes, they're my sister and mother, and they were very excited about the project, but they also believed in its success. In the last two years, my sister has read and reread the book, giving me love and confidence when I needed it, pointing out problems with characters when she thought I needed to rework them. Her personal support kept me going when I questioned my own abilities.

Authors Debbie Rigaud and Robert Rorke gave me tips and suggestions. When I wanted to tear up my manuscript, Robert had yelled, "Don't!"

A girl needs friends, and mine have been there through thick and thin. I can't name all of them, but I especially want to thank Laurie Brickman, whom I've known for over fifty years. She said I was a "real writer" in ninth grade. One of my besties Cathy Kanner, owner of Kanner Entertainment, Inc., has been my friend since the day I was born. Literally. She read the book after the first and last edit and saw it as not only a great read but also something with potential way beyond my imaginings. Longtime colleagues and friends Roberta Caploe and Lynn Leahey had incisive comments and kept me laughing.

Every person I interviewed and came to know as Editor-in-Chief of both *Soap Opera Digest* and *Seventeen* informed my opinions about celebrity, Hollywood, fashion, and media. I loved being a magazine editor. I loved the people, the process, and the ideas we shared. I believe a good magazine can be a leisurely source of information and entertainment for its readers.

Dr. Saud Sadiq and his team at the International Multiple Sclerosis Management Practice in New York were outstanding doctors and helped me realize my disease did not have to get in the way of my work or personal life. A special shoutout to my physician in Florida, Dr. Melissa Rennella Ortega, who is a superb neurologist specializing in MS. She has helped keep this disease at bay and continues to guide me through the challenging journey of living with MS.

Thank you, Lessley Burke, owner of the jewelry studio "Guilded Lynx" in Ridgefield, Connecticut. Lessley is a gifted goldsmith and enamellist. She and other master teachers taught me everything I know about making one-of-a-kind pieces out of gems and precious metals. Her studio provided me with a haven to get to know other jewelers as we helped and supported each other. Thank you, Mary Americo, jeweler extraordinaire. Your friendship, ideas, and the laughter we shared till tears ran down our faces was a blessing.

My character, Susan Gallagher—wholly imagined—taught me so much about the power of self-determination, courage, and how truly sensual good food can be. I'm eating a goat cheese salad and crème brulé tonight in your honor.

If you are interested in seeing the Astor Chinese Garden Court, do visit one of the most glorious museums in the world: the Metropolitan Museum of Art. I think you will be wowed and, hopefully, as awed by the garden as I am.

Jewelry Concepts and Technology by Oppi Untracht (Doubleday) is a magnificent reference book on the making of jewelry.

Special words of gratitude to my children, Greg Berlin, Lauren Berlin Johnson, and Connor Berlin, who always believed their mom was a "real writer" and urged me to complete this project. The love I feel for them is limitless.

To my first grandchild, Summer Madelyn, you've put a stamp on my heart that grows each day. I love you like no one's business.

My husband, Jordan Berlin, acted out certain scenes in this book with me, reliving our first date and helping me to see romance from a man's point of view. As of this writing, we have been married for thirty-four years and never stop loving each other.

To all the unpublished writers out there, here is my advice: don't listen to the naysayers. I'm talking about the people who tell you "writing is hard"—you already know that—or "very few people make it." Be determined. Tell your story.

To my readers, thank you, thank you, thank you. This one's for you. And for all readers of the world, remember we engage in one of life's most pleasurable pursuits. Pass it on.

CPSIA information can be obtained
at www.ICGtesting.com
Printed in the USA
BVHW031204100223
658213BV00005B/642